CROSSING BLOOD

Crossing Blood

NANCI KINCAID

G. P. PUTNAM'S SONS
New York

Parts of this book have been published previously, in somewhat different form,
in the following publications, to which the author offers gratitude: *Carolina
Quarterly, Crescent Review, Emery's Journal, Missouri Review, New Letters,
Ontario Review, The Rectangle, St. Andrew's Review,* and *Southern Exposure.*

The author acknowledges permission to reprint lyrics from "The Wanderer," by
Ernest Maresca (Mijac), © 1960 (renewed) and 1964 Mijac Music. All rights
administered by Warner-Tamerlane Publishing Corp. All rights reserved.
Used by permission.

The text of this book is set in Sabon.

Library of Congress Cataloging-in-Publication Data

Kincaid, Nanci.
Crossing blood / Nanci Kincaid.
p.   cm.
ISBN 0-399-13719-X
I. Title.
PS3561.I4253C76   1992   91-42431 CIP
813' .54—dc20

Designed by MaryJane DiMassi
Printed in the United States of America
1 2 3 4 5 6 7 8 9 10

This book is printed on acid-free paper.
∞

A special thanks for the encouraging words to:
Tilly Warnock, Elva Bell McLin, Penne Laubenthal,
Abby Thomas, Faith Sale, Shannon Ravenel, Susan Ketchin,
and The University of Alabama.

FOR ALI MARIE AND LEIGH ROME

I

Life Is Better Here

W^9E live about as close to French Town as you can get and still be a white person.

After my real daddy left, Mother married Walter and we moved out of the trailer park into a green house on California Street. Ours is the only green house. All the other houses are white and just alike. White crackerboxes, Walter calls them. Little houses on tiny lots with yards so small you can mow the whole thing in thirty minutes on a hot day with a push mower. That's what Walter says. Our house is set apart from the others, the last one on the paved part of California Street. The last house in the white section. We have a big yard and live right on the dividing line. Mother says she always did want to live in a real house. She tells us how lucky we are about twenty times a day.

Mother wouldn't marry Walter until after Benny was born and her stomach flattened back out and she could fit into regular clothes. Walter waited without complaining. Granddaddy said, "Your daddy run off because your mama is expecting again," but she told him to hush and not talk like that in front of us. At night me and Roy listened to Mother cry herself to sleep, and Roy said if he had a gun he would shoot our daddy dead for making Mother cry like that.

Once it was clear that our real daddy was gone for good, Walter, who lived in the blue trailer next door, got friendlier with Mother. In the evening when he came home from work he stood in the yard and talked to her while she took the clothes from the line. Sometimes he set up the water sprinkler in his front yard and said he didn't care if me and Roy played in it. He told Mother one day that she was the prettiest pregnant woman he'd ever seen. He said that in front of me and Roy and Granddaddy, which we hated, but we could tell Mother liked it. He even brought fried chicken home now and then, enough for all of us.

Next thing we knew, Mother was talking a lot about Mr. Walter and what a nice man he was. The next thing we knew, Granddaddy was saying Mother could do a lot worse than Walter Sheppard. The next thing we knew, Mr. Walter was eating supper with us almost every night.

Twice he loaded Roy and me in the back of his truck—we had on our pajamas. Mother laid a couple of blankets down in the truck bed and she popped a big paper sack full of popcorn. Walter drove us to the drive-in, paid our way, parked the truck backwards in a parking spot so we could see good, even hung the movie speaker on the side panel of the truck by us. Mother and Walter sat sideways in the truck cab talking more than watching. Mother was smiling a lot.

When Roy had to go to the bathroom, Walter got out of the truck and took him. It was Roy's first time to go in the men's bathroom. Until then he always went in the women's with Mother and me. You wouldn't think a thing like going in the men's bathroom could make a boy so happy. Walter and Roy came back bringing everybody an Eskimo Pie.

When Benny was finally born it was the middle of the night. It was Walter that drove Mother to the hospital. She was crying when he tried to help her get up into the truck. Granddaddy was crying too. That scared me and Roy, so we also cried. Granddaddy didn't even try to make us go back to bed. He let us stay up and eat cereal and play checkers with him until finally, almost morning, Walter called on the telephone and said Mother was fine. He said she had a big baby boy, more than nine pounds. Grand-daddy said that was good news. He sat down and buried his face in his hands.

After Mother came home from the hospital with Benny she cried all the time, not even trying to save up her sadness for late at night like she'd been doing. It was an unnatural thing to see her lift up that round-headed baby and press him against her chest and cry her eyes out. And Benny was a good baby too, a quiet baby, who hardly cried at all, just slept or lay jerking his legs up and down, looking around at whatever there was. Mother picked him up one hundred times a day and kissed all over his bald head, which did not bother him but always made tears run down her face.

"Good Lord, woman, it's the baby supposed to cry—not the mama," Granddaddy said. By the time a few weeks passed she was over being sad and Walter had asked her to marry him again.

On their wedding day Mother looked beautiful. She always was pretty to me and Roy, even when she said she was a mess. But this day she had on lots of lipstick, her black hair was curled, and she was wearing a blue dress, stockings, and high heels. She had on my dead grandmother's pearl necklace. Granddaddy whistled when she came walking out. Walter said she looked fine. But that wasn't the half of it.

Walter had on polished shoes. He tooted his horn as they drove off in the truck. Granddaddy said he hoped to goodness that Mother and Walter got back home before Benny woke up from his nap and needed fed. He winked at us. "This is really something," Granddaddy said. "First you get a dandy new brother and then you get a brand-new daddy, all inside a couple of months. What do you suppose is next?"

Me and Roy didn't know.

.

But moving to California Street was next.

Granddaddy went home to Alabama. Walter sold his trailer, put money down on this nice house, and we moved in hardly able to believe how lucky we were. Me and Roy hope our daddy finds out how well we're getting along without him. We wish he could see this house. People think Walter is Benny's daddy. We don't explain things to anybody.

Mother loves Walter for getting me and Roy and Benny out of that trailer park, where we didn't have friends to play with or a yard of our own. Walter said that trailer park was no kind of place for kids. It was too full of Yankees, old people who wait until one foot is in the grave, sell their houses and snow shovels, move to Florida and buy a trailer.

Walter says you can spot Yankees without even hearing them say some Yankee thing. You can spot them by their yards, which they don't care too much about. He says they hang out a sign on the front of their trailer that says "Hans and Frieda," and then they go inside and play cards the rest of their lives. They don't get into watering grass or growing flowers. They don't understand about sitting out on a porch rocking. Or about drinking iced tea under a shade tree. Or lying in a hammock with a flyswatter in your hand, thinking. Yankees don't have the knack for relaxing. That's obvious. Walter said that's why they played cards so much, like it was a job or something. Like somebody was paying them to play canasta by the hour. Like some jackass card game was something important. It got to Walter.

Besides old Yankees, we had university people in that trailer park too. Men as old as Walter who still called themselves students, and some who were professors. Walter said he didn't know if universities made people into oddballs, or if oddballs was all they'd let in. Walter swore not a one of those men had sense enough to be embarrassed over himself. "Grown men riding bicycles," he said. "Thirty years old or better, and still never done an honest day's work in their life. Don't have a thing to show for themselves but a bicycle—I reckon their mamas bought that.''

Walter says getting your own automobile is the first sign of manhood. He says you can't be a man without one. It irritated him to death on Saturdays when these pitiful excuses for men jingled by riding their bicycles to the library instead of washing their trucks and listening to the FSU football game. That trailer park wasn't natural.

Life is better here. Me and Roy have friends in the white houses on California Street—Bubba, a fat boy Roy's age, who Walter says looks like a tire that needs the air let out, and his sister Karol, who is my age. Walter says Karol has worms, just because she has dark circles under her eyes. They have a pretty older sister named Patricia, who is in charge of them while their mother and daddy are at work. Bubba's daddy—who is also Karol and Patricia's daddy, but people just call him Bubba's Daddy because they are like the before and after of the same person, both of them fat, sort of handsome, and brown-eyed—is always telling stories. Everybody likes him because of that. But he can get mad too, and when he does, Bubba says, you better run for your life. Bubba says his daddy has whipped him with the buckle end of a belt before. But he is pretty nice to me and Roy. He has bought us cold drinks a million times.

Sometimes we play with Jimmy and Donald, two brothers who have a yard of good bushes for playing hide-and-seek and good grass for standing on our heads. Their old grandmother looks out the window all the time, her face pressed against the glass. Jimmy is Patricia's age and wants to be her boyfriend. Donald is Roy and Bubba's age. People feel sorry for Donald because he wears baggy shorts with an elastic waist and never puts on any underpants under there. Don't ask me why.

Sometimes when we are playing in their yard Jimmy gets

15

the idea to sneak down to Patricia's house and peep in her window. We take turns climbing up on the trashcans so we can look inside and see her bopping wildly with the door-knob of her closet, listening to some sharp music on the radio. *You ain't nothing but a hound dog.* I go crazy over that song. Those seemed strange words for a song at first, but now I think it is the best song in the world. Like it is so good you can listen to it all day and not hear it enough. Patricia says Elvis sings it and the song is sharper than sharp.

Once we looked in Patricia's window and saw her in her half-slip. It was by accident. First she curled her eyelashes, holding a mirror in her hand. Then, out of the blue, she picked up a lipstick, smeared it on, and kissed the mirror. Kissed it. She made little kiss marks and looked them over real close, studying them. She was dead serious about it. Jimmy got mad and made us get down off the trashcans and stop looking. He swatted Donald to make the rest of us stop laughing at Patricia.

When kids come to our house and see Melvina's yard full of colored boys right next to us, they get nervous. "I'm glad I don't live next to niggers," Jimmy says.

"Me and Roy are glad we don't live in such a little tiny white house like yours with such a little tiny yard."

"If Melvina hears you talking about her boys," Roy says, "she'll whip you."

It wasn't true, but Jimmy and Bubba believed it.

Melvina's house was the first one after the pavement ran out and California Street turned into a dirt road winding up into French Town. She lived on the dividing line too, first house in colored town. She had one girl, Annie, and more boys than we could count. We mostly knew her boy Skippy, because he was the meanest one, but also his brothers Alfonso Junior and Orlando, and the babies, Leroy and Nappy. We weren't sure we ever even saw all Melvina's boys.

Mother tried to tell us Melvina was a pretty woman, but none of us could see it. She was big, with shoulders like a man. She was strong and could outwork anybody if she had to. She could keep up with Walter pushing wheelbarrows of sand or grass, and she could lift any heavy thing if Walter wasn't home to do it. We thought she was bossy and too big. Her hand could wrap clean around a co-cola bottle and touch fingers. She had too much oil on her hair and got carried away about any little thing.

On the day we moved to California Street, Melvina came walking down to our house and said to Mother, "I'm Melvina Williams, a good maid. Ask anybody on this street if you don't believe me." That started it. She's been cleaning house for us ever since. Now Mother says Melvina is the best maid in the world, and we have no cause to doubt it.

From the first minute she came walking into our house acting like she owned it, me and Roy have been trying to get Melvina to take us up to her house and let us go inside and look around. But she won't do it. Walter said to Melvina, "These kids are eat up with curiosity about niggers." He said he didn't know what Mother had done to cause it, but he didn't like it. It was clear Melvina didn't like it either.

Once we offered her six mayonnaise jars full of blackberries that it had taken us all morning to pick if she would just let us go up to her house for a little while. She thought it over that time but still said no. From that point on, me and Roy dedicated our lives to getting inside Melvina's house. We make it to the edge of her yard, her dogs start barking, and Melvina shoos us off. "Go back where you belong. No white children don't belong over here." So we leave, but not before glimpsing two or three dead rattlesnakes hung over a fence or a fat 'possum tied to a tree limb waiting to be

17

skinned for supper. "Stay away from here," she yells. "These boys will get you in trouble."

We believed that was the truth. It only made us want to go twice as much. Colored boys were even more mysterious than colored women and the off-limits houses they lived in. The more we wanted to see, the more against it Melvina got.

Granddaddy spanked Roy and me when he caught us on Melvina's porch—nobody home. All we were doing was thinking over whether to sneak inside or not, but Granddaddy acts like thinking a thing is the same as doing it. "It'll never do to cross a colored woman about her house," Granddaddy said as he swatted our backsides. "She might allow dogs to sleep in the kitchen, but she is particular about people."

"But she knows us," Roy said.

"I've seen a colored woman that wouldn't allow her own husband in the house, made him wash up out in the yard at the hand pump, standing in his underwear, or even buck naked, trying to get himself cleaned up enough to go in his own wife's house. Some might say this is a man's world," Granddaddy said, "but the houses in it are women's houses. Isn't nobody more particular about her house than a colored woman."

"Why?" Roy and me wanted to know. That's all. Why? What is it about Melvina's little torn-up house that she never wants us to know? What?

$\mathcal{M}$OTHER never said nigger. She wouldn't even say Negro because it came out "Nigra," which sounded too much like nigger. "The dictionary says a nigger is a lazy person. Any color person can be lazy," she said. "There's times everybody is a nigger. But nobody wants to be called one."

She didn't actually have to tell us not to say nigger, because somehow we automatically knew. When me and Roy said nigger this, nigger that, we sounded stupid and knew it. Some people can say nigger all day and not sound that dumb. They can sound normal. But not us. When I say nigger I feel like I am pulling my pants down and peeing in the yard with people watching. Roy says he says nigger anytime he feels like it but he don't feel like it much, which is a lie.

When Mother said for us not to say it, even though we hardly ever did, we said why not. Everybody else did. Walter and Granddaddy did. "Walter and Granddaddy are Walter and Granddaddy," Mother said. "They're grown and I'm not their mother."

She wasn't our real daddy's mother either. He used to say "Nigra," which got on Mother's nerves too. "Can't you just say 'colored,' Johnny?"

" 'Nigra' is the educated word, Sarah."

"Not the way you say it, it's not."

I pretend I have forgotten this conversation—just like I pretend I have forgotten all of their conversations I remember plain.

I told Mother that Annie and Skippy and them said nigger all the time. They always called themselves and each other niggers. And besides that they called me and Roy crackers. They said, "Y'all two some white crackers." Like soda crackers are white and square and plain. They called us that.

"Well, you're not in charge of what they call you. You're just in charge of what you call them," Mother said.

We tried not to call them anything. We just called them niggers when they called us crackers. But we called them niggers quietly, so they couldn't even hear us.

"Y'all niggers, hush," we mumbled under our breath. Our lips wouldn't move saying it.

Roy said was it all right for him to call me a nigger, like when I ate something of his that he didn't say I could, or when I bossed him around. I said I called Roy a nigger that time at the picnic table when he threw a bowl of potato chips at me. Tried to hit me in the head with it. Could we just call each other niggers since we weren't colored and it didn't hurt our feelings that much?

Mother said no. She also didn't want us saying "shit" or "crap." Some words just aren't fit to use. If she heard Roy call me a fat nigger because I wrote on his face with a blue Magic Marker, she took off her bedroom slipper and swatted him, leaving a red mark that was still there at suppertime. The time I said, "Eeny meeny miney mo, catch a nigger . . . ," she came after me with the flyswatter, got me once, good, on the back of my leg.

This was because of Mother growing up out in Macon County, Alabama, where all there is is colored people. She says she didn't know there were any other white children in the world until she started school. All she ever did was play with Sudie's sister's children, James and Mae. Sudie worked for Grandmother a lot of years, so she and Granddaddy had got used to each other. After Grandmother died Sudie kept coming every day to cook and clean for Granddaddy. Now she is like our secondhand grandmother, almost. Mother loves Sudie. They tell a million stories. James and Mae this. James and Mae that. There's even pictures in Granddaddy's photo album of Mother, James, and Mae—Mother just brown as a berry, Indian brown with her shiny black ponytail, and her and Mae and James standing in a line, grinning, holding up a big string of fish they caught. They look like two black coffees and one with cream.

But I tell Mother just because James and Mae were decent back then, so what? Mother just doesn't know Skippy and

Alfonso Junior like me and Roy do. We try to be nice to them, but they never try back—except for Annie, since she's a girl.

Alfonso Junior is older than Skippy, at least he is bigger, taller. And he has a certain way about him like you'd have to wake him up to say hello. Like he is sleepwalking through those hot Tallahassee days. Like he wants to rest under a shade tree but nobody will leave him alone long enough. Like me and Roy and Mother aren't real. Like we are just cardboard people some fool drew up and cut out and set up next door to him. Just paper people—like every kind of nonsense paper thing when a person can't read. As nice as Mother is to him, he never even notices her being nice, because she is some paper doll, some white-people cut-up thing that he is too busy for. Like it is steady work, him looking for a good tree to sleep under.

It is Skippy that me and Roy pay our attention to. Him calling us soda crackers. Him always carrying on like we ought to be watching him—every minute. Like he would hate to do some little thing and us miss seeing it. Sometimes Skippy wears himself out getting us to watch him. Like once when he caught a snake he carried it way out of the way through our yard, within feet of us, slinging that thing. Being sure we saw he had it. Him and some yahoo snake strutting through our yard. And when we got interested—curious—and came close by, he said, "Who called you over here? Who be telling you to come see this snake? I ain't said nothing about y'all come look at this snake."

And Skippy will pick up a snake as quick as he will a cat. He will let one crawl on his neck and down his arm, a black snake, until me and Roy go crazy watching him. More than once he let me and Roy hold one, which we did, but we had to practically quit breathing to do it. They are not slimy, though.

And then other times when a snake crawls up into the

yard Skippy runs and gets the hoe to kill it. He would chop its head off if he could. Whack it until it is knotted and bent. It all depends. And we don't know if Skippy will do this or that—or what? All we know is he will do something. So we watch. Then he says something like, "I didn't say I need no audience to get this snake kilt. Y'all getting paid to stand out here and look at me kill a snake?"

But what bothered me and Roy most was when Skippy and them went fishing—on a school morning. On dewy, hot school days when me and Roy headed out the door and walked down California Street, to the Billups 66 station, and on across Tennessee Street to the bus stop. Us in our saddle oxfords, carrying our sack lunches. Our hair parted neat. Our teeth brushed. Roy without his boots and me in my stand-out-straight dress with the stiff crinoline under it. The grass would be wet and sometimes turtles were still in the road. And we were clomping off to school.

Then we'd see Skippy over at the ditch, right there by our house, digging for worms. Digging away, right in our faces practically. Getting an applesauce can full of fishing worms. Holding them up in front of his face like he had to study if the worms were good enough for catching fish. Like Skippy was very particular about the worms he fished with.

And then there was Alfonso Junior and Orlando and them. They got cane poles with strings wrapped around them and rusty hooks clamped onto the strings. Some brother in some size had him a jar of crickets. Melvina's wild boys, all just barefoot as the day is long. Not wearing shirts, most of them. Just raggedy shorts and bulletproof feet and their shiny skin and nappy hair with no part. They smiled their heads off.

It made me and Roy feel foolish, like we were the two sissiest things in Tallahassee. Skippy would say, "Look at them crackers be going to school." And we did not say one out-loud thing about him being a nigger and his brown brothers being some too. We acted like we didn't even hear Skippy. And he'd get real loud about he reckoned by the time we got home from school they'd have caught them a mess of catfish, because they had all day to do it. Catch a mess of fish for supper.

Me and Roy hated it, the way we felt like we were going off to church, all dressed up for some holy event that Skippy don't even believe in. So we pretend he is not real. Like we don't even see him at all. Like he is nothing whatsoever.

In the summertime when we played outdoors all day, that Florida sun trying to melt us down into little puddles the way it does a grape Popsicle when you can't eat it fast enough, trying to boil our inside juices so it was more steam than sweat that kept us damp and kept dirt and grass and gnats stuck to us, we'd get to thinking that shade, like under a big oak tree, was proof enough there was a God. And the second proof was those afternoon rains. You know, with thunder and lightning. Kind of a mad rain, like those drops are bullets being blasted from big thunder guns. And me and Roy would stand out in the yard and turn our faces up to the angry sky. We'd open our mouths to the rain and drink.

And if the ditches flooded, washing all the red clay down from the banks, making all the worms come out and swim for their lives, turning the road into a river, then me and Roy felt like rich kids with a swimming pool in our yard. We felt excited, like Walter had driven us all the way to the beach at Alligator Point to swim. It's just as good. Swimming in those red-water rain ditches. Getting cooled off and clean. Being baptized—born again—for the hot night ahead.

Mother let us gallop around in the rain. Flop and slide and splash in the ditches, getting a hard pounding from the rain, like a good beating that leaves us forgiven. But Melvina didn't like it. She said bad weather is what people have houses for, and she was against us taking chances with lightning—and messing up our clothes with red mud.

So when it started to rain, Melvina didn't allow her kids out in it, and Annie would grab up the little children and call the other brothers and hurry them in the house—all except Skippy, who would not go. Melvina let him be, because she had long ago quit expecting him to do right anyway. "Get in this house," Annie would yell, but Skippy wouldn't mind her. He would plant himself in a clear place in the yard, or in the middle of the road, and look up at the sky like he dared a stroke of lightning to try anything. With every crack of thunder he punched the air with his fists, doing a Joe Louis routine, putting on a show better than half the stuff on *Ed Sullivan*. "You ain't coming in this house with them wet clothes," Annie yelled. "Don't come around here soaking wet, saying, 'Let me in.'"

Annie was older than me, but not on schedule with it every minute. She was scared of the dark, and the woods noise, and Skippy's snakes, and she was scared of lightning and I wasn't. I liked it. When it rained, me and Roy would beg her to come outside and swim with us in the ditches or slide down a grass slope on a big piece of cardboard. We hollered for her to watch us, then tried to show her some good example of the wonderful time we were having, like once we tried riding our bicycles in the flooded ditches like they were boats, and once we got a rope and took turns pulling each other down the slick mud hill in front of Melvina's house. And Skippy would get in it with us, whatever it was, and try his best to be the boss of it. If we made boats out of leaves and sticks, Skippy made bombs out of wet pine cones; if we went underwater and held our breath for a minute, he went under and held his for a minute and a half, disappearing until me and Roy think he is dead and we splash into the deep part of the ditch and pull him out, then he spits water and shakes his head like a wet dog

24

and starts laughing. There is nothing we do that Skippy won't try to outdo. He gets right in it with us. But not Annie.

"Come on, Annie," I call. She is looking out the window. "Come outside. I promise no lightning will get you."

"You can't promise nothing for the rain," she hollered back. "You can't speak for the sky, fool."

Then Skippy laughed like I was stupid. If I saved his life I don't think it would matter. If I came into money and gave him half—it wouldn't matter. Nothing I could do would make that colored boy like me. Me, a straggly, yellow-haired, too skinny, big-toothed, scab-legged girl. Me, a wish-we-could-be-friends-'cause-you-run-through-the-rain-like-that girl. And Skippy acts like I am not worth the trouble it would take to spit on me. He has to look at me with his go-fishing eyes that say I am a fool in my stand-out crinoline dress. And he does it. All the time.

But I was not always going to be straggly and wish-I-could. That was the thing. Later on I would be a bright and shiny golden thing, like Mother said. After a few more summers in the Florida sun, that sun with a smiling face that is painted all over every Florida thing—that welcome-to-Florida smiling sun—would turn me golden like a slice of white bread that's been toasted and buttered. That's what Mother said. And Roy, Roy in the summer is so brown you don't know how brown he is until he gets buck naked and goes to get in the bathtub. And there is his white butt. You think you never saw white completely until you see Roy's butt. You didn't know he was so brown until you see how white his butt is. My butt is as white as Roy's, but it doesn't seem like it since the rest of me is not that brown.

In the summertime when we were little, when Mother was in the bathroom making sure we soaped up good, and washed under our arms and behind our ears, and washed the sweat necklaces from around our necks, she would call

Roy her little chocolate drop. Chocolate Roy with his vanilla butt. She looked at the dirt that came off us in the tub water and said it was some of his sweet chocolate that got scrubbed off. She dried him off with a big towel and kissed all over his face, making smacking sounds, and said, "Mmmmm, so sweet I could eat you right up. You little chocolate drop." And Roy squirmed around acting like he wished she would quit that foolishness, stupid kissing and all.

And me, especially close up by Mother and Roy, me, Mother would call her golden girl. Her drying me off and saying, "That old Mr. Sunshine better look out, because right here is a little golden girl that's going to grow up and be shinier than the sun itself. Isn't that right, Lucy?" And I didn't act like Roy about it, like I wanted to get away from Mother's foolishness. No. I believed it. Every word.

Me, a golden thing—and Skippy just still going to be colored. Me, shiny—and him shining shoes or something. Him carrying my groceries. Him mowing my grass. Him holding the door open. I never did want it to get like that, Skippy turning into one them yes-ma'am, no-sir colored men. One those I'm-so-lazy-I-could-die colored men that sat out front of the Snack Shack gas station up there in French Town. It was not me that made up how things would be.

But it was going to happen like that someday, when I got those breasts Mother said I wanted and didn't know it. As soon as I got breasts then Skippy Williams could never look at me again, not out loud. Couldn't be calling his brothers to come over here and feel of my yellow hair. Feel how it looks like some that stringly stuff comes up on top of a fresh-picked corn ear. So if I was ever going to get him to like me I didn't have much time to do it in, because once I got golden—he was still going to be colored.

It was just like Mother and James, back then with Mae. Them rubbing together in the saddle on Granddaddy's horse, and never any black came off on one or any white on the other. Them drinking out of the same tin cup and biting into the same juicy peach. And now Mother sees James, grown and married to Viola. She pats his arm and says, "Hey there, James. How you been treating yourself?" She just pats his arm like he was some one-hundred-year-old man and not that boy that shook a bloody squirrel knife in her face or chased her with a handful of slick fish eyes.

But when Mother sees Sudie she remembers everything. She loves on Sudie. Hugs her neck a bunch of times. Got some presents for her out in the car. Says to us, "Here is sweet, sweet Sudie. Y'all give Sudie some sugar." And we all hug her neck and love on her. But Mother can't be hugging James until he's so old he's about to die. And probably not then.

And it's the same with James. He can't be looking at Mother. James can't say, "Lord, Sarah, you looking good, girl." He can't say, "You some fine-looking woman, Sarah. I'll say that. Fine." Maybe he never did want to say such a thing. Maybe James wouldn't take money to say it. But it doesn't matter. It's not about what he thinks. It's about what he can say. He better not go say some fool thing that will make the world slam on brakes and sling everybody off. All of us. Him too. Nobody told me this. I was just born knowing it.

So I don't know why I bother with it. Skippy Williams. I just get this idea sometimes that I want him to like me. It's crazy and the idea goes away. Besides, I know that deep down Skippy has got to be a hotshot colored boy now, because later on me and Roy are going to be hotshot white people. He can't waste his chance.

I don't even know if Roy knows about these things. Once I tried to tell him how I was someday going to be a bright and shiny golden thing that Skippy never could look at. And he just said, "So what? Skippy don't want to look at you anyway. Shoot. Just because he's a nigger don't mean he's crazy."

I hate Roy.

I'M just beginning to under-
stand the categories. Colored people have their categories
the same as white people.

All whites have is white trash, which is poor people who
are as bad off as colored people but don't have the good
excuse for it that colored people have. So they are sorry in
most everybody's eyes, never will amount to anything and
don't even try to. You can recognize them when you see
them—their long-haired kids got pinkeye, blackened
fingernails, and traces of food dried on their faces. And their
run-down houses, car parts stacked in the yard, gray clothes
hung on the line for days at a time until they look like
weather-warped pieces of wood, and a pack of starved dogs
sleeping in the bald sun. They always leave their front and
back door hanging open so you can look inside and see them
hunched in there sweating. A bunch of white trash are in
prison, Mother says. A bunch of them work on Walter's
prison road crews. Seems like mostly they are skinny, but
sometimes the women are real fat. You can recognize them
in grocery stores especially, and they always have either
torn-up cars or no cars at all. Usually they have something
wrong with their teeth.

Then there is regular white people. Like us.

Then there is the rich white people, which is the kind
everybody wishes they were. You can recognize them too.

Nobody really likes them but everybody has to pretend they do. They talk a lot and never mean a thing they say. It's understood they're liars. But they're very polite about it. Sometimes they live in houses big enough for thirty or forty people to live in. The wives buy china and clothes and get their hair colored. Sometimes they fly up to New York and nobody thinks less of them for it. They have the most greedy, selfish children in the world. They make fun of the migrant children when they come to school dressed like they're about to be thrown in a trash pile. (Migrant kids know they are white trash, so they never speak a single word the whole two weeks they come to school.) The rich kids will not sit by them at lunch. They invite each other to birthday parties held at the swimming pools in their backyards. The rich daddies usually go into politics. They slowly get bald and fat and buy up everything for miles around. When the legislature is in session Tallahassee swarms with them. Mother says half of them have girlfriends put up at the Howard Johnson's.

So there's three main kinds of white people.

It seems like there are three main kinds of colored people too. There is colored, which is the best, and Negro which comes out Nigra, and then the nigger part, where Melvina's husband, Old Alfonso, just barely did fit before falling all the way off the bottom of the scale.

Melvina never was a nigger. She was always colored because of how decent she was. She worked without too much complaining or too much failing to show up. She went to church regularly, which was a good sign. She didn't fight too much, or get drunk, or run loose with men, or go to jail, or be sullen to white people for no good reason. Colored was for people who did things closest to the regular white way. And also, if a person's skin was sort of milky instead of pitch-black, then that helped too. But green eyes and such did not. Melvina was colored, all right. Anybody would say so.

But Old Alfonso, now. No. He didn't qualify. Never held any regular job, drunk up any money he got, went to jail on assorted occasions due to his niggerish ways. Probably carried a razor in his shoe or at least a knife in his pocket, because if niggerism was a club that would be the first rule for getting in. He would lie in a minute, probably steal anything he had sense enough to realize was worth something. Also went around dressed in some way to call attention to himself, like with a stocking on his head, or one of Melvina's kerchiefs tied crazy on there. He would always hide and not cooperate with any white people, like the sheriff when he comes to the house and Old Alfonso hides under the porch like that. Now that's niggerish. And beating up Melvina is too, and most everything he does is. Anybody thinks so. Even Melvina, maybe.

As for Negroes, all that is is the people that fall in between Melvina's goodness and Old Alfonso's sorriness. When anybody talks about a Negro it means somebody they don't know at all, never met him, just seen him or something. We never called Melvina and them Negroes because we knew them better than that. We were personal with them.

No one told me all this. I'm figuring it out myself. The part I'm not sure of is the children. If they have to be what their parents are or not. Like since Melvina is colored and Old Alfonso is a nigger, what does that make their kids? I'm almost certain Annie will grow up to be colored, but I'm not sure about any of those boys.

I know this. White trash is the very worst thing you can be—but nigger lover comes in second. Mother is devoted to us not being one and Walter is devoted to us not being the other.

*T*HE first time we ever saw
Old Alfonso he was drowning dogs. We didn't know then
that Melvina had a husband for sure, so we took the
bent-over colored man to be a robber. He circled Melvina's
yard, snatching up stumbling puppies, slinging them into a
croaker sack.

Melvina was cleaning down at our house, but we didn't
go get her, yelling, "Melvina, somebody is stealing your
dogs." We just watched this colored man, like an inside-out
Santa Claus chasing the rolling-around puppies, grabbing
them by the back of the neck, dragging his sack behind him.

His presence had cleared Melvina's yard of kids, except
her boy Orlando, who was watching and crying. Roy and I
eased up as close as we could. In a minute Annie came out
on the back steps, saying, "Daddy, make Orlando come
inside the house." The old man looked at Orlando a couple
of seconds, sharp, like his eyes were bullets ready to shoot
out. He didn't say a word to the boy. Orlando went in the
house. He walked right by Roy and me with his nose
running. "Is that Old Alfonso?" I asked Orlando.

He ignored me.

"Is that y'all's daddy?" I yelled to Annie.

"Hush," Roy said.

"Are you Melvina's husband?" I hollered to the man. He
did not even look at me.

"You two go home," Annie ordered from her porch,
hands on her hips, chin jutted out like the toe of a shoe.

"We don't have to," Roy yelled back.

I don't know how many puppies it was, seven or eight,
most of them golden, a couple spotted, all of them looking
like sweet names—Honey or Butterscotch—snatched up
and pitched in a burlap sack, yelping like crazy. "What's he
doing?" Roy says.

Old Alfonso turned on the water spigot, filled up the washtub until it was overflowing. He slung the sack of puppies into the tub, squatted, and held the sack underwater, those puppies struggling and jerking.

Even with Old Alfonso sitting dead still, the water in the tub kicked and slapped up over the edges. Old Alfonso wrestled the sack, his muscles knotting under his skin. A couple of times it seemed the struggle was over, then the croaker sack lurched up again. "He's drowning those puppies," Roy whispered.

I watched Old Alfonso with the same stupidness I use watching Walter clean fish. I pretend I understand the sense in it as good as he does. I look at those scared fish that keep their eyes wide open and make kissing motions with their mouths right up to the second Walter slams the knife down and cuts off their heads.

"Skippy!" Old Alfonso's voice was so hateful it made me and Roy jump. He drew out the dripping sack of dead dogs and sloshed it to shake out the water. Skippy came out of the house. "Take these dogs," Old Alfonso said, "and bring me back my sack." He handed Skippy the neck of the dripping bag. It was heavy, but Skippy didn't drag it. He lifted it, straining, his eyes looking away, like if his eyes didn't see, his brain wouldn't know. He started across the back corner of our yard towards the woods. He should get a shovel, I thought. How can he bury them without a shovel?

"What are you going to do with those puppies?" Roy yells. Skippy looks away. The sack is too heavy, he can't keep it lifted, he lowers it to the ground and drags it. "Can I see them dogs?" Roy takes off running after Skippy. "I never seen drowned dogs."

Roy's grief is nothing long and drawn out.

Walter killed a cat once.

He was not married to Mother then. He lived in the

trailer next door to ours. Roy was too little to have good sense, and when a scramble-colored cat wandered into our yard he grabbed it. It clawed him to ribbons. Instead of putting it down Roy held tighter. The cat hissed and threw a fit. Roy started screaming but would not let go until Mother ran outside hollering, "Rabies!" When the cat got loose from Roy it made slow semicircles and sidestepped around. It had runny sores where the fur was gone. Mother was shrieking. So Walter came outside to see if World War III had started.

He looked at that cat and went and got his gun. While Mother poured Mercurochrome on Roy's scratches Walter shot that cat. One bullet. One loud, quick blast. He put the dead cat in a croaker sack and slung it in the back of his truck and hauled it off. A croaker sack is an animal coffin. It can be a dog or a cat coffin, either one. Walter keeps a pile of croaker sacks in the back of his truck.

So Walter has killed a living thing too. But he says he was putting something out of misery instead of into it. Besides, all Walter killed was a cat, but Old Alfonso killed dogs. And that's the difference.

People had a way of bringing stray puppies to California Street. They'd drive past our house to the edge of colored town, right in front of Melvina's house, and dump out litters. Sacks full. Cardboard boxes full. Puppies and kittens. In the rain sometimes.

Melvina said she didn't want the half-starved, mangy things straggling over to her house, she had enough kids and dogs already. So Melvina's boys gathered the abandoned litters, put them in a box, and wearing big grins, went down California Street to the white people's houses, giving the puppies away. Sometimes me and Roy tagged along.

Skippy was the best at getting rid of animals. In fact, that's how we got one-eyed George. He wasn't a puppy or even half cute-looking. Mother says beauty is in the eye of the beholder, but we never knew any beholder who could see beauty in George. Skippy came to our house carrying George in his arms. Roy and me were in the yard and saw him coming.

"Whose dog is that?" Roy asked.

"This fixing to be Jesus' dog," Skippy said.

"Jesus?"

"This dog's gon die today—or maybe tomorrow. He's an old dog. See here." He showed us George's gray, whiskered face. "Don't nobody love this ugly dog," Skippy said.

"I do," Roy said. "He's not so ugly."

But he was. George was about as ugly as a dog could be. Besides him being old as the hills, his color was scrambled up black and white, with a speckled face. He had one crooked leg. He looked like he had been a nice bulldog in the beginning, with a smashed-in face and bowed legs, but now he was just an old mess. The worst thing about George, though, worse than his nasty mouth full of missing and broken teeth, worse than his fleas and sore spots, was the fact that he was missing one eyeball. He had an empty hole in his head. You could poke your finger in there and he wouldn't even twitch. A creepy dog with a hole in his head like that.

Skippy stood in the yard. "Only the kindest people can save this old dog. He ain't been treated good. Look. Some mean kids poked his eye out with a stick. They watched that eyeball roll around in the dirt. They kicked it."

"They kicked it?" said Roy.

"You don't know that," I said. "You're making that up."

"What you think?" Skippy said. "This dog was walking down the road and that eyeball just fell out his head?"

"No," I said, "but . . ."

"I'm just showing y'all this dog before I take it down the street," Skippy said. "There's a white lady wants this dog bad. If she don't take him the dog catcher's gon kill him. Feed him poison or shoot him with a gun."

If Roy's eyes had gotten any bigger his skin would have split. "We're kind people," he said. "We are."

"Boy, your mama won't let you keep this dog."

"She will too."

"She might," I said. "Roy, go in the house and ask Mother if we can have a dog. Go on."

Roy sprinted in the house.

"And bring out some food," I yelled.

I stood looking at the ugly dog, thinking about how we could fix him up. Put some of Walter's black shoe polish on his gray face. Maybe put a big marble in his eye socket; probably couldn't find a brown marble that would match—but a big blue marble wouldn't be bad. We could glue it in. We could make him a collar out of clothesline wire and hang a bell on it. We could teach him tricks, like how to fetch the *Tallahassee Democrat* and bring it to Walter and how to stand on his hind legs and beg for a Vienna sausage. We could even sneak him in the house and let him sleep in the bed with us. With a little fixing up we could turn this half-dead bulldog into a pretty decent pet.

Mother came outside carrying Benny, with Roy at her heels. "Hey, Skippy," she said. "What you got?" Benny began to squeal and make little fists trying to reach for the dog. He leaned so hard Mother nearly dropped him.

"I just found this old dog here, ma'am."

"Poor thing." Mother fingered a place where a flap of the dog's skin hung down in a fold.

"That ear got bit off," Skippy said.

"Poor old thing," Mother said.

Skippy smiled. He knew he'd made the sale.

We named our pet George. It sounded old and respectable. He mostly wanted to lie in the sun and sleep, but we insisted he have some fun. We fed him bologna and tried to get him to drink milk, but he turned up his nose. We looped a rope around his neck and tied him to a shade tree in the yard. We said this was in case anybody came along and tried to steal him while we weren't looking.

That afternoon when Walter came home he saw old George in the yard. He saw pine straw piled up with a nice towel on it in case George, who was lying in the dirt, wanted to sleep in a soft spot. He saw the tin pie plates set around with food and water. He saw Roy and me, hairbrush in hand, back-combing George's fur, looking for ticks.

"What the hell?" said Walter.

"Mother said we can keep him," Roy said.

Walter looked at George sprawled out on his stomach, four legs extended north, south, east, and west. "Couldn't you find one no uglier?"

"We're going to fix him up," I said.

"The only thing that'll fix that dog is a shotgun."

"Walter!" we screamed, afraid we would have to run in the house and get Mother to tell Walter she said we could keep old George.

"George can learn stuff," I said. "This is just his first day." We looked at the sleeping dog. He didn't budge, just an occasional twitch to chase off a fly.

"Well," Walter said. "A dog that ugly ought to scare off salesmen and preachers. Shoot, he'd scare me off if it wasn't broad daylight."

Mother came out on the steps and hugged Walter's neck. Me and Roy liked it when she did that. Walter liked it too. His face turned blood red.

"It's okay with me," Walter said, "as long as he eats scraps and don't cost money." Me and Roy smiled like crazy.

"You're going to have to wash up good after fooling with that old dog," Walter said. "He's liable to have worms and who knows what all. You're going to have to wash with soap."

We felt happy, Mother hugging Walter—and us with a

new dog we could keep. Roy and me sat out under the tree for the longest time petting old George, our own dog, while he slept, his pink tongue hanging out the side of his mouth, making a pool of slobber in the sand.

At supper we told Walter about Skippy bringing George to our house. That mean kids poked out George's eyeball with a stick, that the dog catcher was going to shoot him, that George needed kind folks—which was us. Walter kept eating and shaking his head. "Too bad that boy is a nigger," he said. "He could sell ice to the Eskimos. Hell, if they wouldn't buy it, he could sell it to your mama."

Walter was right about Skippy. Me and Roy watched him enough to know that. When white kids on California Street saw Skippy carrying a cardboard box from house to house, they took off in a tear, bunches of them, yelling, "Go ask my mama," and, "Where you get all them dogs from?" It would be a lie if I said I didn't think much of it.

One hundred times I asked Skippy to let me help carry the boxes of puppies when he and Orlando started down the white end of California Street. One hundred times I begged to pet a sick puppy or carry a scared yellow cat with his eyes crusted over. "Hush, girl," Skippy said.

"Please, Skippy." I strung a chain of pleases all the way down California Street, one please for every step we took, until Skippy could not ignore me any better than he could a barking dog, and he did me the same way you do a barking dog, ignore it first, then sling something at it, like a handful of mean words.

"Just because you got one half-dead dog don't mean you know nothing about puppies," Skippy said.

"Old George is not half dead."

"Might be all the way dead, old as he is."

"He's not dead. Take that back."

"How do you know that dog ain't laying dead in your

yard and all you care about is worrying me about some puppies?"

"George is not dead. I don't care what you say."

"Then where's he at?"

"At home, sleeping."

"Sleeping sure do look like dead."

Skippy drives me crazy saying that. Like he's an expert on death since the time Old Alfonso sent him to the woods with the sackful of drowned dogs. It was Skippy's job to bury them—but he didn't take a shovel with him. I think about that. Burying something with no shovel to dig the hole. I picture Skippy laying the blond puppies in a dead row and clawing out graves for them in the soft dirt by the stream, using his bare hands. Were the puppies' eyes open? I've asked him, "How did you bury those dogs with no shovel?"

As sure as I am that George is in our yard asleep in the sun, listening to Skippy I'm not sure at all. I have to go home and see. Is George dead or alive? I run home, getting more doubtful and breathless by the minute, picturing George on his back with his four stiff legs pointing at the hot Tallahassee sky. I run barefoot on the gravel, through the sandspurs, home. My eyes search the yard for old George. I run from tree to tree, look under the car, under the house, in every flower bed. It's up to me to stop death. I am an angel of mercy, believing that I can keep George alive just by laying my eyes on him. Just by seeing him asleep in some shady spot, and poking him gently with a stick or calling his name so he will lift his head and be saved. I run into the yard screaming George's name.

It's not hard to locate him. George sleeps like a rock in the coolest shade he can find. I know all the places to look. Under the picnic table, behind the back steps, on the cool water hose, coiled and wet after Walter has unhooked it from the sprinkler. I always find George—he's never dead.

•

I bet Skippy goes to sleep at night laughing at me. I bet he thinks we are crazy white people the way we love an ugly dog like George. I bet he thinks he could give us a dead dog and make us glad to have it. I picture him carrying a mangled, bloody dog, just run over by a car, and all of us gathering around him, begging to keep it.

I sit in the shade beside old George and pet him while he sleeps, running my fingers gently around the hole in his head. He'll let me stick my finger in there, but I don't like to. Sometimes his hind leg starts to jerk like he's scratching something. I think he's dreaming of running fast.

I wish Skippy liked me. I picture him dragging the croaker sack into the woods and burying those puppies. He says I don't know anything about puppies, but he's wrong. Some nights when I go to sleep I put my mind in that croaker sack where it is dark and helpless, and I feel how it is to struggle against something that has you closed up in it.

*T*HE *Tallahassee Democrat* came in the afternoon. Mother always read the letters to the editor out loud. They were mostly about integration and said things Roy and Benny and I didn't want to hear. I never could tell if Melvina wanted to hear the letters or not. She only listened while she ironed Walter's shirts. Sometimes after a particularly stupid letter she said, "He must of been behind the door when God was handing out brains," or she'd say to Mother as she read, "If you're singing that one in parts you can leave mine out."

Four o'clock in the afternoon, right when Popeye came on

TV, Mother sent Roy out to get the newspaper. She read each letter out loud, commenting on it, while we watched Popeye and Brutus beat each other half to death. They pounded each other with hammers, ran over each other with cars. Melvina ironed, listening. I polished my toenails. Mother said, "Can you believe a preacher would write such a thing? A preacher now?" Most of the letters said integration would never work. They quoted the Bible. I believe if our preacher at Trinity Methodist had written an anti-integration letter we could have got out of going to church for the rest of our lives.

ROY sneaks to the Snack Shack anytime he can come up with a little pocket change. He goes up there in the middle of all those colored people and buys baseball cards with bubble gum, or fried pigskins and RC Colas, or candy cigarettes. I know because he brings that stuff home to eat in front of me and make me wish I had some. He goes so much I guess they know him up there. Regular Roy. Mother and Walter don't have any idea about it because they don't allow it, same as they don't allow Roy to do half the stuff he does.

A few times I'd been to the Snack Shack with Walter when he went to get some chewing tobacco. A few times when I was younger, Mother let me walk up there with Annie and Skippy to get her some dishwashing soap, and we bought ourselves Popsicles. But then Walter got to where he didn't like it, me and Roy up in colored town, running around with Skippy, and he quit allowing it. I haven't been a time since.

It makes Roy hate me when I do things right. He has no respect for it. He starts acting like he knows more than I do, even though I am a good two years older than him. So sometimes I have to let up, and that's what I did one day in August when the sun was frying Tallahassee in a skillet. It was so hot all I could think about was a cold drink or an ice cream sandwich. It got on my mind like water gets on somebody's mind when they are lost in a desert. So I said to Roy, "Let's sneak up to the Snack Shack and get us something cold to drink."

We got on our bicycles to do it and rode them behind Melvina's house, which, of course, we didn't have to worry about Melvina catching us, because she was always down at our house, eight to five, Monday through Friday, cleaning for Mother. All there was at her house was Annie and a yard full of kids who didn't pay us any more mind than they would have two dogs crossing the yard. "Where y'all going?" Annie said, hardly looking up from where she sat running a comb through Leroy's hair while he hollered his head off.

"Nowhere," Roy answered.

We pushed our bikes through a path on the other side of Melvina's house until we were out of sight of our own house. Then we pedaled up the dirt road and around some curves, with dogs barking at us. Roy rode a good ten paces ahead of me to make it clear who the leader was. It's not that far, but we were breathing hard when we got there because it was so blasted hot, and uphill all the way.

We parked our bicycles out front, at least I did, leaned it on its kickstand, but Roy just slung his down on the ground like he didn't have no idea what a kickstand was for. We went inside and started poking through the cold-drink box, taking our time. Some old colored men sitting on the bench outside, all they did was nod their heads at us and sort of look me over since I was not a regular like Roy. It was dark

inside the store, and too hot, but they had a window fan
going.

Before we made up our minds good on what to buy, a car
pulled up out front and stopped. Two colored men got out.
They were young and one had on eyeglasses. He was the
first colored person I ever saw wear eyeglasses. They walked
inside the store, had on white shirts and neckties like two
Jehovah's Witnesses, and they had a bunch of papers in
their hands.

"Afternoon, sir," one man says to Daddy Joe behind the
counter. They call him Daddy Joe because he says he feeds
half the women and children in French Town on credit, it's
like he daddies them, so people call him Daddy Joe. Roy
told me that, but don't ask me how Roy knows. Anyway,
one of the men says, "Afternoon, sir," to Daddy Joe, and
me and Roy stopped to look at him—besides, it feels good
to stand in front of the drink box with the lid open, that cold
air slapping our faces.

"Mind if we put up this notice in your store?" the man
said, handing a paper to Daddy Joe. "We're putting them
around in all the stores. It's about a meeting is all. Over at
the Good Shepherd Church."

"What kind of meeting?" Daddy Joe asked, not reading
the paper, just holding it in his hand.

"A unity meeting, sir. We got a speaker coming all the
way from Atlanta. An important man with important things
to say."

The man talking sounded strange to me. He talked just
like a white person. Even Daddy Joe noticed it. I could tell
by his eyebrows shifting up when he listened. It was white
talk.

"It's time the black man armed himself with a political
organization, sir," the white-talking colored man kept on.
"The black man must . . ."

Black man? Calling hisself black? It's the pot that calls the kettle black, I thought; now it's the colored man that talks white calling hisself black. I had never heard it before. I heard colored people call themselves niggers, and that was bad enough. Mother never would let us call colored people black. "How would you like it, Lucy, if somebody called you black?" she had said. I knew, of course, that I wouldn't like it. And furthermore I thought that if anybody ever called Melvina black I would argue the point for her, saying she is only brown as a berry, shoe-polish brown.

The man with the papers said things about a black army to march for liberty, and it gave me shivers, but I could tell Roy liked the sound of it—an army, guns and bombs and those metal canteens you get to carry your water in, like the one Walter got Roy that he carries in the woods with Kool-Aid in it. Roy is crazy about war equipment.

"The black man is going to have to vote his way into freedom. It's time we got us some of that 'liberty and justice for all,' " the man said.

Daddy Joe didn't look too sure he wanted such talk as that plastered up in his store, so then the two men threw Jesus into it, making it sound like the meeting was really a gospel sing and the speaker was going to talk about the colored man's Christian duty. So then Daddy Joe understood—and I felt better myself. Nobody in Tallahassee is going to say no to any doings that concern Jesus. Daddy Joe let them tack up one paper on the windowsill and one on the front of the counter by the cash register.

"I'll leave some of these right here that you can pass out," the man with eyeglasses said, and he set a stack of papers on the counter. Then he walked outside handing each old man on the bench a copy. I bet one hundred dollars they couldn't read a word between them. Then, after smiling and saying, "Good day, sir," the two fancy colored men were in their car and off down the road.

"A couple of Florida A 'n' M boys," Daddy Joe said,

"that's all." He is like Walter—the way they explain strange behavior by pointing to the nearest university.

The dust hadn't settled good when up came another car screeching to a stop out front, five or six boys in it. White boys. Two of them got out and came in the store. The first boy, with hair so blond it was white, pointed to the paper in the window, then snatched it down. "Looks like somebody been leaving trash laying around your store, don't it, Daddy Joe?"

Then the other boy, small and long-haired, saw the paper tacked on the counter. "If there's anything I hate," he said, "it's somebody messing up a man's store with garbage." He pulled the paper off and tore it up.

I guess they would have left then, because their car motor was still running and those other boys were out there waiting, except for seeing me and Roy standing there. "Well, looka here," the white-headed boy said. "What we got here?"

All me and Roy did was walk over to the counter to pay for our cold drinks. We didn't say nothing. I wanted to get some of those miniature wax co-cola bottles that have grape drink in them, but I forgot about it, I guess, and Roy put the few pennies change in his pocket.

"Does your mama know you're up here in nigger town?" the white-headed boy said, stepping too close to us. We eased by him, drinks in hand, and on through the doorway outside. I was nervous, like when the teacher makes you stand up and read out loud in front of everybody, their eyes crawling all over you, making little prints on your skin. It's a prickly feeling, and it makes me hurry up. It makes me read too fast and slur. Now it made me scramble down the steps too fast. I stumbled, sloshing RC on my leg.

The two boys laughed at me. It felt like somebody had struck a match inside my chest. I looked over at the car with the other boys in it. One of them had his hand out the window slapping the fender to a radio song. I looked at them one second, and I thought I saw Jimmy, Donald's big brother, who lives four houses down from us. I felt better for an instant, but the instant faded because I wasn't sure.

"Don't be coming up here." The white-headed boy leaped out of the doorway and grabbed my bicycle handlebars. "You hear me? This ain't no place for white kids."

"You're here," Roy said. He was about to pick up his bicycle from the ground, but the long-haired boy slammed his foot down on it, making Roy drop it and spill his cold drink too. "Look what you done," Roy yelled. "You owe me for that cold drink."

"I don't owe you nothing, boy. You better get out of here before I decide I do."

"You're not the boss of me." Roy shoved his hands into the boy's chest. He laughed and shoved Roy back. Roy fell over the bicycle and landed on his butt.

"You better get on home before you hurt yourself," the long-haired boy said.

"You ain't the boss of me," Roy yelled again, trying to jerk the bike out from under the boy's foot. Roy's eyes were ready to spill. He will all but kill a person before he lets them make him cry—he once half killed me with a baseball bat and it took Walter to stop him. He can be something when he's mad, little as he is. He grabbed the empty drink bottle lying spilt at his feet and jumped up slinging it back and forth in front of him, striking at the long-haired boy. "Holy shit!" the boy said. Roy was mad and trying to crack him in the ribs with the bottle, and he can be mean enough to do it. The boy stepped back and Roy held that bottle in his hand like it was a gun. "Your hair is so long you could put a ribbon in it," he said. He leaned over, picked up his bicycle, and was on it and pedaling before I could think.

"Come on, Lucy," he said, but the white-headed boy still held my handlebars. "Come on!" Roy shouted again, like the trouble was I hadn't heard him.

"He's got my bike," I said.

"Let go of her bike!" Roy yelled, but the boy made no move to do it. Roy reared his arm back, hollering again, "Let go of her bike!" Then he slung the drink bottle at the boy, but he was off aim and hit the long-haired boy instead—whacked him across the shin. He dropped to the ground, cussing. The white-headed boy let go of my bike and leaped down to grab the bottle and chase Roy with it. I tried to get on my bicycle but my kickstand was stuck, and I dropped my RC struggling to kick it up. The boy threw the bottle at Roy, who was fast-pedaling down the road. It made a crashing noise when it hit his bicycle. Then Roy was out of sight.

"Let's go," one of the boys yelled out the car window. He honked the horn a few times and yelled again, "Them niggers are halfway to Georgia with those papers and you out here messing with kids."

The long-haired boy hobbled on over to the car, mumbling. But the other boy stayed. He held my arm tight, cutting into my flesh with his fingernails. "Where you live?"

"Down there." I nodded.

"Well, you come on and we'll ride you home in the car."

"No."

The boy yanked my arm, and my bicycle fell to the ground beside me. "No," I said again.

"Let go the girl," a boy yelled from the car. It sounded like Jimmy.

"We're going to ride her home." The white-headed boy was dragging me. "Ain't safe, a white girl up in nigger town like this."

I'd heard stories about girls who got in cars and were never seen again. Terrible things happen to a girl in a car full of strangers. The boy jerked my arm. My knees went limp and I squatted, pressing my feet into the road like bad brakes. But he kept pulling, my feet like two raw skis across the red dirt. I used my free hand to try and unpeel his fingers. "Please," I said.

There was a thud and the boy sprang loose from me. I dropped flat down. He yowled, put his hands on his head, and I saw blood. Something else hit him, a broken piece of brick, and another one and another one, hitting his chest and his back when he turned to run. I scrambled up. Clumps of cement and chips of brick were flying. "Over here, Lucy. By the trash barrel."

It was Skippy.

I ran to him. The white-headed boy was hopping all over the road trying to get to the car, Skippy slinging stuff at him. "Get behind the store," Skippy hollered, and I ran to do it. He grabbed a drink bottle and hurled it as hard as he could just as the boy got into the car. The bottle hit the windshield and shattered, making a crack in the glass. Skippy grabbed my arm, the same arm the other boy had just let go of, and we started to run through the woods behind the store.

I don't remember running at first. I remember being pulled, Skippy's hand clasped on to my arm. In a minute I could feel my legs, the briers that slapped across my face, and how hard I ran, harder than I breathed, my crying suspended in front of me like the thing I was running to, like a reward when I got there.

No words passed between us. Just the rustle of bushes and slapping tree branches, just twigs and sticks snapping under our feet. The woods splashed around us unevenly, like an ocean of green. We ran where there was no path, stumbling through vines and jumping underbrush when we could, so that it seemed we were running through a rolling green tunnel and very soon would be spilled out the end of it. My fear of being chased was so strong, the sound of the slamming car doors and the yelling boys who had come bounding after us, the sound of their thrashing through the edge of the woods, me almost unconscious at first, like a flimsy paper kite Skippy held by a string. I had only a sense of foreign territory, of running far beyond reasonable limits into woods for colored people only. I knew in my heart that no white person—certainly no white girl—had ever been this deep into the colored people's woods. I ran as hard as I could, as fast as I could, into the most forbidden place imaginable. It pleased me in my pain, that flash of seeming to be chasing Skippy, rather than being pulled by him. That sense of running faster than it's possible to run.

Twice I fell. Once because my foot got caught, tangled in a sticker vine, and I fell so hard I scraped the skin off my knee. Skippy yanked me up and we ran twice as hard until we stopped hearing the voices, until the white boys abandoned the chase and the only noise was our own furious breathing as we crashed through the woods. I fell the second time because I was too tired, my green lungs threatening to burst. My legs folded under me and I collapsed on the ground, my heart stomping like a grown man kicking me in the chest again and again. Skippy didn't pull me up. He sank beside me and breathed with his head between his knees. We were loud breathing. I thought I was crying at first, but I wasn't. It was sweat running down my face. Sweat poured off Skippy too, down his neck and bare chest. I don't know how long we stayed like that, gasping, lying still in a dark woods that continued to swirl.

"What are you smiling at?" Skippy looked at me hard.
"I don't know."
"Well, stop smiling."
"I'm sorry."
"There's nothing to smile about."
"I know." But there was something to smile about. I was deep, deep in the woods for colored only—a place not even Roy had ever been. We had outrun a whole carload of boys together, Skippy and me, making us—this one time in our lives—on the same side. I liked it more than I can say.

Skippy rolled over on his back. He was drenched. He was the darkest boy I'd ever seen in my life. I always pretended he was just another barefoot colored boy going around shirtless in a pair of ragged shorts. I pretended I didn't see his face any more than I saw his whitish brother Orlando's face, or Alfonso Junior's ugly face, or the faces of sweet little Leroy and Nappy. But in all the time I pretended not to be looking at Skippy, I had memorized him. He had a small chip off his front tooth, and when he smiled, lines cut into his face, curving from his cheekbones to the sides of his mouth. His hair coiled into tiny circles above his ear, individual hairs making individual circles. I always wanted to touch his hair. Stuff got stuck in it. Right now he had bits of pine needles and dried leaves in it where he laid his head on the ground. He almost never looked at anybody unless he was mad. I'd learned that about him. I told myself that he never looked at me the same thorough way I never looked at him. And for the same reasons. His skin shone. I liked him. Of all the boys in the world, he was the one that I most wanted to like me. And he was the one most resistant to doing it. But we weren't in that world now—we were deep in the colored woods, deep.

"Skippy," I said. "Are you afraid of me?"

He leaned up on his elbows. "Why would I be scared of you?" He looked like he was thinking about laughing.

I reached for his hand, keeping my eyes on his. His hand was bigger than mine, the underside as pink as the inside of a seashell. He held his hand up. I fit mine against it. "I've always wanted to see how our hands would look."

"You satisfied with what you see?"

"I've always wondered."

Skippy took his hand away and slid back so that he was sitting against a tree. I moved over and sat next to him. "You're crazy if you think I'm scared of you." He placed his open hand on the ground between us. "Here."

Nobody ever tells you that fear is soft and ticklish. Certain kinds of fear. This kind. I put my hand on top of his.

It didn't look the way I wished. There was dirt under my fingernails and spots of clear polish that hadn't chipped all the way off yet. But I liked the feeling.

"Your hand is shaking," I told him.

"No, it's not."

He was right. It was my hand.

We sat in silence until a rabbit hopped within two feet of us. Skippy sprang after it, nearly catching it. The rabbit disappeared into the thorns.

"Let's go, girl."

We made our way through the pathless woods, slowly this time, Skippy leading the way, stopping to hold a branch now and then so that it didn't spring back and slap me. Sometimes he held a tangle of briers down with one foot so I could step over it more quickly. My legs were raked with bloody scratches, long red lines that welt up on the skin and look like the work of cat claws. Crisscross scratches. One of my knees was scraped raw and bleeding. The gnats liked it, clustered to it, forming a scab themselves.

Because it was August, I had my summer feet. Good tough-bottomed feet that come from a summer of going barefoot on hot pavement, gravel, and sandspurs. Feet that gradually become leather-bottomed, sturdy as the sole of a shoe. My feet were all right but I hobbled because of my knee.

I didn't see a scratch on Skippy, although he must have had scratches. Dark streaks of dirt obvious on me and like a dusting of ash on Skippy. The dirt looked black on me and white on him. The bottoms of my feet were darker than the rest of me, and the bottoms of his feet were lighter. Nothing about us ever matches.

"My legs are all scratched up."

Skippy looked at them.

"I'm not allowed to go to the Snack Shack," I said.

He was expressionless.

"I'm so glad you were . . . you know . . . when everything happened . . ."

Skippy said nothing.

We slid down a slight ledge to where a trickle of stream ran through the underbrush. Canopied oak trees umbrellaed the spot. It was almost cool, the sun blotted by layers of branches above us.

"Get a drink," Skippy said, scooping the water up in his hands, drinking it, rubbing his wet hands over his face.

I copied him. Kept scooping the water up trying to drink enough before it all ran out the leaks between my fingers.

Then we walked on. We were quiet and the quiet was comfortable, like an honest conversation—one step up from words. We didn't look at each other. But as we got near the dirt road again, the alert set in, the listening for voices or footsteps. Each time a car drove by, we backed into a dark place in the green, a safe shadow, and watched to see that it was not the carload of boys still searching for us. We dodged in and out of the edge of the woods, staying just out of sight and enjoying it in a strange way—our escape.

There was possibility in the for-colored-only woods that I never felt in the woods that circled my own house like a life preserver, cushioning us from all the things that loomed beyond. "Skippy . . ." I said.

"Shhhhhh." He motioned for me to duck as a slow car went by. We passed the Snack Shack, just peeping at the back of it as we snuck along behind it.

"I need to find Roy," I said.

We darted across the dirt road and hurried down a path until came up behind Melvina's house. "Wait here," Skippy ordered. In a minute Annie came out of the house with him, carrying a bowl of water and a rag. "Wooooooo," she said, "you a mess, girl." She handed me the wet rag, and Leroy and Nappy came close by to watch anything that might be worth watching.

"Most of this blood will wash off," I said, rubbing the rag up and down my legs, making mud riverlets that puddled around my feet. "Don't tell Mother," I said. "Or Melvina either."

"I ain't," Annie answered.

My legs were stinging from the washing. The scratches reddened when I washed the dirt off. I dabbed at my bloody knee.

"What they chasing you for?" Annie looked at Skippy.

"It was me," I answered. "They said I didn't belong at the Snack Shack."

"It's a free country last I heard," Annie said.

"Well, they're right," Skippy said. "You don't belong up there."

I looked at him, disbelieving.

"You ain't supposed to be up there. Roy neither. Look what happens when y'all go up there."

"Roy goes up there all the time. You know that."

"Look what happens when he takes you with him."

Skippy was ruining things.

"You should have seen that girl run." He made a wild-looking gesture, waving his arms and legs crazy, mimicking me. Annie giggled.

"I kept up with you, didn't I?"

"Shoot, I say. Felt like I was dragging a log."

"Shut up," I said. "Why don't you shut up."

He smiled, satisfied. "Just don't be going up to the Snack Shack no more, or I'll tell your mama."

"You will not."

"Might tell her right now if you don't watch out."

My face flashed hate.

"He ain't going to tell nothing," Annie said. "He's just running his mouth." She took the rag, dipped it in the water, wrung it out good, then handed it back to me.

I folded it on my raw knee. It was stinging and my eyes

watered. Right then Roy clanked up into Melvina's yard on his bicycle. "I been looking for you," he said. "What happened?"

"Nothing."

His eyes took a quick inventory.

"Where's your bicycle?"

My bicycle? I had forgotten all about it.

When Walter got home I was sitting out on the picnic table, next to Roy, swinging my legs in an ordinary way. I had a Band-Aid on my knee. Mother had insisted when she saw I had fallen and scraped myself.

There seemed no way to get back to the Snack Shack for my bicycle, besides which I felt afraid to go up there after it. Maybe I would go back for it tomorrow. Maybe I would say it had been stolen. If worse came to worst I would tell Walter the truth, I guess. But Walter would hate it so bad—with him it wasn't true, that saying, "The truth will set you free."

Walter drove into the yard, got out of his truck, and slammed the door behind him. He looked over at me and Roy on the picnic table. He took off his hat and ran his hands through his summer-wet hair, then put his hat back on and walked towards us.

"What y'all so quiet about?" he said.

"Nothing," we answered in unison.

Walter studied us a minute, then put his hands in his pockets. "Lucy?" he started. "I don't guess that was your old blue bicycle laying up there at the Snack Shack, was it? I passed it on my way home and said to myself, 'That looks like Lucy's bicycle, but I don't guess it can be.' "

I didn't answer.

"No way for it to be your bicycle, is there?" He looked at me from beneath his hat brim.

I was thinking as hard as I could of a good lie, but I

wasn't fast enough with it and it left a blank space. Walter was patient.

"Was that your bicycle, Lucy?" he asked me.

Just as I was about to confess, to say yes because there seemed no alternative in the world that Walter would believe, bouncing down the road in front of our house, bouncing that flying bicycle until the chain rattled, came Skippy. It was the most noise a person could make riding a bicycle. He fast-pedaled it into the yard, across the grass, and over to where we were, slammed on the brakes one second before too late, skidding to a halt.

"Brung your bicycle back," Skippy said to me.

"What's Skippy doing with your bicycle?" Walter asked.

"He went to . . ."

"I borrowed it," Skippy said. "Rode it to the store."

Walter looked doubtful. "Is that right?"

I nodded yes.

"Did you tell him he could borrow it, Lucy?"

"Yes, sir, she did," Skippy answered for me. "You know I wouldn't take this bicycle and don't ask nobody."

"I didn't think you'd care," I said, "if he borrowed it."

Roy was dead silent the whole time, which was part of why Walter was suspicious.

"Just don't let me catch *you* up at that store. You hear, Lucy?"

"Yes, sir," I said.

Walter started walking towards the house, but about halfway he turned and said to Skippy, "You know that's a girl's bike, don't you?"

Skippy looked at the bike beneath him the way a person looks at the underside of a cat to see if it is a boy or a girl.

"Seems like if you wanted to ride a bike you'd have sense enough to borrow Roy's." With that Walter was gone in the house.

Me and Roy looked at Skippy straddling my bicycle and

started laughing. Skippy jumped off the bicycle like a bareback rider thrown off his horse, and slung it to the ground, making the back wheel spin. He slung it hard, like he hoped it would break into a million pieces. "Stop," I yelled. "You're tearing it up."

I walked over, got the bicycle, and leaned it up on its kickstand, the way it should be. Skippy is as bad as Roy. Neither one of them knows how to take care of anything.

*C*ARS with Confederate flags cropped up all over Tallahassee. A few colored people rode through town with freedom signs taped on their cars. Sometimes the cars were so nice nobody believed they were colored people's cars. People said they belonged to rich college kids from up North who came to Tallahassee to take colored people for rides in their fancy cars for the express purpose of making them unsatisfied with themselves.

We saw a particularly swank car—a long black Cadillac we thought must be the governor riding around, surveying the situation. Melvina was with us because it was Saturday, grocery day, and we were in the parking lot at Winn Dixie. Walter saw the car first and whistled like men do when they see a good-looking woman, only Walter always whistled over cars, nice tractors, and heavy equipment.

"Whoaaaa," he said admiringly. The car drove right through the parking lot where we stood. When it got closer, we saw that it had a sign on it that said "Freedom—It's now or never." Inside were six serious-faced colored people.

We stared like we thought it was the FSU homecoming

parade going by. It disgusted Walter so bad he spit. He glared at Melvina square in the eye and said, "Don't look to me like nobody in that car needs set free." He slammed the grocery bags into the trunk. "Niggers are free to pack a sack and catch the next Greyhound out of here," he said. Melvina stood like she was listening, but she wasn't. "They can free theirselves right on up to Detroit or where the hell ever it is they go. I wish they would."

Walter's head was fire red. He was sweating under the arms. We all got in the car silently. Melvina didn't say a word in the backseat and Mother didn't in the front seat. They both looked out the window the whole ride home, both of them pretending Walter didn't exist—like he was just part of the automobile, no different from the rubber tires, the small hood ornament, or the rear bumper.

Melvina sat next to me. I tried to squeeze her hand—a code message that said: Do not pay attention to Walter. She snatched her hand away from mine so furiously I was stunned. All the heat in my body rose to my face and tried to burn my ears off.

𝓕ROM the start they were like a mystery to us. Seemed like they were all keeping secrets or something. Like they knew something they weren't telling. I wanted to know it so bad it like to killed me sometimes. The colored people's secret.

It had to do with the Blue Bird, which was the main thing in French Town. The Blue Bird was like Melvina's house in a larger way—how you wanted to go in it, but felt nervous about it and plain unwelcome. It was nothing much to look at, a gray cinder-block box with a messy sign above the door that said "Blue Bird Cafe." It had what looked like a blue chicken hand-painted on it. And no windows. Not a single window. Walter said it was because those people wouldn't do anything but break them out first thing, just bust them things right out. He said you'd have to sell a heck of a lot of booze to keep a place like the Blue Bird in windows. But I knew the truth—that there were no windows because they didn't want white people to look in and see what was going on. There was a beat-up old wooden door that led inside, into complete darkness. And there was some music. Walter said all you could say about that kind of music down at the Blue Bird was that it was loud enough. And it usually was.

Colored people were always gathered up around the yard at the Blue Bird, talking, laughing, whispering. Once in a while fighting and yelling. Whenever we saw fighting going on we knew for sure it must be Old Alfonso. Walter would drive right by in a calm way, like he never even noticed. Me and Roy would be hanging out the window trying to watch. We were never clear on what went on at the Blue Bird—or why they called French Town French Town. We were never clear on anything that had to do with colored people.

It wasn't just Old Alfonso and the Blue Bird. It was Melvina too, who we saw practically every day of our lives, who was in our house rummaging through things as much as any of us. Melvina and her kids and her crazy little fall-down house next door. Walter said one good hard wind would blow that house clean across town and he wished it would. But not me. I liked that house close by. It was my best chance to find out things, colored-people things. I watched that house like a hawk. There was always a lot of screaming and yelling at Melvina's. There were all those kids, Melvina, and sometimes Old Alfonso, all staying in that little two-room house. There was hollering all the time, and dogs barking.

When Old Alfonso got good and drunk, Melvina locked

him out of the house, and then he got mad and turned mean. It was always at night. Some nights we could halfway see Old Alfonso stumbling around on the porch and could more than halfway hear the screaming and crying. "I'm gon kill you, woman," Old Alfonso would roar. "I got me a knife and I'm gon cut you up. I'm gon slice your ugly face, you no-count woman." Inside, the children wailed like a chorus of terrified crickets.

Melvina tried to hush them so she could hear where Old Alfonso was and what he was doing. He tried to crawl in a window, but Melvina banged him on the head with a stick or a shoe or a rock. Then the biggest boys grabbed something to hit him with. "You ain't gon hurt Mama. You old drunk dog. You a dog."

Some of Melvina's real dogs would take offense at this and start yelping and baying and yapping at Old Alfonso's heels. Once he sat outside cussing his head off and throwing rocks at the house. Sometimes he'd yell for Melvina to come outside so he could show her something. "I got something you sure do want to see. Come on out here. I ain't gon do nothing to you." Melvina would just sit inside very still. I could picture all her little children huddled up around her, listening. "Mama, you ain't gon go, are you? Mama, don't mess with him."

Sometimes Old Alfonso got mad and passed out in the yard. Melvina left him there all night, and in the morning he'd be laying like a dirty dog with his tongue hanging. Melvina's dogs would be right beside Old Alfonso like a pack of old wolves worn out from a night of trying to kill sheep and little baby lambs. Old Alfonso was just like the old wolf in all those wolf stories.

Once on a rainy night he was drunk and talking about what he was going to do with a razor. Melvina locked him out, and for a while he circled the house like a vulture, his arms waving wildly in the darkness. We could see his silhouette when he passed in front of the window or got under the porch light. The rain hitting the tin roof of the house was loud enough to make Old Alfonso's yelling useless. From time to time his legs gave way to his swaying body and he slipped down in the mud. He disappeared from sight for a while, then in a little bit here he would go again. He had to be getting tired when a bolt of lightning cut through the night like a jagged saw blade, and thunder followed—loud thunder—that shook the ground under his feet. He disappeared then, and for just a minute it crossed my mind that maybe he had got struck down by the lightning, had dropped dead in the yard someplace. That maybe God had had enough of Old Alfonso's doings and went on and called his number right then and there with one fiery stroke. But no. Twice more we saw him, both times making a run for the porch and standing out there pounding on the door.

Later on Melvina told us that when he seemed to disappear all it was was him crawling underneath the porch, and that her yard dogs had gathered around him under there, licking and scratching him. She said every time he rolled over, one of the dogs yapped and moved out of the way and Old Alfonso splatted back down in the mud like a half-dead fish. He wanted her to give him a quilt, but Melvina wouldn't do it. She said she never saw no kinda pig-in-the-mud that slept with a quilt. Then Old Alfonso said tomorrow he was gon get the wood ax and chop off Melvina's head. He said she was a dead woman tomorrow for sure.

But she wasn't. She was down at our house like always. The only difference was that she was about a half-hour late since she wouldn't let the children outside until Old Alfonso was gone. She said he didn't wake up good until way after daybreak and that the children watched out the window while he crawled out from under the porch, mud on his face

59

and clothes like dried paste. Said his hair was caked with mud too, and he looked like an old gray ghost, like a spook or a haunt. The children watched him wander up the road with the muddy dogs trailing behind him, their fur matted in tufts and points. She said they watched as wide-eyed and quiet as kids who had just seen the devil hisself rise up from hell.

Me and Roy watched this stuff too, as much as we could, before Mother would come and try to shame us for it, try to make us find something better to do, as she put it. Shoo us off and then stand at the window herself and watch. Mother and Walter had got used to the uproar next door. Some nights Mother sat in the kitchen listening and worrying about it. She listened to all those little boys screaming while Old Alfonso banged on the door and tore things up. Walter usually went on to bed. He said he was not going to let the likes of Melvina and them keep him up half the night. He had a day's work to do tomorrow. "That's just the way niggers are," he told Mother. "No use in sitting there worrying about it. They ain't happy unless they're into a fight. It's their way," he said. "You might as well come on to bed." But Mother wouldn't.

Walter tried to tell Mother that Old Alfonso was mostly talk, that he was like one of them dogs whose bark is a lot worse than his bite, but that was just because Walter never did see the looks of Melvina after Old Alfonso beat her. He never saw her half tore to pieces like Mother and us did—and I didn't guess he ever would, since Melvina would not allow it, a white man like Walter in her personal business. She said she could tolerate a lot of things, but not that.

So Mother knew better than Walter about the actual fighting itself, because whenever Old Alfonso got ahold of Melvina and beat her up bad, then she'd come down to our house the next morning as soon as Old Alfonso and Walter both were gone off. When we saw her coming me and Roy hollered for Mother, who would meet her at the door. Then me and Roy would freeze solid like a couple of useless nothings, like we were paralyzed, like we were just a couple of sticks of furniture in the room. We'd get as still as two dead children, couldn't do nothing with us but bury us. And Melvina would go along with it, us not being real, the way she walked past us—all bloody and beat up—and would not look at us same as if we were invisible. Her just crying and crying. And goodness knows Mother got to crying right with her, and then she'd send us out to play or off to school, and if we could we would get somewhere close by and be real quiet and listen to Mother and Melvina. Sometimes outside under the kitchen window.

Mother would say, "Melvina, next time he comes around up there I'm calling the sheriff, and I mean it."

Melvina would practically swoon. "No, Mrs. Sheppard. Don't you never do that. Don't never call the sheriff. Alfonso'll kill me for sure." Mother would get some ice for Melvina's eye and a warm rag to wipe off the dried blood, and pour Mercurochrome into her cuts, which made Melvina start crying again.

"If I had a gun I'd shoot Alfonso Williams myself," Mother would say. "I would, Melvina. He is no good. I swear you'd be better off dead than living with a man like that."

"Alfonso don't hardly give me no money."

"He ought to be shot, Melvina." Mother spoke like somebody spitting. "I mean it."

"He stay drunk," Melvina would say.

Mother would pour coffee and say, "Do you love him, Melvina? Are you that crazy?"

Melvina would shake her head. "It ain't his fault."

This all happened a hundred times and Mother always ended up promising not to call the sheriff—not ever. And

Melvina always went home cleaned up and cried out. And then me and Roy got back to normal.

After a while Walter laid down the law about Annie using our phone to call Old Alfonso home for supper. He said Mother ought never to have got that started. He said no way in hell was Melvina going to keep calling Old Alfonso home from the Blue Bird. "She ought to let him starve. She ought to hope he just stays there and drinks hisself to death. I swear Melvina is as much a fool as he is."

"We don't understand," Mother said.

"The hell we don't."

"We can't understand," Mother said.

"Understand what?" Walter said. "Tell me that. Understand what?"

One night late Old Alfonso got going again. Only worse this time. He was striking matches, threatening to set Melvina's house on fire. I woke up, not because of the racket up at Melvina's, but because Mother woke Walter over it and he yelled so much he woke me.

"I've got a mind to get my gun," Walter said. "I'm sure as hell calling the sheriff this time." And he did, without Mother even trying to stop him.

Down at our house Mother turned on every light. She lit it up like a Christmas tree. She wanted Old Alfonso to know we were awake and watching him. But it didn't seem like he noticed. Walter was walking around in the yard with his flashlight, old one-eyed George beside him. If Old Alfonso noticed Walter, he didn't pay him any mind either.

I sat in the kitchen and Mother let me. It wasn't too long until we saw the sheriff's car go by, and we knew exactly when he pulled in at Melvina's because the yelling and crying stopped. There was dead silence up there. The red light on the sheriff's car flashed like a big heartbeat in the sky.

Walter went on up to Melvina's as soon as the sheriff got there. Melvina wouldn't open the door. The sheriff said he'd have to knock it down if she didn't. So she cracked it, just enough. Walter said the children sat still and quiet, the little ones crying.

Melvina told the sheriff she didn't know where Old Alfonso was. She said they were not having any kind of trouble and there was no need for the sheriff to bother hisself with them. She said she could look after herself and her kids.

The sheriff and the man with him found Old Alfonso up under the porch, mostly because of the dogs. Walter shined his flashlight under there for them. "Boy, if you don't come on out of there by yourself, I got a dog can convince you," the sheriff said.

Melvina stepped into the doorway, her shoulders reaching almost from side to side and heaving up and down with each breath she took. She was quiet.

Old Alfonso came on out, and the sheriff and his man led him to the car, his hands cuffed behind him. He drug his feet when he walked as if they were tied to something heavy at the end of a rope. His head hung forward and his eyes stared down at the dirt. In the night, with the red light flashing, Alfonso looked old and small. Not like something to be afraid of.

As soon as the sheriff's car drove off, Walter came on home and made me go to bed, but I could not sleep a wink for thinking about it. Old Alfonso gone. And Melvina—her just standing there in the doorway like that, and Walter said she did not act one bit grateful. He said he guessed she would like it better if he had just let Old Alfonso go on and burn the house to the ground—and all of them with it. "Guess she'd appreciate that better." He said Melvina stood right there and told the sheriff a bold-faced lie like only a nigger can. I couldn't get away from thinking about it.

Melvina was quiet about things afterwards. Mother too. Melvina came to our house the next day as usual. She didn't seem any different to me. She seemed the same. Any secret Melvina's got is safe forever. I see that plain. Nothing going to make the colored-people secrets come loose from Melvina.

Walter said being rid of Old Alfonso felt like when you finally run off some old dog been getting in your trashcan night after night, making a mess you got to clean up over and over again. He was satisfied with it—Old Alfonso gone. But I kept wondering what the sheriff did with Old Alfonso after he got him. Did he hang him? Walter said he hoped they taught him a lesson he'd remember. Mother said she guessed they put him in jail for a while. Melvina said when Old Alfonso came back we better all watch out.

I was minding my own business, thinking my own sad thoughts, when Skippy came towards me. He was walking his bounce walk, messing with a pocketknife, opening the blade, making sure I saw it.

"Where'd you get that knife?" I asked.

"Somewhere."

"Melvina know you got it?"

"Maybe."

"What you fixing to do with it?"

"Don't know. Might get who it is been making you cry."

"What?"

"You sitting here crying. If somebody bothering you, say who it is and I'll get them with this knife." Skippy spit on the blade and rubbed it on his shorts.

"What do you care if somebody is bothering me?"

"Don't care. Just said I'd get them."

"Well, nobody's bothering me. Except you."

Skippy made a snorting noise and picked up a stick and started cutting on it, sharpening a point. I watched him. "One day I'm gon get me a gun," he said.

"What you need with a gun?"

"You can hunt with a gun. You can go around with a gun and won't nobody mess with you. You can protect yourself."

"From what?"

"From everything, girl."

"What makes colored boys so crazy about guns? I never saw anything like it. What makes y'all love knives and guns so much?"

"What makes white girls so stupid?"

*S*KIPPY couldn't stand Elvis. When he caught me sitting in Walter's truck listening to "Jailhouse Rock" on the radio, he said, "If you want singing, Chuck Berry can sing. Little Richard is a thousand times better than Elvis," which just proved Skippy's ignorance as far as I was concerned.

"Who do you think is best," Skippy said, "Elvis or Little Richard?"

"Elvis," I said. "Little Richard is foolish with all that makeup on his face."

Skippy moaned, stumbled back like he'd been shot in the heart by my stupidity. "Who do you think is smarter," he said, "Martin Luther King or George Wallace?"

"I don't know what that has to do with anything."

"Answer me, girl. Who you think is the smartest?"

"What difference does it make?"

"You won't admit it," he hollered. "You won't admit a colored man is smarter than a white man." Skippy reached inside the truck and turned the radio up full blast. Elvis was screaming about how *they said you was high-classed, but that was just a lie.* I reached to turn it down, but Skippy wouldn't let go of the knob. We wrestled each other for it. "You won't admit it, will you?" he yelled. "Never will admit it." I jabbed my fingernails into his skin to make him stop.

He squeezed my hand so hard he nearly broke my fingers. "Stop," I screamed. "You're crazy."

Skippy pulled his hand loose, pounded his fist on the side of Walter's truck, and bulldozed across the yard. If a tree was unfortunate enough to be in his path he would have up-ended it and kept on. I turned the radio off. *Wait a minute, Skippy. Come back,* I thought, *please.* I watched him shoulder his way out of my yard, furious. What I wanted to know was—Who in the world is George Wallace?

*I*T seemed like Melvina being our maid was not enough. She wanted Mother to get Annie to hang out the wash or do the ironing. Something Annie could get paid for.

"Annie's got enough of a job watching after that yard full of children while you come down here and work, Melvina,"

Mother said. "If Annie needs to be doing something, she needs to be going to school."

Me and Roy knew Mother's education speech by heart, how the educated person didn't have to be afraid, how the educated person can change things. Me and Roy and Melvina hated it. Everybody did.

"I can't keep the girl in shoes," Melvina said.

"If Annie had an education she could buy herself all the shoes she wanted." Me and Roy gagged. "If Annie had an education she could change the world."

"You educated," Melvina said. "I don't see you changing nothing. If it's the same to you I'll let somebody else's girl change the world."

Mother thinks it is pathetic that Melvina cannot see the value of a good education. "Lack of education is what's holding the colored back, Melvina. Can't you see that? I swear, you can't see the woods for the trees."

"I ain't trying to see no woods. I'm trying to get out the woods. Chopping down one day at a time."

"What about the big picture? What about tomorrow?"

"I got today standing in the way of tomorrow," Melvina said, which is why it was a paying job she wanted for Annie. Nothing less. We are just regular white people, but Melvina acts like there is no end to the money we got. She wants Walter to pay Skippy to mow the yard, Alfonso Junior to clean pine straw out of the gutters, and Orlando to wash the truck. Walter never will do it, though. So Mother is Melvina's only hope. Since Mother went to FSU two years, she is more educated than Walter and acts accordingly. Walter says Mother majored in changing the world when secretarial school would have done her more good. But Mother takes her education seriously and Melvina knows how to make her prove it.

Melvina hit on the idea of Annie baby-sitting me, Roy, and Benny some night when Mother and Walter went out.

But Mother and Walter hardly ever went out. So Melvina started saying, "A man like Mr. Sheppard ought to take his wife out once in a while." And Mother started to believe it too. "Mr. Sheppard makes good money, don't he?" Melvina asked. "He can afford it, can't he?" And pretty soon Mother had taken up the cause—Annie baby-sitting for us one night while Mother and Walter went someplace nice.

"She's not going to boss me around," is all Roy said. "I don't have to mind a colored girl, do I, Walter?"

Walter made a noise in his throat and said to Mother, "Annie's no baby-sitter."

"I'll write down the fire department, the police, and the hospital numbers, Walter. I'll set them beside the phone."

"I don't like a thing about this," Walter said, and then gave up.

When Skippy heard about Annie baby-sitting us, he got one of his stupid ideas. He said as soon as Mother and Walter left home for us to let him and Alfonso Junior and all the rest of the brothers come in the house to look at television. He said they would watch for Walter's car to go off down the road, then they'd come down to our house, and for us to let them in.

"Baby-sitting is a paid job, and I'm going to do it like a paid job," Annie said.

It was the craziest idea I ever heard. We cannot have a house full of colored people with Mother and Walter not home. Not colored boys all up in our house.

"We ain't gon hurt nothing," Skippy said.

"That's right," Annie said. "You ain't gon hurt nothing, because you ain't gon be there."

"A colored girl is all right," I explained to Skippy, "but colored boys cannot go around in people's houses. Tell him, Annie."

I do not even know how colored boys look on furniture. How do they look in an indoors room? I tried to picture it, me and Roy sprawled out to watch a little television with

Annie and a room full of moving-around colored boys, stepping over us on the floor, sitting here one minute, there one minute, picking up everything we have to look it over, setting their bare feet up on everything, handling everything. What if they decide they will go off with some of our stuff, like they unplug a nice lamp and walk out the door with it, or Skippy shoves Walter's favorite chair across the floor and squeezes it out the door and hauls it off? Who will stop him? Who will say, "Skippy, you put that chair back. You know better than to go off with a chair that doesn't belong to you"?

"We are just as sorry as we can be," Annie says, her hands on her hips, "but you cannot come in that house to watch TV." Annie turns into the Queen of England telling it. Her part is grand. Yes, I will be in those white people's house eating some of their supper, drinking their cold drinks, bossing their kids, watching TV, and making all matter of important decisions. "You mize well forget it," she tells Skippy.

"You gon be sorry," he says.

The night Annie baby-sat us everything was going fine. Mother had put Benny to bed before she and Walter left for the catfish restaurant. Annie fixed me and Roy peanut butter crackers, and we were watching Jack Benny with Rochester when the doorbell rang. And rang. And rang. It was pitch-dark outside and at first we were all three thinking the same thing—that it was Skippy and Alfonso Junior and every other colored boy in Tallahassee lined up out there to get in our house and watch TV.

"Make him quit it, Annie," I said.

She peeped out the window, but it was too dark to see. "It's not Skippy out there," she whispered.

Me and Roy froze. We like to know *exactly* what it is we are afraid of. "But it's got to be him," I said.

"No such thing as got-to-be," Annie said. "How you

know it ain't white men heard I'm keeping y'all by myself and come to get me? How you know it ain't some crazy body seen us in the window? It could be any crazy body out there." Annie made good sense.

"It could be drunk niggers breaking in the house," Roy said, wild-eyed.

"Or people escaped from Chattahoochee," Annie said.

"Or somebody that just broke out of jail," Roy said.

Annie turned off the living room light. Complete darkness. That darkness that has little spurts of color shooting through it. "We got to hide," she whispered. It sounded like the crickets surrounding the house had gone hysterical. At Annie's command we caravaned into my bedroom and crawled under the bed—all three of us—with Annie in the middle. The bed skirt hung down and covered us up. "Can't nobody see us now," Annie said.

We lay there in terror. The dizzy kind. The kind that feels like a bird is set loose in your belly. I'm scared because I think a bunch of colored boys might get in the house and do who knows what. I think of drunk niggers in the flower beds looking in through the windows, and carrying knives in their pockets and wearing scuffed-up, raggedy shoes. They try to kill me with smiles on their faces and their white teeth showing.

Annie is mostly scared of white men. It doesn't have to be a bunch of them, it can be just one crazy white man lurking around in the night, looking for a colored girl he has heard is baby-sitting white kids for the first time in her life, and him coming after her with soft pink hands and a red face and probably a tattoo on his white belly. And in his pocket he has got chewing tobacco and keys to his tore-up pickup truck. Tears go down her face telling it.

"I heard about this colored girl walking down the road not bothering anybody," Annie says, "and a white man stops his truck and says does she want a ride." Annie is telling this slow and quiet. "The girl got in that truck and vanished from sight. Nobody saw her again until they found her body floating facedown in Lake Jackson."

Me and Annie hold hands now. Tight.

"That's nothing," I tell her. "I heard about this colored man that killed a white girl and didn't know what to do with her body. He didn't have time to dig a deep grave. So he got a saw and sawed off her arms and legs, sawed her up into manageable pieces and just scattered them out all over the place."

"He did not?" Annie said, squeezing my hand.

"He did too," I said. "People are still finding her pieces. And she couldn't get a decent funeral since all her body wasn't collected. And nobody could prove nothing, so the man is still on the loose."

"The police didn't catch him?" Annie whispered.

"No."

"And he was colored?"

"He sure was."

"Then why didn't they catch him?"

"Don't ask me."

Then Annie said, "One time I knew this real pretty girl that white men got ahold of. They doused her with kerosene and set her on fire. She started running, and everything she touched caught fire too."

"Is that the truth, Annie?" I said. "Do you swear that's true?" It scared me so bad just to hear it, because I am more scared of fire than anything. That's the main reason I don't want to go to hell. Because you just keep burning in a fire forever and nobody comes to put it out. "Do you swear to God that's true?" I said.

"It's as true as this world," Annie said.

I pictured myself in flames, running through a dark Tallahassee night when everybody was asleep, going

71

through yards like a blazing torch, dogs after me, barking and trying to bite.

"You know what some white men will do if they get ahold of a colored girl?" Annie said very quietly.

"What?"

"Take her clothes off."

"Then what?"

"They bother her," Annie whispered.

"Shut up!" Roy says. *"Y'all shut up!"*

It got hot up under that bed. The three of us lay with our legs tangled together, Annie's skinny arms wrapped tight around me and Roy. And ours around her.

Our fear carried us just as far as it could before flipping itself over. Soon we were all dead asleep.

*T*HERE used to be safe places, where nothing bad could reach us. When we were little it was our mother's bed, and later our own beds in a house where people loved us. Granddaddy's farm was like that too. It was better than roasting hot dogs at Alligator Point or riding glass-bottom boats at Wakulla Springs. At the farm we could climb on the garage roof and jump off, lay in the barn loft and eat hot-off-of-the-vine watermelon, spitting seeds on nervous jerk-necked chickens below, listen to the afternoon rain on the tin roof—like God spilled a change purse of coins that flashed silver when the sun hit.

Granddaddy always saddled his old horse, Minnie, gave Roy and me each a dime, and we rode a hot mile to a nothing gas station store. Roy rode in the saddle going, I rode behind him, and we traded places coming back. Glory, glory, hallelujah. On Minnie's back with a dime to spend. Me stuck to Roy. Minnie sweating white foam after a while. Roy and I got quiet and went deep inside ourselves.

More than once a particular feeling came over me that I never told anybody about—one I never got in church in my life, but it came in the yellow heat on an Alabama red dirt road. Nobody else knew it, but hiding in the trees where I couldn't see clearly, floating along with me just out of sight, was Jesus himself. That's why I didn't tell anybody, because it sounded crazy. I couldn't exactly see him. It was a feeling, the way being too hot is a feeling, or too cold—when it happens to you there's no doubt about it.

This was an orange summer day, heat shimmying up out of the baking earth. I didn't exactly sing out loud with Roy there—he'd have had a laughing fit—but inside I sang, with no words at all. The singing was so loud my ears rang. Only Jesus heard me, because he was out there too, behind the bushes or up in a high tree. I say it was Jesus because I don't know what else could it have been?

We tied Minnie to a rail in front of the store. Old men were gathered on the bench outside. They sat there all day every day, waiting to die. It seemed like a good way to finish a life. A couple were white and a couple were colored. They played dominoes or cleaned their fingernails with a knife blade. Always, they spit chewing-tobacco juice, wet splotches like bird droppings, on the ground around them. When we rode up they said, "It's the Wilcox grandkids." They said, "Howdy, partner," to Roy, who was decked out in a world of cowboy stuff the likes of which they'd probably never seen.

A dime in Tallahassee wouldn't be worth going a mile to spend. That would call for at least a quarter. But a dime at this Alabama country store was plenty. We got a nickel co-cola and shared it, and fifteen pieces of penny candy. It took us thirty minutes to spend our twenty cents if we selected the candy piece by piece.

On the ride to the store and back we passed a tarpaper house sitting at the edge of the cotton fields. It didn't have a tree anywhere near it, which made this a strange place for a house. Out in the bald sun. Lots of colored kids lived there. The most kids you ever saw at one house. They stayed in the yard mostly. The youngest ones went naked, so me and Roy stared. The older ones were about our age and walked to the edge of the road when they saw us coming on horseback. They looked us over shyly but thoroughly, like we might be for sale and they were thinking about buying us. We were glad because then we could look them over too. I mean study them from head to toe. Try to memorize them. Our shared embarrassment took the form of excessive smiling. We tried to be friendly in a magic way that didn't call for anyone to say or do anything particular.

Roy and me up on horseback, pockets full of candy, them standing at the roadside—the littlest ones with no clothes on. I felt like an accidental princess, high on horseback, prancing my way someplace. I thought they must wish they could do it too, ride the horse, eat a dime's worth of hand-selected candy. If I were a princess in real life I'd kill myself, the specialness is so terrible. They made me wish I was walking down the road with a stick in my hand going to do some necessary errand instead of buying myself candy which I'd have gobbled up before supper.

We stopped Minnie. "Y'all want some candy?" we said. Maybe they nodded yes. When they spoke they were hard to understand, because they were country on top of being colored—and not Tallahassee colored either. Especially the littlest children. Roy and I laughed because it was something we'd never heard before, the sounds of their words, the extra mouth they put into speaking them. "What?" we said. "What did you say? Say it again." They laughed because we were too white, too deaf, too Tallahassee to understand what they all understood. They seemed to like that about us.

Maybe, since the facts all pointed in that direction, I was supposed to believe that I was in the United States of America, on a road in Macon County, Alabama, riding my granddaddy's slow horse—but I wasn't. Not really. I knew then and I know now that I was someplace else. Maybe on the road to heaven but I don't think so, maybe in Africa, maybe in someone else's life that they lost and I found for a minute. I was someplace important, every place at once—my heart shot up suddenly with the force of a missile, flying towards the hot sun, nearly yanking me off the horse, nearly making me fly upward too. I gripped the saddle to keep from flying away. The world was watching. Not the walk-around world. The other world. Nothing was as it seemed. Jesus himself wore a camouflage outfit like a soldier at war and dodged in and out of the trees.

The colored children touched Minnie, jumped back if she snorted, touched the saddle, Roy's boots, and some of the mosquito bites on my leg. They laughed and pointed to my dirty feet where I had remaining splotches of pink polish on my toes. This was how it worked. If they laughed we laughed too, if we laughed they joined us.

There was a girl my age. We looked at each other hard and long, smiled shyly at each other half a dozen times, intent on making the smile take. *There, can you feel that, can you feel it?* I saw to it that I was the one who handed her her candy. She saw to it that she took her candy from my hand, not Roy's. We wanted so much from each other—but didn't know what it was or how to get it. I always looked for her face first in the crowd of faces. Her name was Reedy. I was jealous of the things she knew.

Soon we were asking Granddaddy for an extra dime. Once I spent the whole thing on a Payday for Reedy.

Roy was furious. "That's not fair," he said. "You can't

give her a Payday and everybody else just a chocolate Kiss."

"Yes I can."

And I did. The little children squealed for the Payday when I pulled it from the sack, but I handed it ceremoniously to Reedy. *Here, Reedy. Here's the world. Unwrap it and gobble it up.* She took the Payday, slid it up under her shirt, and took off running. I pictured her sitting alone eating it, no one asking her for a bite, no one watching her.

As young as we were, I believed even then—maybe especially then—that Reedy was my other self. I was her other self too. That's why we watched so hard and with such amazement and fear. She didn't know how it was to be yellow-haired and prance down the road on a horse. I didn't know how it was to dip a bucket in her mama's well and drink the warm water from it. I didn't know how it was to have to look at the world through the pores of your skin. Was it like never getting to take off a pair of sunglasses, even at night, even when you sleep? I knew almost nothing about her, but I knew one thing: If I hadn't been Lucy in this life, I'd have been Reedy.

The next several years Roy and I saw the same colored kids in Granddaddy's yard in the early mornings, trampling dew, fussing because they didn't want to go in the fields to pick cotton all day, but their mama made them. Reedy was as tall as I was now, but thinner, and she had breasts. She had got sullen-faced, and had her hair tied in a kerchief like her mama. I could hardly get Reedy to look at me. Something had happened to her eyes. Every time she blinked it made me think of doors slamming. It seemed like her eyes stayed closed even when they were wide open. It was like they erased everything they looked at. Especially me. She erased me all over the yard, up on the porch, on the tree stump, in the swing under the pecan tree, on the garage roof. Anyplace I was, she looked there, saw me, and I was erased. I felt my arms and legs go first, then my face and my belly. She never erased the place my heart was because she didn't know there was such a place. I only knew it because it ached. It wanted to jump out of my body and be somebody else's heart.

Roy and me wanted to go in the fields with the colored people to see what it was like, picking cotton. We begged like fools. We cried in front of that yard full of early-morning colored people, half awake. They sipped coffee and watched Roy and me get wild and red-faced begging. But Granddaddy wouldn't let us go. Period. Reedy and the other colored kids were mad because they had to go, and we were mad because we couldn't. A line was drawn at the edge of the cotton field. There was no crossing over.

The white part was not as bad as the colored part. But the white part was not wonderful either, like Reedy probably thought. Those times when the cotton had to be picked and everybody was in the fields except Sudie in the kitchen and Granddaddy on the porch, where he sat watching the little children because he was too old to go in the fields anymore. James was in charge now, and half the children in the yard belonged to him. A yard full of colored babies and also me and Roy, as old as we were, up at the house with all those bare-bottom, raggedy-shorts kids, mad, embarrassed to the depths of our small souls. We acted hateful. We did the meanest things we could think of, got in as much trouble as we could, because we wanted those colored children to know we were just as real as they were. We wanted Granddaddy to get out his strap and beat our rear ends. We wanted them to stop picking cotton in the fields, stand up straight and listen to our mournful screams as Granddaddy slapped his leather strap across our white flesh. We wanted to suffer pain that was noticeable so the colored children wouldn't go around thinking we were lucky and hating us for it because they had to.

I could see the cotton fields from the top of the garage.

Reedy was reduced, like everybody else, to a dot of color in a row of green. Which one was she? What was she thinking? *Reedy, if I had a gun I would kill the world for you. I would blow the head off this stupid world.* I laid on the hot corrugated-tin roof and imagined Reedy dressed for church. I imagined her at a dance with all the boys lined up waiting their turn. I imagined her standing before a microphone in front of a throng of thousands, saying, "I'd like to thank my best friend, Lucy Conyers, who gave me my first Payday." The crowd cheered and lifted us up on their shoulders. Reedy and I waved our clasped hands in the air.

One summer I walked down to Reedy's house by myself with a Hershey bar I'd brought all the way from Tallahassee. When I gave it to her she threw it at me. I grabbed her hand and tried to make her take it, but she wouldn't. I think if she'd been lying in the yard starving to death she'd have slung that candy bar into the hog pen and listened to them snort and squeal and eat it up, wrapper and all.

This summer I didn't see Reedy. Granddaddy said she had a baby now, but I knew that couldn't be true. He's old and mixed up. She didn't live in the trapper house anymore, though, or if she did, she never came outside.

*T*ALLAHASSEE colored people were mad. They started having sit-ins at the Woolworth's lunch counter. They marched in front of the State Theatre. Colored people would get on a city bus and sit slam up-front, throwing the driver into a stir—whether to go on with his route or just sit there and refuse to go. The police came, and it was in the *Tallahassee Democrat*. Finally the buses decided to continue running, but for a while not many white people rode them.

We did once. Mother and us. Our car stalled while we were downtown, and Walter couldn't get to it until after work and didn't want Mother to pay anybody at a filling station to do what he could do himself. So we left the car where it was, and caught the bus that let off on Tennessee Street. There were colored people riding in the front of the bus, and still lots of colored people riding in the very back. We just got on and sat in the middle. It wasn't much.

Once we saw picketers marching with signs in front of the State Theatre. White people, mostly boys about soldier age, circled them and said, "I smell something. Do you smell something?" They poured Evening in Paris perfume all over the sidewalk where the colored people were walking. A scuffle started. We saw some of it—we were terrified that Mother would get in it. Roy and I pulled her away, saying, "Let's go home. Let's go home." We could imagine her picture in the *Tallahassee Democrat*. The caption would read: *Sarah Sheppard, mother of Roy and Lucy Conyers, and nigger lover, in a common street brawl in front of the picture show. Her husband, Walter Sheppard, had nothing whatsoever to do with it. He has filed for divorce. (It will be Mrs. Sheppard's second divorce.)*

It was a good thing Mother didn't believe in guns. I'd hate to think of all the people who would be dead if Mother had had a gun. I was torn between wanting her to kill them and wanting her to go home and fix us a delicious supper.

WHAT we liked to do after supper on California Street when the weather was nice and the grass was green was go sit out in front of the house with our unfinished glasses of iced tea. Just sit out there, all of us, and talk some or play something. Walter and Mother sitting on the steps and me and Roy and Benny in the grass, tumbling and flipping and standing on our heads. Us outside in the evening air waiting on darkness. Waiting on the lightning bugs to come out, and the mosquitoes—lying in the grass with the chiggers, itching from head to toe but paying it no mind because we're so happy out there, gon get us a soapy bath later. The air is nice. The grass Walter sprigged all around has taken hold good, and almost our whole front yard is green and bouncy, feels like walking on a bed mattress instead of the regular ground.

Walter made a million Saturday trips in the truck out to country roads and two-lane highways to dig up grass. That Florida grass that grows like something crawling, spreads by sprouting arms and legs and reaching until it feels another grass hand to hold or leg to cross, grass spots hooking up with each other, thick and bouncy. It'll grow right up over the edge of the highway if anybody lets it.

So Walter goes in the truck to dig it up, takes us with him, and sometimes takes Skippy or some of them. Lets them ride in the back of the truck in the blowing wind, but makes me and Roy sit up front in the cab with him. We complain about it, but Walter says it's our mother that gives the orders and he's just minding her, like we better do. And off we go.

We usually stop somewhere at a gas station on the way, and Walter gets everybody a cold drink and gets himself some salted peanuts and pours them into his co-cola. Hardly drinks a gas station co-cola without salted peanuts dropped in it, making a sizzling sound, fizzing up. Walter tells us not to drink all our drink, to save some because we're gon be mighty thirsty when we get out on the highway and go to digging up and loading sod. We've done it enough to know he's right.

Walter drives us to just the right spot and gives Skippy a shovel, and he takes a shovel and goes along digging up good sod grass. He scoops it up in squares and patches and it's me and Roy's job to carry it to the truck bed and load it. Sometimes it gets so hot that we are soaked to the bone. Especially Walter, whose clothes will be wringing wet, water pouring off his head, hand slipping on the shovel handle. Gnats and grass and dirt on him and on us too. We get so nasty that nothing will do but to hose us off when we get home—Skippy and them too. Hose us off good before we so much as think about going in the house.

Sometimes, out digging up grass on the roadside, we take a break and finish our now warm cold drinks. Try to find some shade to get under, but sometimes we can't, so me and Roy and Skippy and them lay up underneath the truck, climb under there and lay in the dirt because we want the sun off us that bad. Walter sits in the back of the truck with the grass, says we look like Oreo cookies the way we're all smashed together under there—trying to drink our drinks without spilling co-cola all over us. We rest until the gas smell starts to bother us and Walter hollers for us to get back to work.

When we've got enough grass to suit Walter we go on home. Skippy and Orlando in the back with that wind blowing like a fan, cooling them off, drying them off. Me and Roy and Walter up in the sweat-box truck cab, just miserable. Past miserable.

We get home and Walter makes us unload the grass sprigs. Tells us where to put them, how to arrange them. When we're finished he hoses us off good and we go on. He stays out there digging the sprigs in and watering each one a long time, and then putting the sprinkler on them after that. It's an all-day job. By the time he's done he looks worse than one of those chain-gang convicts been digging ditches all day. He takes a bath. Then Mother rubs his back because he is slam worn-out.

That's how we got our nice grass, and Walter's proud of it. Mother says he likes to sit outside after supper just to watch that grass grow. Says she believes he thinks he can actually see those sprigs crawling, matting together, making us that nice bouncy grass floor to play on. It's one of our favorite things. All the family together after a good supper, drinking iced tea out in the yard. Playing swing the statue, doing tricks, and standing on our heads.

This one night Walter is watching me and Roy show off, or try to. Us saying, "Look here, Walter. Watch this," and all of a sudden Walter says, "That's nothing. You call that standing on your head? Good gosh. I can stand on my head all day long if I want to. Matter of fact, I can walk on my head—you ever see anybody do that? Walk on their head? Probably not, because ain't nobody can do it but me. I can walk across this yard on my head."

Me and Roy laugh. Know Walter is up to some foolishness, but we love it when he does like that. "Can't do it," we say. "It's impossible for somebody to walk on their head!"

"Maybe for some regular person," Walter says, "but not me. This ain't some ordinary head sitting up on these shoulders."

"Okay, then show us. Come on, Walter. Prove it."

Benny pulls on Walter's arms for him to get up off the porch steps and show us. Mother is laughing too.

Walter stands up and walks out into the yard, acting out his part so good. He taps his foot on different spots of grass, says he has to have the exact right grass spot to do head-walking on. Finds a nice bouncy spot, gets on his hands and knees, twitches some like he's getting ready. He sets his head down in the grass and slowly kicks up his feet, but not high enough and they fall back down. So he does it again, me and Roy and Benny and Mother laughing and squealing at crazy Walter. This time he kicks up his feet just right, way up high, got his legs apart, scissor style, and he is standing on his head. Seems like the ground is shaking with Walter's nervous legs up in the air and us all laughing so much. There is Walter on his head. His shirt falls down over his face, showing his big stomach and chest, got all that hair all over it, this big furry chest and some legs look like they are slow-walking up in the air.

It is the funniest sight there ever was, Walter upside down like that—and not even thinking about falling over. Got his legs walking up in the air. Us rolling in the grass over it. And Mother notices this car coming down the street, an old car, driving kind of slow. She just notices it because she thinks it will embarrass Walter to death, people driving by the house and him out in the yard on his head—his face covered up by his shirttail, his hairy stomach for the world to see, his feet still slow-walking. But Walter don't care.

That car slows down to almost a stop, just creeping by. Only a driver in there, looking hard, leaned across the car seat looking. As Mother looks back she gets a nervous, hot-stomach feeling, because she sees that driver. I know because I see him too. I get that same hot feeling. She looks at his face, him looking up in the yard so hard. A person might think he's just looking at Walter, but he's not. Looking at everybody. His eyes catch Mother's eyes and they lock together a second. Mother is upset, because driving by the house out there in that slow, old car, leaning across the seat looking, is Johnny Conyers, our real daddy.

Mother is frozen for a minute. Seeing that face she knows every line of, every expression, every angle. Here he is,

riding by her house, looking at her children, and her husband, and her house—and her life that she has got going
good without him.

Walter has rolled down in the grass now, all three of us
climbing on him, sitting on his stomach like people sit on a
horse. Walter has never noticed the car.

"Time to go inside," Mother says. "Right now. Come
on." She gets up and hurries into the house, the rest of us
not making any particular effort to hurry.

It was unsettling, seeing our real daddy alive and well in
this world. Seeing him like a ghost—him seeing her,
knowing she saw him. Mother said she couldn't sleep that
night, just lay in bed wondering. Feeling like our daddy was
everywhere, outside looking in the window, in the closets
hiding, in the hall looking in on her children as we
peacefully slept. Even trying to lie in between Mother and
Walter, in that little space between them. Daddy's memory
edging itself in there. And Mother clinging to Walter most
of the night while he slept, snored even. Her wrapped
around him like a blanket on a cold night.

I do not look one thing like
Mother. Maybe just have some of her face. How her cheeks
sit out there like round biscuits of flesh that got put on last,
as an afterthought, once the rest of the face was finished.
My cheeks did like that too, looked added on. My hands
and feet were like Mother's too. Square and neat. No
fat-looking fingers or toes. We could pick up most anything
as good with our toes as with our fingers. A marble. A

thumbtack. Mother could hold two armfuls of grocery sacks, pick up the car keys off the ground with her toes, bend her knee up, and hand the keys to Roy. It was a natural thing. Walter said Mother must have some monkey in her. But I could do it too.

I had some of Mother's ways, but not much of her looks. It was Roy that had those. Brown Roy with his black, shiny, almost wavy hair. Roy who could have dirt all over his hands and face, and it wouldn't even be noticeable hardly. Not on his brown self.

It was funny how we were. Roy brown like Mother. Me golden like my real daddy, which is not what somebody said, but I just saw that. How he had this straight yellow hair like me. And we had those blue eyes and those white eyebrows that go away, invisible, all summer long and come back in the fall and winter. And then Benny looks like Walter. Kind of, he really does. He's like me and our real daddy about his white hair and skin. But like Walter in his build, which is big. Thick. Husky. And like Walter in his quietish ways. It was not unusual for folks to say, "Lord, that boy takes after his daddy." Meaning Walter. People who didn't know would say that. "You sure can't be denying that child, Walter Sheppard."

When folks told Walter that Benny was exactly like him, just him made over, Walter smiled and said, "That's one lucky boy there. Damn lucky." He'd wink at Mother. It was just generally recognized how Benny was Walter's spittin' image.

Walter's people lived in Valdosta. That's in Georgia, not too far off. There's a bunch of Sheppards there. Walter said he had more cousins than you could shake a stick at. He said every other person you'd meet on the street in Valdosta was a Sheppard, or married to one, or lived next door to one. "There's such a thing as too much of a good thing. That's why I came down to Tallahassee. That, and because I had a chance at a right good job with the highway department."

None of us ever laid eyes on any of Walter's people. He never said much about any of them. Just his brother, Hugh Henry Sheppard. He was Walter's little brother, grown now. Walter liked the heck out of Hugh. But that was about all.

Mrs. Sheppard, Walter's mother, was very disappointed that Walter didn't make a better marriage. She called Mother the *divorcée*. When Walter was fixing to marry Mother he called to tell Mrs. Sheppard about the wedding to see if she could come. She could not. Because it broke her heart, Walter marrying a divorcée. One with kids. She said Walter deserved his own-flesh-and-blood kids. Here he was going to be bringing his hard-earned paycheck home to somebody else's leftover wife and another man's kids. It broke her heart. There wasn't any need in her coming clear down to Tallahassee to cry her eyes out at such a terrible mistake of a wedding. So Mrs. Sheppard had never seen Mother, or any of us. We didn't think she ever wanted to. Walter said we were not missing one thing. He said he'd seen enough of the woman for all of us.

Then out of the blue she calls up Walter and says she's coming to visit. She's taking a Trailways bus to Tallahassee and can he pick her up at the bus station. She says her conscience cannot rest until she sees Walter and meets his divorcée wife. She just has to come, because she can't rest until she does.

Mother went into a frenzy over the idea. Not mad exactly, just a nervous wreck, worrying about what to fix for dinner. Does she like biscuits better than cornbread? Does she like sweet pickles in her potato salad? Mother wished we could go on and paint my bedroom. It had been needing it, so she wished we could paint it. She wanted Walter to mow the grass, and wash the car and his highway truck, and fix the tear in the screen door. She wanted Roy and Benny to get a haircut. She wanted to clip our fingernails—and our toenails. She did speeches on us acting nice, not just yes ma'am, no ma'am, please, and thank you, but also chew with your mouth closed, put your napkin in your lap, do not pick your nose, don't scratch, say excuse me, no yelling, no slamming the screen door. Walter's mother coming was nothing like when Granddaddy came.

We had the feeling we were in a contest to see if we could be nice enough to win Mrs. Sheppard so she might want to be our grandmother or something. She was the Grand Prize if we won the niceness contest. If we could be good enough.

Walter tried to calm Mother down, because she was about to wear herself out, and us too. Walter said it wasn't the Queen of England coming, just his mother, Emma Sheppard. There wasn't no sense in trying so hard to please her. But you couldn't tell Mother that. On the day Mrs. Sheppard was coming, Mother changed clothes a half-dozen times. Brushed the curl right out of her hair. Got all the rest of us nervous too. She burned the first batch of dinner rolls she put in the oven. Walter told me to go get Melvina. Mother didn't know one thing about dinner rolls. He said, "Get Melvina in the kitchen before it's too late." Mother went in the bathroom and brushed her hair some more. Melvina came in the kitchen mumbling and took her shoes off.

When Mrs. Sheppard finally came walking in the house with Walter one step behind, carrying her suitcase, she was not exactly what we were expecting, because we didn't know what we were expecting. Walter standing there behind his Grand Prize mother. Everybody, including Melvina, gathered around her and stared like she was an outer-space creature. Mrs. Sheppard in her pillbox hat with the flowers on it, her silver-blue curled hair, and her seashell earbobs. She was a regular grandmother type. She didn't look so bad.

"Mama, I want you to meet Sarah here. My wife."

Mother reached out her hand. "Mighty glad to meet you, Mrs. Sheppard. Walter has told me an awful lot about you."

Mrs. Sheppard did not shake hands with Mother, but just stood with her hands folded across her stomach and let her eyes fix on Mother. "You are a pretty thing. I'll say so. Walter, she is a pretty thing. How is it a pretty girl like you come to be a divorcée?"

"Mrs. Sheppard, meet the children." Mother put her arms around us. "This is Lucy, and Roy, and little Benny." She didn't add that at that moment we were the three squeakiest-clean children in Tallahassee. But she could have. She didn't say, "Look here, Mrs. Sheppard, look behind these kids' ears, clean as a whistle. See that?" She did not make us show our teeth, how toothpaste-white they were, or make us hold out our hands for Mrs. Sheppard to check how our fingernails were clipped so neat. She didn't do it, but she could have.

We said, "Glad to meet you." Then Mrs. Sheppard told Walter she was tired and thought she would lie down and rest. That was how the visit started. And it never got better.

Mrs. Sheppard went and laid down on the bed in my room—with her flower hat still on her head. She laid on her back with her hands still folded over her stomach, her shoes still on her feet. She looked like somebody about to get buried in a grave.

Mother put a Tennessee Ernie Ford religious record on the record player. She thought some music would help Mrs. Sheppard rest better and would drown out any noise me and Roy and Benny made, which wasn't much. Mother told Melvina she could go on home, since supper was under control. But Melvina didn't want to. She said, "I ain't come clear down here for nothing." That was because if there was something good left over from this company dinner she was gon take it home with her. She always did that. Fix her a big plate and take it up to her house. Meanwhile she was gon sit in the kitchen with a flyswatter in her hand and wait.

Most of the afternoon passed with Mrs. Sheppard laying in my bed. Finally Walter went in and woke her up to come eat supper. Mother made him do it because she didn't know how much longer the three of us could keep being so good. She was afraid our decent behavior was going to run out just about the time we sat down to eat. Roy and me would chew with our mouths open and grab food. Benny would start crying and rub Jell-O in his hair. She wanted to get supper over with before our goodness ran completely out.

When we were all seated at the table, Benny in his high chair by Mother, we bowed our heads and Mother asked the blessing, like she always did. Sometimes she let me or Roy ask the blessing, but on an occasion like this, with Mrs. Sheppard eating with us, Mother said it herself. She meant every word of it, you could tell. We started passing the food around in a quiet way. Mrs. Sheppard looked at Mother and said, "What church do you go to?"

Walter made this noise in his throat.

"Well," Mother said, "I was raised Methodist and I'm raising the children Methodist."

"What is the name of your Methodist church?"

"It's right in downtown Tallahassee," Mother said. "Trinity Methodist. It's a nice church."

"Walter was raised a Baptist," Mrs. Sheppard said.

Walter kept on eating.

"Walter never missed a day of Sunday school when he was growing up. Did you, Walter? If the door was open the Sheppard family was there."

"There's not too much difference between Methodist and Baptist," Mother said. "They're pretty close."

"World of difference." Mrs. Sheppard put spoonfuls of sugar in her already sweetened tea. "If it was good enough for John the Baptist, then it is good enough for me. Baptizing is. Real baptizing, like the Bible says. Underwater, head and all, washing away those sins, getting reborn right on the spot. Wet as a newborn baby."

"Mama," Walter said, in his please-don't-get-started-with-this voice. The same one he used on Mother sometimes.

"It's so," she said. "Methodists might think sprinkling a little dab of water on their heads is baptizing. But they're wrong. Sprinkling is not baptizing. It's sprinkling. God doesn't care one thing about a few drops of water on your head—not even enough to mess up your hair. There's a world of difference."

Mother acted like she needed to cut Benny's pork chop for him and wipe off his mouth with a napkin. We could tell she was biting her tongue.

"Walter is baptized proper. Aren't you, Walter? Didn't I take you and Hugh Henry and get y'all baptized? Because if the Bible says it, then I believe it."

Mother was watching Walter eat. Her eyes were beating on him. If her legs could reach him, she would have kicked the daylights out of him as a signal for him to say something. It looked like she was chewing her food, but really she was biting her tongue.

Me and Roy had not said one word. We had not spilled our milk or dropped food in our laps. Since we didn't know much about grandmothers we just sat there watching Mrs. Sheppard. She was our first close-up look at a real grandmother.

"So," she said to Mother, "where is your first husband?" Mrs. Sheppard smashed her Jell-O square with the back of her fork. That Jell-O shook like crazy. "Your first husband. Where is he?"

Mother darted her eyes at Walter. "Mrs. Sheppard, we ought not to talk about this at the dinner table with the children."

"Sarah don't have a first husband and a second husband, Mama. All she's got is one husband, and that's me."

"I was just asking a harmless question, Walter."

"We're not gon talk about this now, Mama."

It was quiet a long time, us sitting at the table eating. Us using nice manners. Sometimes somebody said pass this or that and somebody would do it. Sometimes Walter cleared his throat. All there was was knives scraping across plates and forks tapping, and ice cubes melting and clanking in the glasses. Then Mother said, "Does anybody want some dessert?" Me and Roy did. Everybody did. So Mother fussed around the table moving the plates.

Mrs. Sheppard put her hand on Walter's arm. "Son, it's normal for a mother to have curiosity about her boy's wife."

"Don't the Bible say something about curiosity, Mama? It's bound to say something on the subject."

Mrs. Sheppard looked at Walter mean-eyed. "Well, I'll tell you one thing, Walter Sheppard, the Bible says plenty about a divorced woman. It says, *Submit unto your husband,* which means your one and only husband. It doesn't say one thing about trade this one in for that one."

Mother carried the dinner plates into the kitchen. They were piled up with forks poking out between them, and they rattled when she walked, like skeleton bones banging together. She closed the door with her foot.

Walter pushed back his chair from the table and it made a loud scraping noise. Walter made some loud scraping noises of his own, saying, "Let me tell you what!" He was about to speak to his mother, but then he looked at me and Roy with our wide-open eyes and Benny with Jell-O in his hair and he stopped. "Lucy, you and Roy take Benny on out in the yard awhile. You'll get your dessert later on."

We didn't like the idea.

"Right now, I said!" We could tell Walter meant it. We pulled Benny out of his high chair and went on outside. We got under the dining room window as quiet as we could be—like we did when Melvina came to see Mother because

Old Alfonso beat her up. We got up there because we wanted to hear.

"Let me tell you something, Mama," Walter started. "This is my house. And Sarah is my wife. This can be any kind of house I want it to be, and I want it to be a Methodist house. You hear me? If you and John the Baptist don't like it, it's plain too bad!"

We wanted to look in the window so bad and see if Walter was making his mother cry. "And another thing, Mama. You cannot come in my house acting like it's your house. You cannot be talking that divorced-woman trash to Sarah. Do you hear me?"

"You never used to talk to me like this." Mrs. Sheppard was crying her words. "Not before you married her."

"For Lord's sake, Mama."

"I just want what's best for you, Walter. That's all I ever wanted. For you a Christian home with a wife of your own and kids of your own. You can't blame a mother for that. I just wanted you to have a good wife that appreciates you."

"Mama," Walter said calmly, "I'm going to be picking out my wife, not you. And I picked Sarah. She ain't making me into a Methodist any more than you ever made a Baptist out of me."

Mrs. Sheppard blew her nose.

"You don't know one thing about Sarah, Mama. Not one thing she's been through, and you ain't never gon know because it ain't your damn business."

"Walter," she cried, "you never used to talk like that."

It got quiet. Walter sitting there, his mama crying into her paper napkin. "Do you think I'm blind? Do you, Walter? Do you think I was born yesterday?"

"Mama, what are you talking about?"

"When I got here this afternoon and your wife said meet

the children—and I saw that littlest boy. Walter, I cannot tell you what it did to me."

"What the . . . ?"

"It was like you standing there, Walter. Why, he couldn't be any more yours if you named him Walter Sheppard, Junior. Did you think I wasn't gon notice that little boy looking like your spitting image?"

Walter chuckled.

"It just come to me this afternoon, standing there seeing that little boy—you made over."

"What did?"

"Why you married that divorcée."

"Mama . . ."

"Don't deny it. I know you like a book. I laid in there on that bed, thinking how it was me that raised you that way. Honorable and all. You from a good Baptist home. Some men would be long gone when a divorcée comes up expecting a baby."

Me and Roy were still in the flower bed under the window. We did not know what to think about crazy Mrs. Sheppard.

"You're dead wrong, Mama. Do you hear me? This is my house and I'm saying you're dead wrong."

Mother opened the kitchen door. She and Melvina must have been listening in the kitchen same as we were listening in the flower bed. We got brave enough to look in the window. Here comes Mother carrying Walter and Mrs. Sheppard plates of pound cake and ice cream. She set Walter's down in front of him, but when she went to set Mrs. Sheppard's down, Mrs. Sheppard said, "I'm sorry, but I do not believe I can eat this. I have lost my appetite. I think I'll just go lay down awhile." She stood with her balled-up paper napkin pressed against her nose and went in my room and laid on the bed. Again.

Mother sat down at the table with Walter, who was

eating his dessert like on any ordinary day. Putting a spoonful of ice cream in his mouth and letting it melt. "Is she all right?" Mother asked.

"She's okay."

"It seems like we should do something, Walter."

"Like what?"

"I don't know, go in there and talk to her or something. Get this thing straight."

Walter was eating his pound cake and ice cream like he was enjoying the heck out of it. Like it was one million times more important than his mother laying like a corpse, crying because she had come down with the fatal truth.

"Well, we can't have her go around thinking Benny is yours and I tricked you, Walter. I don't want her to think that. I'm no tramp. It bothers me, Walter."

"Look on the good side. It's not you being a tramp so much as it is her Baptist boy being one hell of a lover."

"Walter." Mother smiled at him like she did when he would not take a serious thing serious. Like it could be the end of the world and Walter would sit and eat a plate of cake and ice cream, slow and relaxed. If bombs were going off Walter could sit still and feel good about himself.

In a minute he got up from the table and walked by Mother, patting her shoulder. "Good supper," he said, "for a Methodist divorcée." He walked on into the living room and sat in his regular chair over by the picture window.

When me and Roy and Benny came back in for our dessert, we saw Mother crying with her hands over her face, and Melvina patting her like she was a child. She turned from us and hurried down the hall to her bedroom. Mother in her room crying and crying, and Mrs. Sheppard laying in my bed doing the same. Some people might say Walter didn't have much of a way with women.

Nothing can take away a child's appetite like a mother crying her eyes out. Me and Roy sat at the table sort of jabbing at our cake, but not eating any of it. Melvina came in and stood by us, saying very quietly, "Y'all allow your mama to be sad, now, you hear? Don't she allow you to be sad when you need to?"

We looked at Melvina, and she reached out both hands and took our serious faces in them. Her hands were soft and warm, and wrapped most nearly from ear to ear under our chins. "God wouldn't have give folks no teardrops if he hadn't of meant for them to cry some, now would he?"

We nodded our heads no.

"And Melvina wouldn't of give y'all no dessert if she didn't expect y'all to eat it." We half smiled at her. She smiled too, and gave our faces a squeeze. "See can you eat your ice cream before it melts all over the table."

The next day Walter took his mother back to the Trailways bus so she could get on home to Valdosta. We said good-bye and nice to meet you like Mother told us to. We felt disappointed for Mother because she wanted us a grandmother so bad and could not get us one no matter what. Me and Roy tried to tell Mother we didn't need a grandmother. Not some blue-haired woman who just sleeps all the time with her shoes on. It was sort of like when you enter into a contest and try your absolute hardest to win, and then find out that the prize is something you never have wanted in your life. Just some contraption that's gon stay broken and tore up, and don't work good when it's fixed. We told Mother never mind about Mrs. Sheppard, but that made her sadder than ever.

Later on, when Walter saw how funeralish we were acting, he said his mother would not know a good kid if one bit her. In fact, he said, if she ever came back that's what me and Roy should do. Bite her. Bite her right on the leg. Me and Roy laughed our heads off. Walter is so funny.

*T*ROUBLE erupted in Birmingham and Montgomery. We saw it on TV one night, and Mother was never the same afterwards. She was in love with Martin Luther King. Everybody else's mother was in love with Frank Sinatra—but Mother gave him up completely when she saw Martin Luther King. If Walter died and Martin Luther King's wife died, Mother would have gone to find the man and marry him. It was the truth. I think she believed she'd finally found a man who understood something. She never expected it to happen—to find a man who could speak the things right out of her heart. She'd have thrown Walter and my real daddy both into the Gulf of Mexico if she'd thought she stood a chance with Martin Luther King.

Melvina didn't get as excited over him as Mother did. "As crazy as he's talking, he's going to get hisself killed."

"What's wrong with you, Melvina? The man's straight from heaven," Mother said. "Can't you see that?"

"Can't a colored man talk to white people like that and them listen. He must don't know white people like I do."

Mother shot her a look.

Every time Martin Luther King was on TV, Walter took his newspaper into the bathroom to read it.

One night they showed the Montgomery police chasing colored people with sticks, their teeth in a snarl while they hit the colored people again, again, again. Police dogs were set loose, and everybody knows colored people are afraid of police dogs. They were running and screaming. Montgomery is less than thirty miles from Granddaddy's farm, and when Mother saw a colored woman fall to the ground in the fighting and a policeman strike her across the head with his stick, the woman bloody-headed, screaming to Jesus, Mother cried and said, "That could have been Sudie. You know that, don't you?"

She acted like it was Roy's and my fault. Like it was Walter's fault. Like she was seeing her own family on TV trying to beat colored people to death with sticks. She was furious with all of us over it.

Martin Luther King said things on TV the way colored preachers always said things, like he was really singing it, very slowly, so it was clearly understood. Everything he said, Mother whispered, "Amen," to herself out loud, just like *she* was a colored woman.

Suddenly everybody in Tallahassee had things to say about integration. Another civil war, people said, this time between colored and white. There were places colored outnumbered white, and wherever the colored needed a hand, people said, Yankees would come down and fight on their side, because they wanted the colored to get happier in the South so they'd stay down here and stop dragging up North and messing up all the cities up there. Yankees wanted the southerners to treat the colored better so they'd stay where they belonged—down here with us. Bubba's Daddy said, "When the colored start carrying guns and getting up an army, it's a sign of the end times. The Bible says so." I couldn't sleep good anymore because of it.

"If the colored man is going to have a gun, then the white man better have two," Bubba's Daddy said. So now he kept a gun in his car, and he didn't care who knew it. Bubba showed it to Roy, a little gun that fit underneath the seat on the driver's side. Roy wanted Walter to get one like it for his truck because he couldn't stand for Bubba's Daddy to outdo Walter in anything.

We had a book about World War II. Mother ordered it from *Life* magazine, and Roy and Benny and I had studied it until the spine was broken. Dead babies, torn-up cities, bombed buildings. Blood splattered on everything. It was the worst book in the world. We studied the wounds and the nakedness with equal terror. Silently imagined ourselves in the pictures. We looked at it by the hour, until Mother took it away from us. Those war pictures were in my head, though, and Roy's too. So when people started talking about integration it scared us. They said it was going to be integration or war—and nobody was sure which would be worse.

I started to wonder if Melvina hated us. Did she go home in the evenings, curse our name, count up all the rotten stuff we said and did? I pictured her sitting at her supper table saying to her kids, "That stupid Lucy, she's the stupid one. Mr. Sheppard's underwear is gray as pitch. Roy is a born liar—be in prison before he's sixteen. Mrs. Sheppard busybodying herself into the grave. Does she think I want to listen to all that talk?" What does Melvina say? We thought she loved us. Really. Like the time we came home from school and found Melvina asleep on the sofa with little Benny in her arms. It looked like love to us. I thought it was.

Now I wondered if Melvina held us accountable for every bad action a white person ever took. Did she think white people were all the same? Mother didn't hold every niggerish thing that happened against Melvina. She didn't blame her for what went on at the Blue Bird, all the drunken ruckus. She didn't even blame her for the way colored people seemed to have way more children than they could look after right. Walter said, "The colored have more kids than they do good sense." But I don't think Mother blamed Melvina for that.

ANNIE was pinning Melvina's wash on the line out in her own yard, and I was in my yard practicing cartwheels in the grass so I could try out for cheerleader. I was flipping all over the place. "Annie, watch this," I said. "See if my legs are straight?"

Before I could get a running start Annie hollered, "Do your granddaddy stay in Alabama?"

I stopped mid-step, looked at her, nodded yes.

"They're killing niggers up there," she said, pointing a clothespin at me, looking me square in the eye. I think she was waiting on me to come up with an answer of some kind.

SUDIE had moved to Grand-daddy's house. He said so on the phone. It was the sensible, practical thing. She'd been living in a little fall-down house up the road for as long as anybody could remember, but the house wasn't hers. She just lived there because she always had, and so folks called it Sudie's house. Her brother, James's daddy, used to live there too, until he died. He farmed the land, cotton. The white man that owned the land wanted James's daddy living in the house while he was working the land, doing a good job of it. Then he died. Besides that, farmers started using machines to do what it took a bunch of niggers to do back then. So nobody said nothing. The white man never told Sudie and her two sisters, Yes, you can stay in the house, and they never asked him whether they could or not. No man to work anymore, just a bunch of colored women growing old, so the white man let them be. Then the sisters moved off different places, one to Montgomery and one to Jackson, Mississippi. After that people called it Sudie's house. *You turn right down there at Sudie's house like you're going to church. Somebody around here needs to take some pine planks and a fistful of nails to Sudie's house while she still got a house.*

But there was no sense in it. Sudie needing chopped wood, and too old to chop. Using a kerosene lamp. Walking the hundred yards to the outhouse. The roof falling in. The porch rotten. And her well water was so rusty she's got to boil it first. Sudie is too old to boil a tub of water in the yard, scrub her clothes on a board and hang them on a fence wire to dry. That's how the idea started. Sudie bringing her pillowcase of dirty clothes to Granddaddy's to wash them in his washing machine, the easy way. She ironed them there. She hung them in a closet, took home each night what she would wear back the next day.

Sometimes she would lock the door to Granddaddy's bathroom, run herself a tub of warm water and bathe. Granddaddy coming home and Sudie's locked in the bathroom taking a slow bath. He yells, "That's not what I'm paying you for, woman, to come to my house and take a all-day bath in my bathtub."

It just started to make sense—Sudie moving to Grand-daddy's house, out of that by-herself rattletrap house that was too cold in the winter and too full of bugs in the summer and lonely all the time and Sudie's getting old.

It made good sense for Granddaddy too. His breakfast on the table when he gets up in the morning. No need to warm up the truck and drive to get Sudie every blasted day. Somebody to play checkers with after supper and to watch the fights with on Saturday-night TV, and somebody to listen to him talk. Even Sudie, who thought most of what he said was dead wrong, could listen to him say it, shake her head in disagreement, and keep him happy. And Sudie liked to fish too, could sit on the pond bank from morning to night, napping and fishing, and not tire out a bit faster than Granddaddy did.

So Granddaddy and James took the truck up to Sudie's place on a Saturday and loaded it up—one load, that's all. Left the stove such as it was and left the washtub and two chairs that made sitting down too much trouble the way you'd sink down, deep, and have to climb your way back out of them with their rotten springs and loose stuffing. Sudie just left them. Just took her personal stuff, said get this, carry this, load this, and handed James and Grand-daddy whatever was worth keeping. And she called her cats. Two of them. She climbed up in the truck cab, her cats on her lap, and Granddaddy and James tied her stuff down with some rope in the back. Granddaddy mumbling and groaning about Sudie moving in was bad enough, but two cats was just plain too much. Said he needed two cats like a hole in the head.

Sudie didn't seem sad about leaving the place that had been her home most of her life, the only home she remem-bered. Her leaving it and moving in with Granddaddy, mov-ing in Mrs. Wilcox's house, the house she'd been keeping clean for as long as she could remember. Spent more time there than at her own house, and now it is her own house— sort of.

Mother tried a hundred times to get Granddaddy to bring Sudie down to Tallahassee with him when he came to see us, but Sudie wouldn't do it. She said she couldn't ride for no five hours straight, said if anybody wanted to see her they would have to come to Alabama to do it.

7 know all about George Wallace now. Walter says, "He's the only politician I ever credited with having any sense." Mother says he is the smallest little man she ever saw. When Granddaddy came for Easter he had George Wallace stickers all the way across the back bumper of his truck. Skippy didn't miss seeing them.

OTHER hadn't told us a thing about it. She opened the *Tallahassee Democrat* one afternoon and shouted, "My gosh, here it is. It's in here." She read her own letter out loud: " 'A neighbor is not just the person next door but all the people who share the world with you.' " She read the whole thing right down to her maiden name, Sarah E. Wilcox.

"You wrote that letter?" Melvina said. "Let me see it."

Roy and I leaped up from our places on the sofa and went to look. There it was. Our mother's name in the newspaper. Then Walter drove up.

"I had to do it, Walter," she said, "so I can live with myself."

"You don't live with yourself, Sarah. You live with me, remember?" He slung his hat across the room, missing Melvina by inches. Roy and Benny and I ducked, belly to the floor, and he hit Walter Cronkite right between his television eyes.

"I swear to God, Sarah." Walter slumped into his chair. "Are you trying to get us all killed?"

"Walter, I just . . ."

"Don't talk to me. There's nothing you can say that I want to hear. Damn it, woman."

"But Walter . . ."

"Shut your mouth, Sarah. I mean it. I've heard enough

out of you to last me the rest of my life." He picked up the newspaper, held it in front of her face, and tore it in half.

For two weeks afterwards, we tiptoed around him, doing our best not to set him off. If Mother asked him something he nodded yes or no. She couldn't get a real reply out of him. He sat in his chair and thought about something—we were scared to guess what. Mother fixed Walter's favorite suppers three nights running. She got Melvina to make a lemon icebox pie. If he wanted her to, I know she rubbed his back, because Walter liked a good backrub before going to bed.

I'd have paid money to see Walter hug her in the kitchen or pull her down in his lap when she walked by with a load of clean clothes. One hundred dollars to hear him tease her about the snake in their bed. But he had stopped that.

Everybody on California Street knew Mother had written that letter. They knew she was a Wilcox as much as a Sheppard—maybe more. Miss Margaret Ann, next door, said, "You want Lucy going to a school full of colored boys? They carry knives, Sarah."

Bubba's Daddy saw the letter. Now he thought we were nigger lovers because Mother was. I wanted to tell him we only knew one nigger—that was Old Alfonso, and we sure didn't love him—but there was no sense in trying to say it.

My mother's name in the newspaper—I liked it so much it scared me. I had gotten the newspaper out of the trash—Walter had not injured Mother's letter in his rampage. I had cut it out neatly with the kitchen scissors. I read the letter alone in my room at night: *It is sad to realize the church is perpetuating segregation and racism. Is the Southern church really the hotbed of ignorance and hatred that the editorial page would lead us to believe? The only thing that redeems the word "Christian" in recent months is Martin Luther King. He brings it dignity.* I shivered when I read this, overjoyed.

The rest of the time I was mad at Mother. I felt sorry for

Walter and wondered if Mother knew that he sat out in his truck at night and drank whiskey from the bottle he kept in the glove compartment. I saw him out my window, sitting with the door open, one leg in the truck and one leg out, his elbow on the steering wheel, looking straight ahead at nothing.

II

Looking for Something to Save

$\mathcal{I}$T has to do with your blood and how it's changed after he just walks out late at night, letting the screen door slam behind him, thinking you are probably asleep, but not thinking enough about it to look in and see, he doesn't say good-bye, you hear him go, but don't believe it, pray to God it's a dream, like you are paralyzed in your too hot little bed with your brother, who is paralyzed too. Neither of you gets up to go see, because then it might be true. So me and Roy laid in bed like we were dead, and we wished it, while we listened to the sounds Mother made. She didn't scream. So we didn't. In the morning we unparalyzed and Mother's eyes were gone, swollen off her face like two slits someone had stuffed large marbles into and sewn closed with catgut. She was ugly-faced, our own mother, and something inside us broke at the sight of her and spilled into our blood, like splinters, tiny, sharp points of glass, and it stayed that way, making it hurt to breathe, making it hurt to have a pumping heart. But we didn't cry.

This was before Mother found God. Back when she *was* God. Mother was not like any other mother, even later, after she married Walter, who was a normal man.

We didn't have a mirror in our house until Mother married Walter and he couldn't find anyplace to look while he parted his hair in the mornings and he mentioned it, and then we all knew for the first time. No mirrors. How did me and Roy know what we looked like? How did Mother know

107

if her lipstick was on straight? Walter was amazed but thought it was a nice quality, a woman who wasn't busy looking at herself, fixing, painting, and curling. But the truth was that Mother didn't need a mirror to see herself, because she saw herself in every other person she looked at. It was like she went inside them, felt what it was to be them, and then came out shining and knowing—looking good. At least in our eyes. I think she wanted to raise me and Roy and Benny to do the same, see ourselves in everybody we ever looked at, but we weren't good at it.

"Mother's crying," Benny said one day when Roy and I came walking home from school. He pedaled down the driveway on his toy tractor, dragging one of my old naked dolls at the end of a rope behind him.

"Benny," I said, "what are you doing . . . ?"

"I'm riding her. She likes it."

Roy and I went in the house and found Mother closed up in the bathroom making what sounded like vomiting noises.

"Is Mother sick?" I walked to my room, yanked my dress over my head, and pulled on a pair of shorts. I kicked the dress under the bed and went to stand outside the bathroom, where Roy was leaned against the door, his ear pressed to it.

"What's wrong?" Roy says to Mother. "You sick?"

The toilet flushed for the second time.

"Your daddy come around here today," Melvina said. "He came looking for you."

Our daddy had not been mentioned since Mother married Walter and we moved to California Street. Not once.

"Your Mama been locked in that bathroom ever since your daddy come."

"What do you mean, looking for us?" Roy said.

"Y'all kids. Get away from that door, Roy. Quit leaning against it." Roy stood up straight. "I never seen a woman so scared of a man, as your mama is your daddy."

"She's not," I said.

"What did he do to her?"

"Nothing," me and Roy answered.

"He must have done a whole lot of nothing—because she ain't quit crying all afternoon."

It didn't seem right for a colored woman like Melvina, whose own husband beat her up every time he got drunk enough, to be asking a question like that. Melvina started back toward the kitchen, the heels of her shoes slapping at the floor. "Ain't no law against crying," she said. "Y'all get away from that door and let the woman cry."

But we didn't. We remained planted outside the bathroom, eventually pressing our bottoms against the wall and sliding down against it until we were sitting knees-up on the floor. Neither one of us said a word. We listened to Mother flush the toilet twice more. I bit off the uneven edges of my fingernails and made a little pile of the paper-thin half-moon strips in the fold of my shirttail. Roy's eyes scanned the wall behind me, working their way up and down the planks, counting the number of knots in the wood.

Melvina said, "Come in the kitchen if you want something to eat." But we sat until Mother jiggled the bathroom doorknob and unlocked it. She opened the door and stood looking at us, her face bright pink, a sour red smile stretched across her face. "Guess what?" she said.

It was like somebody had nailed us to the floor.

Mother squatted eye-level with us. Her blouse was wet under her arms. "Your daddy has been missing you two."

We nodded, our eyes locked open.

"And he wants to see you. Because . . ." The muscles around Mother's mouth quivered. Her eyes puffed into slits.

Roy put his hand on Mother's knee. She folded over us,

pulling our faces against her wet blouse. She kissed the tops of our heads, then cleared her throat. "Because your daddy loves you a lot, you know." Her voice shook like something broken in a wrapped box.

Me and Roy leaned into Mother as hard as we could, trying to soak some of the sadness out of her, feeling her misery juice up in us, and being glad, as if any unhappiness we could absorb relieved her of some. Her heart squeezed like a fist, opening, closing.

"Everything will be fine." Mother pulled away from us and stood up, rubbing her hands across her face, trying to smooth her skin back into place.

"What about Walter?" Roy said. "Does Walter know?"

"I don't see nothing to him," Melvina said, "your daddy."

"You don't know him," I said. "That's why."

"Y'all don't know him neither. He's the same as a stranger."

But that wasn't true. I remembered things about him. I knew Roy did too. It was only Mother that tried to forget everything. She had Walter now.

Walter didn't like to see Mother torn up over anything. To come home and see she'd been crying herself sick. Didn't like Mother's other husband—the one supposed to be gone forever—coming around unexpected, like something that fell out of the sky. Like a bomb. Mother, with slit eyes and a Kleenex knotted in her hand, saying to Walter, when he came in from work, before he could even get his hat off, "You'll never guess what." Then all the rest of it. Mentioning our real daddy in the living room in front of all of us. Walter listened, didn't say a word, watched Mother bend over to wipe vanilla wafer crumbs off Benny's mouth with her wadded-up Kleenex and hurry out of the room. Walter didn't like it. His wife closed up in the bathroom again. Johnny Conyers's name mentioned in our house, the house Walter Sheppard had bought and paid for.

"Mr. Sheppard's worried," Melvina said, looking out the window at Walter, who had walked out to the yard and was watering the grass, the same spot again and again, jerking the neck of the hose back and forth absentmindedly. "He's worried it's not you children your daddy wants time with. He thinks he hears your daddy saying your mama's name."

"He does not," I said.

A couple of days later, while Melvina cooked supper she made me slice tomatoes and put them on a plate and dot each one with a spoonful of mayonnaise, and I was having trouble because the mayonnaise slid off unless the tomato was exactly level on the plate. I tried to get the mayonnaise to point at the top like a Dairy Queen ice cream cone, so it was hard. While I was working at it, Mother sat on the kitchen stool reading the newspaper, or at least staring at it.

"I swear it is just like Johnny Conyers to show up out of the blue like this." She crushed the paper closed.

"What you worrying about?" Melvina asked.

"He wants to see the children, Melvina. You know that."

"That ain't what's worrying you."

"I guess you know what's worrying me better than I do, then?"

"You jealous."

"Jealous? Jealous of what?"

"Him wanting to see the kids, ain't said nothing about wanting to see you."

"Melvina Williams, you're crazy. Crazier than crazy. What Johnny Conyers wants doesn't mean a thing to me. You hear?" She was shouting. "If he'd stop cropping up out of nowhere then I could forget the man altogether, because he means less than nothing to me." Mother stomped out of the kitchen.

Melvina turned to me and said, "Well, all who believes that stand on your head."

Daddy came to see us after he and Mother got the arrangements made. It was on a Saturday. Walter had taken the truck out to dig up some grass, and to get away from the house and the confusion. Skippy didn't go with Walter. He said he had to stay home and do some work for Melvina— and Walter was crazy enough to believe that. But what Skippy really wanted to do was hang around our yard, him and Orlando, waiting to get a look at our real daddy, waiting to see what kind of shoes he wore and what kind of car he drove and all the stupid stuff colored boys pay attention to. Skippy didn't fool me one bit, showing up when Daddy was supposed to show up, making me holler out my bedroom window, "Curiosity killed the cat, Skippy Williams!"—which didn't bother him at all. In fact, he smiled, which made me want to scream.

Mother got us cleaned up but was quiet about it, not calling out a list of manners to remember like usual. Then she locked herself in the bathroom, and me and Roy thought she was vomiting some more, or crying her eyes out again, but when she came out she didn't look a bit sad. She had taken the pin curls out of her hair and put on lipstick and clean shorts and even had on that My Sin perfume Walter gave her for Christmas. She kept looking at the clock and tucking in our shirttails again and again and looking at herself in the full-length mirror Walter had hung in the hall. When our daddy came to the door she took a big breath, stiffened, and herded us out to him.

Me and Roy were cautious, but not Benny. Mother put her arms around Roy's and my shoulders and said, "Lucy and Roy, you remember your daddy, don't you?"

"Yes ma'am," we answered.

"Hey, Lucy. Hey, Roy. It sure is good to see you." Our

daddy was smiling. "You two sure have been growing. Hey there, Benny boy." Benny ran over and took our daddy's hand, which made me and Roy feel stupid, our own hands hanging so useless. "Thought we'd go get some lunch and then I'd take you over to my house for a while. Okay?" He didn't wait for us to agree. He was nervous as a cat, and Mother quiet as a mouse. "Run on out to the car. Let me talk to your mama a minute," he said, and we minded him.

"Sarah, this is going to work out. I want to thank you for being fair. I know you could have made this into a mess if you wanted to."

"Thank Walter."

"You thank him for me."

"You said three o'clock. You'll have the children back by then."

"Promise." Our daddy turned to leave, then stopped and looked at Mother. "Don't guess you want to come with us?"

Mother shook her head a slow no.

He came out and got in the car. Mother stood on the porch waving good-bye to us, not smiling.

I didn't know what to think about our daddy. Something made me want to like him, like it's a rule that a girl should like her own father. Something about the same blood pumping inside both of us, and me looking almost just like him. Walter says he's a paper-shuffling fool that makes Mother cry. Walter calls him a hide-and-seek daddy that doesn't play by the rules. He says, "Sarah, I swear Johnny doesn't know a thing in this world unless it's written down in a book." Mother doesn't argue.

Walter says, "The man doesn't have a lick of good sense. What did you used to see in him, Sarah? What the hell was it?" He asks her that all the time, and she never answers him.

113

But I don't think of that now. I think only that Daddy and I have the same color hair, blond, with no curl at all. I think he is probably sorry for everything. I think Walter is wrong. I decide I'm going to love Daddy if it kills me.

"Should we call you Daddy?" I ask.

"That makes good sense to me." He smiles.

It was quiet almost the whole ride to the restaurant. Nobody could think of anything to say. Finally, I got my nerve up. "Well, Daddy," my voice came out like it belonged to some other girl, "how has your life been going?"

Daddy busted out laughing. His laughter made Roy and Benny laugh too, sitting in the backseat quieter than they had ever been in their lives. "Lucy, you are your mother made over."

I took that as a compliment.

We went to a nice sit-down place with half-dollar cheeseburgers and little miniature jukeboxes at every table. Daddy gave us each a quarter and let us pick out five songs apiece, and by the time all of those songs had played, well, then lunch was over.

I picked the hound-dog song because it reminded me of Skippy, and the jailhouse-rock song because it reminded me of Old Alfonso. I picked Connie Francis singing "Where the Boys Are" because I saw that movie, and Eddy Arnold singing "Lips Sweeter Than Wine," and Tennessee Ernie singing "Sixteen Tons" because it was Walter's favorite song. Roy and Benny just picked out a bunch of mess, stupid songs nobody ever heard in their life and never wanted to hear again.

Later we went to our daddy's apartment. Roy and Benny ran through the place like wild Indians. They watched TV and opened up every drawer and cabinet in the place. But Daddy didn't seem to care. Smiled at every mess they made.

He tried to read us some stories, but Roy and Benny

wouldn't listen long enough. They stayed keyed up and running wild. Finally they went outside to see what they could get into. I stayed inside and listened to Daddy read. Not three-pig stuff and all that Goldilocks mess. Nothing like that. Stories he wrote himself about grownups doing stuff crazier than kids could ever think of. Sometimes he'd read along and then leave out a part. He'd say, "Your mother wouldn't want you hearing that." He'd wink at me, like it was a nasty part, and skip that section.

Those were some stories. One was about children hunting their father with guns in the woods the way a person hunts a rabbit. The father is thinking like a scared rabbit thinks. But it's his own kids doing it, stalking their jackrabbit-type father. It was pure strange.

Another story was about a woman going crazy on a Greyhound bus, always on her way someplace but she never gets there. She turns into an old woman; then she realizes she's been on a bus her whole life, looking at the world out dirty-fingerprint windows while that bus zoomed along. The bus stopped a million times and opened its doors. But for some reason she never got off. So she goes nuts on the Greyhound heading for Atlanta.

And a story about a man who sees a beautiful woman always walking by his house in the afternoon and he tries to meet her. He waits for her on his steps and walks over to her when she comes by. He talks to her, but she can't see him or hear him and walks past him like he is not even there. This goes on for days, until the man finally realizes that he's invisible, can't even see his own self in the mirror anymore. Tries to put his voice on a tape recorder but no sound comes out on the tape. By the end of the story he finds out he's a dead man—has been dead a long time—but never was bad enough to go to hell or good enough to go to heaven, so he just got left here on earth—dead and invisible. I am talking a weird story.

That's the kind of stories Daddy wrote, and read them to

me like they were picture shows. I loved hearing his half-crazy stories. Was thankful that it was me hearing them and not Walter. Just one of those stories would have Walter convinced that our daddy belonged in Chattahoochee. Walter would think any grown man who spent time writing such foolishness didn't have enough work to do. "Idle time can addle the mind," Walter always says. So I was keeping Walter out of it. Besides, I liked the crazy stuff.

Daddy asked us about Mother like it was just chitchat. "So does your mama hug Walter a lot?"

"Walter don't like hugging," Roy answered. "She would be hugging him, but he don't like it."

"What did Walter get your mama for her birthday?"

"A crown," Roy answered. "One of those crowns with diamonds in it. You know."

"A crown?" Daddy smiled. "Where in the world does your mama wear a crown?"

"Church," Roy said.

It's embarrassing. Roy doesn't like Daddy to talk about Mother. Every time Daddy asks a question Roy tells a lie answering it. "Walter might buy her a deep-freeze too." He gets these ideas from watching *Queen for a Day* with Melvina.

I get mad at Roy because he is lying his head off. But Daddy is polite about it and goes along with him. And keeps right up with the questions. "Do Walter and your mama dance in the kitchen to the radio sometimes? Do they sleep in a double bed? Does your mama have a nickname for Walter like Sweetie or something?" Questions were stuck inside our game of Old Maid. Questions ambushed us when we washed up before going home. He did not know he was giving us an upset stomach asking so many questions.

When Daddy brought us home Mother was in the yard. She and our daddy sat on the picnic table. It was nice. They laughed and Daddy said a bunch of good things about us, their children, that Mother had done a good job of raising. Then Walter drove up in his truck.

Mother rushed over to Walter, who walked right in the house without looking her way. She had to practically run to catch up with him. Daddy stood there like somebody caught sneaking past a "No Trespassing" sign. A look came over his face, watching Mother run after Walter like that. Daddy, who is ten times handsomer than Walter, looking like he has just broken something he always meant to take good care of. It's like for a minute Daddy doesn't understand that everything is his fault in the first place. I go over and walk him to the car, like I am his mother and he is the child.

"I'll call you next week, Lucy," Daddy says. "We'll do this again real soon." He looked over my head, staring at the closed door of our house. "I promise." Then he got in his car and drove off, looking straight ahead.

I knew he was not coming back.

The part I hate about this, the embarrassing part, is that Melvina and Skippy both act like it is their business too, us and our daddy. Colored people are so nosy, I've always noticed that. "I don't have nothing good to say about a pretty man," Melvina said. "What good it do for a man to be so girl-faced? It make him love hisself too much."

"He's not pretty," I said. "He's handsome."

"Same uselessness."

"Why don't you shut up, Melvina!" Roy said. Mother popped him on the butt, hard, with her houseshoe and sent him to his room.

"If you ain't careful, that man will rub off all over those children," Melvina said.

I should have noticed something strange about Mother afterwards. A jumpiness. The way she vanished into her own thoughts and floated them up over our heads like puffs of cigarette smoke people blow at the ceiling.

She looked over her shoulder like she suspected someone might be sneaking up on her. She left the lights on all night, saying the next morning that she forgot to turn them off. Just forgot for some reason. We ate our breakfast not listening to it. Mother could have just as easily whistled Dixie as made up explanations none of us were looking for. Walter never suspected a thing.

But I knew why she wanted the lights on. She didn't want anything hiding in a shadow, like a man she used to love, once, before she came to her senses.

Sometimes I wished I had run after Daddy, hugged his leg like a boa constrictor, stuck to him like a Band-Aid, locked myself around him like a ball on a chain, like I was the law and he was the prisoner. I pictured myself hugging Daddy so tight he had to call Mother to come and get me loose, but she couldn't do it either.

Daddy floated in and out of our lives like a ghost. And a ghost was something you weren't supposed to believe in.

Afterwards I drove Mother crazy. I bothered her like a song stuck on your mind that makes you hum and say the words all day long—you are sick to death of it—but you can't stop. I kept after her like a refrain, or a spinning record that hits a snag on the best line in the song, *Do you love him or not? Do you love him or not? Do you love him or not?* I said I wanted a yes or no. But she knew it was only a yes I wanted.

"When I see your daddy in you three . . . I love the parts of him that are in you," Mother said.

Loving him in us was no good. I wanted to know if she loved him by himself—like he was. I looked like him, yellow-haired and blue-eyed, Roy didn't like to do things right, the same way Daddy didn't, and Benny was bookish, studied pictures like he had to take a test later. But all that was no good.

I think Mother wished she could say what I wanted to hear, but was afraid to say it because it was true—or because it wasn't true. Since she couldn't say what I wanted to hear, she said other things, coming as close as she could, trying to hit on something that would suit me almost as well. "Your daddy is a handsome man, Lucy."

She hardly spoke one sentence about Daddy without putting us in the sentence too, Roy and Benny and me. Divorced from Daddy meant never say his name again. No sentence where she was alone with him—the two of them together in a private sentence of their own. No, only chaperoned sentences. I just wanted to know whether she loved him anymore.

"If I hadn't loved your daddy I never would have married him, would I? I wouldn't be the mother of his children if I hadn't loved him, would I?"

"I guess not," I said, unsatisfied.

"When a woman has a man's children, Lucy, it's like they get tied together by a rope. A knotted thing that keeps tugging on them the rest of their lives."

"And? And what else?"

"It was your daddy that cut that rope—slung words like an ax and cut himself loose."

Mother wasn't answering the question I had asked. She took a sock out of the laundry basket, dug around looking for the mate, then laid one on top of the other and rolled them together into a ball. They stayed together like that, couldn't get separated or lost.

"You know those metal tags Granddaddy staples to his cow's ears?" she said. "He used to burn his initials into their hide, so anybody who found a stray knew who it belonged to. It only hurts a minute, branding, but it lasts forever.

"Having a man's baby is like that. Don't roll your eyes at me, Lucy. The way a woman's body is, after a baby, like she's branded herself. Her stomach softer, like putty. Remember that putty Walter put in there around the window, and y'all wrote your name in it with your fingernail? Remember?"

I remembered.

"Like that. Stretch marks on a woman's stomach that read like a memorial plaque to the father of the baby. Like it's his name written across her in Chinese letters. Right there in her skin is a message that never was there before—and a woman can look at her skin and read the man's name, plain. Don't look at me like that, Lucy."

"So you've got Johnny B. Conyers written on you?"

"In a way, yes, I do. Like Granddaddy's cows. You look at their hide to see who they belong to."

"You're saying you belong to Daddy?"

"Sometimes when I take a bath, naked in the hot water, I look at myself and see your Daddy's name. Nothing will ever change that. It's like I'm an autograph book and he signed his name on every page. There's nothing I can do to erase it. What's written is written."

I still didn't know the answer. Was it yes or no? Did she love Daddy or not? When she said things about love it sounded angry—not like I thought love should sound. It was exactly like when Roy or Benny or me did something we should know better than to do and she got after us with a bedroom slipper, spanked us, and we cried. She grabbed our shoulders, shook us hard, and looked in our faces: "Now, I love you. I wouldn't spank you if I didn't." She said it like no way could she mean it, and we only believed it because we wanted to. That was how she talked about our daddy and loving him, like she had that bedroom slipper in her hand.

"Does Daddy know his name is written all over you?"

"Probably not." She was holding a blue sock but couldn't find the other one.

"Does Walter know?"

"Probably does."

"Does he care—that it's Daddy's name and not his?"

She gave up on the missing sock, stuck the one she had in her pocket, and loaded the clean clothes back into the laundry basket so she could carry them from room to room and put them where they belonged. She paused and said, "That's one of the reasons I love Walter, Lucy. He doesn't have to have his name written all over every possible thing. He's not like your daddy about being in love with his own name.

"Your daddy's got to look at things—like the stories he writes—and see his name on them. That's the only thing that makes him happy. Don't you understand, Lucy?"

I shrugged. Maybe I did and maybe I didn't.

"I do," Mother said. "I understand it, but it's sad to me. And Walter isn't like that. You could write his name up in the blue sky with one of those writing airplanes and I don't think Walter would so much as walk outside to look up and see it. He isn't in love with his name that way."

"So you love Walter. Do you love him more than Daddy?"

Mother lifted the laundry basket. "I've got good reasons to love Walter," she said. She started down the hall to put our clean clothes away, each item in its proper place.

Good reasons. That's what Mother said. She said she had *good reasons* for loving Walter. I already knew that.

*M*E and Karol and Patricia would get on our bathing suits and lay out on a quilt in the backyard. We'd get some cold drinks and Patricia's transistor radio and Patricia's movie magazines, which we had to hide from Mother because she didn't want me getting wrong ideas.

Me and Karol thought Patricia was a knockout in her two-piece bathing suit. That top filled out exactly right, just barely overflowing. How she would lie on her stomach on that blanket in the yard and paddle her feet up and down like she was swimming, that movie magazine opened up in front of her. Every song that came on the radio, she knew it and sang with it, and bounced her head and swung her long, all-day ponytail, and snapped her fingers with those pink fingernails. She chewed gum just as natural as a heartbeat. When I was by myself the songs that came on the radio were about me, but when Patricia was around then they were about her. Every song on the radio was written for Patricia, and I think she knew that.

Those long Saturday and Sunday afternoons with us out laying in the sun would be the very time Skippy would pick to mow the grass. He and Walter had this deal where Skippy could use Walter's big highway department lawn mower to get him some grass-cutting jobs down on the white part of California Street. He mostly worked at it in the cool of a morning or the late afternoon, and Walter said he made right good money too. Then Skippy cut our grass for free in exchange for use of Walter's mower. It was my job to carry him a cold drink. "Lucy," Mother would holler, "come take this iced tea out to Skippy," which I did, running alongside the mower, the ice cubes jingling like bells in the glass, the cold tea spilling on my leg. "Here," I shouted until he noticed me. He paused. The roar of the mower sounded hollow when it stood still, trying to cut what didn't need to be cut. Gripping the lawn mower handle with one hand, Skippy took the glass of tea, smiled at me—his jaw flexing square—and drank the whole glass in one gulp while I watched and he watched me watch. Mother makes the best iced tea. It's half lemonade. He reached into the glass, took out an ice cube, and rubbed it over his face. "Tell your mama thank you." He handed me the glass and went back to his mowing.

Like I said, about half the time he picked to mow the grass when me and Karol and Patricia were set up to lay out in the sun, and it was too hot and unsensible for anybody to be cutting grass. He'd start up that mower, it spitting cut grass all over us, sticking to the baby oil we smeared on our skin, and we couldn't hear the radio, or each other, or ourselves think. I would wrap a towel around me and walk over to him, hands over my ears, and shout, "Do you have to do that now?"

"Now's as good a time as any," he'd say, never altering his pace. "Look out." The mower was headed straight for my feet. Sometimes I had to jump to keep him from mowing off my toes.

We'd complain to Walter, who always said cutting grass was a necessity and sunbathing was a luxury, so he'd have to side with the grass cutting.

But our yard was big, so we'd move over to the other side of the house, away from where Skippy was running the mower. He paid us no mind. Acted like he hadn't noticed us laid out in our bathing suits on a bright-colored quilt. He ignored us like we were just more pine trees in the yard. But I knew he could look and look like he was not looking. He could lower his eyelids the way you pull a windowshade on a sunny day and leave it cracked just enough to still see out.

I bet he didn't miss watching a move Patricia made, especially when she unhooked her bathing suit top to keep from getting strap marks, and those times she forgot about it and rolled over or sat up. It could take your breath away. Her breasts were pure white—sitting there like a couple of snow cones before they pump the cherry flavor on. I know the sight put a swerve in his lawn mower. I bet Skippy thought me and Karol were ridiculous sprawled out on a quilt with the likes of Patricia.

I kept aware of Skippy in our yard, but I don't think Patricia and Karol did. Like as far as they were concerned he was nothing more than one of those pine trees he pretended we were. But they meant it. A colored boy pushing a lawn mower—about the same as a pine tree. Only noisier. They had never even noticed his face. The way his jaw flexed. How straight his teeth were. Nothing. And that time Patricia hosed the baby oil off herself sticking the nozzle of the water hose between her legs, and making all these thrusting gestures that made me and Karol squeal and holler for her to quit it. "Nobody's watching," she said. "Nobody's even out here."

"You think she's pretty, don't you?" I said to Skippy, who was latching the wooden door that led up under our house. He had just rolled the lawn mower under there and was fiddling with the lock. "I see you looking at her."

"She look all right."

"I know you can't take your eyes off her, out mowing the grass in hundred-degree heat, when half the time the grass don't even need to be mowed. Her daddy would have a fit. You know that, don't you?" I shivered to think what Bubba's Daddy would do.

"Ain't no law against cutting grass."

"You think she's pretty. Admit it."

"Some white girls look all right."

"Is that what you say about me?"

"I don't say nothing about you."

124

"Here"—he tossed me the keys to the door he had just locked—"give those to Mr. Sheppard, and don't forget."

"It would kill you to say something nice, wouldn't it?"

"It might," Skippy said. He made me want to scream. I watched him walk across our yard towards his own house next door, where Melvina had the porch light on. I just stood there like an idiot.

Me and Karol learned everything from Patricia. The telephone rang off the hook at her house with boys calling. Inside her pocketbook were about one hundred notes that she got at school. Sometimes she locked her bedroom door and let me and Karol read them out loud. Mostly they were from Jimmy. They told about dreams he was having. He had the notes dated, and every one started out, *I had another dream about you last night.* Then he went on to say amazing things like, *You were locked in a room at my grandmother's house. Don't ask me how you got there. But when I got the door pried open you wouldn't come out because you didn't have any clothes on. Last night I dreamed we were swimming in Lake Jackson and it turned into a bathtub. You look pretty good in a bathtub. I can't tell you what I dreamed after that. You'll get mad and slap me.* I had never read anything like Jimmy's notes. They were better than any movie magazine. He had an advanced way with words. He said, *You're beautiful. I sincerely mean it.* He said, *I think about you all the time, so I hope you don't charge by the minute.* It was wonderful stuff. Me and Karol knew Patricia was something special because of it. I thought it must be hard on Karol being Patricia's little sister. The pressure.

After school me and Karol and Bubba and Roy trailed Patricia and Jimmy home, watching them whisper and slap at each other in a romantic way. It was beautiful, I thought. But Roy and Bubba thought Jimmy had got so foolish they lost their esteem for him. How he carried Patricia's books sometimes, and how when a bunch of boys were supposed to be playing tag football in the yard after supper Jimmy drifted off, got in a mood—what Roy called a mush mood—and he laid in the grass chewing on sweetweed and staring up at the sky like he was watching a turned-off TV set. Roy hated to see such a thing happen, anybody to ruin like that, over a girl. I think Roy believes Dale Evans is Roy Rogers's sister or something. I don't want to be the one to break the news to him.

I always thought Patricia should go to Memphis and get Elvis Presley. She could do it if she wanted to, walk down the street swinging that ponytail, and Elvis Presley would see her and screech on his car brakes and break out singing a song right to her face. I bet she could marry him if she wanted to. She knows how to drive a boy crazy by acting like she doesn't know she's driving him crazy—so he has to act crazier and crazier to prove it to her. It's just like the Elvis Presley picture shows. Patricia knows all the same stuff girls in picture shows know. She says Elvis Presley would not give a hoot about a Tallahassee girl like her—but that's a lie. The only way he could keep from it was if he was dead.

But the truth is, I didn't actually want her to go off to Memphis and catch Elvis's eye and make him fall in love with her, because that's what I wanted to do myself when I got a couple of years older and a little further along. By that time I would know what I needed to know and my hair would be long.

One day when Patricia is telling us how cute Jimmy is and every cute thing he says, me and Karol start to ache listening. We start to wish for boys of our own to lay around in the grass thinking about us and dreaming of our exquisite nakedness in a bathtub. We want the same sort of love and adoration that Jimmy showers Patricia with. It is a kind of yearning that feels like a queasy stomach. And before I know it I am telling Patricia about Lamar Forehand. I don't know what made me do it. Lamar is no prize-winning boy or anything. I don't hardly like him and have never paid him two cents' worth of attention, and then out of the blue he starts to write me these notes at school. It's the notes I like.

Patricia and Karol acted so interested in my notes from Lamar that I brought them outside and they took turns reading them and screaming. Lamar does not have near the romantic flair that Jimmy's got, of course. There is no mention of what he dreams about—which is probably for the best. His notes are practical and sane. In one, he says he wants to take me to ride in his uncle's new car, then goes on for two pages describing the car's souped-up engine. In another he lists the baseball teams in the order he thinks they will finish the season. His notes pale alongside Jimmy's lewd love letters, so after just the first few minutes I was embarrassed to have shown them. Lamar is not that good a speller.

"Every girl has to start somewhere," Patricia said.

"Start what, exactly?"

She thought I was kidding.

One day when Roy and I came home from school Skippy was sitting in our yard. Leroy and Nappy were playing with Benny up underneath the picnic table. "What are you doing?" I said.

"I got something belongs to you." Skippy dips down into his pocket and pulls out some folded paper, dirty, faded.

I reached for it. He snatched it back like he wasn't going to give it to me. Then he slowly unfolded it—and when he did I recognized it was one of Lamar Forehand's notes.

"Where'd you get that?" I demanded.

"Found it." He waved it in my face like a red flag in front of a bull.

"Found it where?"

"In the grass when I'm mowing." He has it all the way unfolded now. "It's a letter somebody wrote you."

"I know what it is. Give it to me." The more I reached for it the more he dodged and waved the paper.

"Finders keepers," he said.

"Skippy, give it to me."

"Say who wrote it."

"None of your business. Nobody you know." I am yelling so much that Leroy and Nappy come out from under the picnic table to watch. "You read it, didn't you?" I screamed. "Nosy as you are, you read it."

Before I had finished speaking I remembered. It was like I had spilled something hot and it was getting all over both of us. Because I'm not sure. Can Skippy read or not? I stand there like I'm sorry. It's worse than saying "nigger." He knows it and I know it. When I try to act sorry, like a nice white girl feeling sorry, then he hates me. He glares at me with them mean-colored boy eyes.

"I know who wrote this is somebody stupid," Skippy says. "Dear Lucy . . ." He holds up the paper like he will read it.

I snatch at it and rip it, and get ahold of it and ball it up in my fist. Skippy laughs. "I know can't no ugly girl like you have a boy."

"Well," I said, "I don't see no colored girls lined up at your house after you. So why don't you shut up."

"Lucy is in love." He laughed.

"Shut up," I screamed.

"Lucy got her a little sweetheart."

"I hate you, Skippy. Do you hear me? I hate you." But he will not hush, so I am swinging my arms at him like I will hit him if I can.

He grabs my arm, yanks it, and squeezes it so tight it hurts. "You don't," he said. "You don't hate me, girl." He flung my arm loose and smiled. "Ain't no sense to tell a lie."

I watched him strut across my yard like he owned it. He had never been more wrong in his life, because for a moment there—one split second—I hated him so bad I practically jumped out of my skin over it. Probably can't even read, I thought. Probably don't have no idea what that note from Lamar Forehand said. So what am I so worried about? Skippy could get ahold of every note I have hidden in my bottom drawer and it wouldn't do him one bit of good.

"GET ready, Lucy," Mother said, "because here you go." She proceeded to tell me the facts of life—even though I never asked to know them. "I don't want life's facts sneaking on you like they did me," she said. She only said "blood" once. The rest of the time she called it "time of the month." Like payday. Payday is a time of the month. "Don't call it bleeding, Lucy. That doesn't sound nice."

I didn't see why it should sound nice. Bleeding is what you do when you're shot by a gun or stabbed with a knife. It's what happens when you're in a car wreck and almost die. I don't know what it has to do with being a woman. It seemed cruel. Mother says it's God's plan. He makes women bleed because he's still mad at Eve, who ate that apple a long time ago. He won't forgive her. All women have to bleed to make up for it—even me. There is not one thing I can do to stop it. Since Mother is religious, God's plans make sense to her. But not to me. I think surely an all-powerful God could have thought up something better than this.

And sex. Mother told it too. Not the same way Patricia did—so outrageous it made me and Karol scream she's a liar and her eyes are crossed, Patricia telling too crazy, nasty stuff, me and Karol laughing because we don't believe a word of it. Not like that. Mother told it as nice as such a thing can be told.

"You will know you're in love, Lucy, when the idea of sex doesn't disgust you anymore. The right man, when he comes along, can make you think like that."

Mother is crazy sometimes.

WHEN summer came Roy and I would go spend a week with Granddaddy. One time he took us to a rodeo in Lee County. After a sizzling day, bucking horses, charging bulls, men slung into corrals of manure, Granddaddy in the shade talking farming, Roy and me eating a barbecue overdose and listening to fiddle music—we started back home. Roy was totally satisfied with the world, as though he'd finally stumbled across his proper place in it. Why hadn't anyone ever told him you could ride bulls for a living?

It was late, and dark. Roy and I settled down to sleep in the truck, but about the time we succeeded, Granddaddy slammed on the brakes. "What the . . . ?" he said, and skidded to a stop in the road.

We woke up to singing and saw lights shooting from the windows of a colored church. The place was lit up like a pointed star in the black night. Cars were parked around it.

One had an Ohio plate, two said New York, and another one said Illinois. Granddaddy read them out loud like he was reading tombstones of people he didn't know had died. A voice like, Good Lord, somebody should have told me. We could see through the windows, a swarm of people, clapping, talking, carrying things. The brightness was terrifying.

"What are they doing?" Roy said, but he knew the answer.

"They're about to start the most trouble you ever saw in your life," Granddaddy said.

I wanted to get far away from there, home to Sudie, because I thought, What if those colored people see us stopped out here in the road and they come outside and shoot us cold-blooded dead for it?

It felt like spying while the enemy planned war tactics—secretly, late at night, way out in a country church so nobody saw them. On a Saturday night too, which was colored people's favorite night, the one they usually used for whooping it up somewhere. A colored church lit up on a Saturday night. It chilled my blood.

"Let's go," I said. "Let's go." We rode home nervously because it was in the air that something big was going to happen. That night Roy slept with Granddaddy and I slept in the bed with Sudie, who was colored too, but she was used to things and too old to get mad now.

WHEN Granddaddy brought us home from Alabama, without asking anybody he also brought a wire cage of white rabbits in the back of his truck.

Mother threw a halfhearted fit when she saw them, because she didn't want to fool with them. But Granddaddy said me and Roy and Benny could raise rabbits and sell them—make some money. Benny was thrilled out of his mind. So we kept them. I named my rabbit Elvis. Roy named his Trigger. And Benny's rabbit was Mopsy. It was ridiculous, but it made Granddaddy happy.

*I*T was the first week in September, still hot as blazes. School was getting ready to let in and Mother loved getting us ready, getting Roy new dungarees and me plaid dresses, a couple of writing tablets, some yellow pencils, and always new shoes. She made a to-do of it, which we liked. But Melvina's kids weren't going to school too, which drove Mother crazy. She couldn't stand for us to carry our packages in the house in front of Melvina, our new Sears saddle oxfords and the J. C. Penney's bag with my back-to-school dresses in it and our school supplies from Woolworth's. She made us leave everything in the trunk of the car until after Melvina had gone home. Then she slipped the stuff in the house and put it all away like a reverse criminal.

When Melvina found things, she said, "I see you got Roy and Lucy they new school clothes. How many dresses you get Lucy? Roy been needing socks." She wanted to see everything, she wanted to know what it cost, and she went looking through the drawers and closets to see what all Mother had bought us. Sometimes she laid everything out on the bed, just to look it over. Sometimes she carried each individual thing into the kitchen, where she commented and arranged it on the kitchen table, making a display. "Let's see," she said, "when did Roy grow to a size eight? Look at these underpants, what's this?"

"It's the days of the week," Mother said.

"You don't mean it?" Melvina looked at the panties closely. "Seven pair," she said. "You mean each day has its own panty?"

"You don't have to stick to it," Mother said.

"Wait," Melvina said, laying the panties out side by side, "they ain't seven. They's just five pair. What days is missing?"

Mother looked at the panties. "It's just Monday through Friday," she said, "school days." She talked like the idea was stupid now, but at J. C. Penney's she thought it was cute.

"What's a child supposed to do on Saturday and Sunday," Melvina said, "go bare-bottomed? They ought not to leave none the days out, most especially Sunday. I wouldn't of bought none of these unless it was a full set."

But Mother was hardly listening, because she was going inside Melvina—me and Roy knew it—and she was feeling things. If you knew her you could see it happening. She could be Skippy's mother as easy as ours. She could be Annie's mother, and Orlando's, and Leroy's and Nappy's and even hateful Alfonso Junior's mother. She could go into Melvina and be a colored woman with a houseful of kids—which as Walter said was a houseful too many—and she could live in Melvina's fall-down house and feel how it was to sweep a dirt yard day after day and look at her delicious children knowing full well this world was going to eat them right up first chance it got. Mother could be Melvina and love Melvina's kids every bit as much as she loved me and Roy and Benny. In fact, we suspected she could love them more. She looked out in the yard and saw

Melvina's boys all over the place. She saw Annie giving orders nobody was minding and the boys bare-chested and brave. They were pop-bellied just like Roy and Benny, skinny-legged that way. Melvina was saying, "How much these tablets run?" but Mother couldn't hear Melvina because she *was* Melvina. "They're . . ." she said, and paused.

"What?" Melvina said, realizing Mother was talking about her very own children.

"Shoeless," Mother said.

"Oh, that," Melvina said, disappointed, wanting more, wanting beautiful, or strong. "Don't need shoes in the summertime."

But Mother got it in her head that shoes were the answer. Shoes were what would get Melvina's kids a good education. Then they could change the world. Shoes would save them. Skippy and Orlando would give up fishing. Alfonso Junior would give up troublemaking. Annie would learn to read, old as she was—if they just had good shoes.

Suddenly Mother believed in shoes like some people believe in the Bible and some people believe in telling the truth. Mother said there were people so poor they had to join the army to get a pair of shoes. You couldn't join the human race without them. Life, liberty, the pursuit of happiness—and a sturdy pair of shoes that fit good.

Me and Roy hated it when Mother got like this, tried to make us ashamed of having something that we didn't even particularly want. Like Roy wanted boots and I begged for Mary Janes, but no, we got saddle oxfords. Then Mother got mad at us: "Just look next door at Melvina's kids and think what they wouldn't give for new shoes."

The next thing we knew, Mother took the September grocery money Walter gave her and bought Melvina and all her kids new shoes. "Get them a little bit big so they'll last," she said. Mother herself drove Melvina and that carload to Sears. She had to make two trips. Me and Roy and Benny went both times.

Skippy got red tennis shoes. The rest of Melvina's kids got black shoes that Melvina said wouldn't get too dirty too quick. But not Skippy. Fire-engine red. Seeing him in those shoes like seeing somebody with a couple of red people on his feet. Alive like that.

I knew it wasn't going to be good from the minute I saw Walter's truck pull up in the yard, his wet hair creased where he wore a hat all day. It was too hot for Mother to be telling Walter news he wasn't expecting. I knew that by the way he walked into the house and let the screen door slam.

Mother fiddled with her hair, putting her bobby pin in her mouth. "You have a good day?" she said, but her voice didn't sound right. My blood started rocking. "Guess what?" Her voice did like a bird flitting from branch to branch, too high up.

"You think I'm out there busting my butt for the month of August so I can buy half the niggers in Tallahassee damn shoes?" Walter's voice had a shake to it. Me and Roy had gone stiff, listening. Walter's voice rattled like a snake's tail and Mother stood like a woman who was watching it coil, and waiting.

"Do you and the kids ever want for anything?"

"No," Mother said, squinting.

"You're damn right you don't. But I ain't going to be daddy to that litter next door, Sarah. Goddammit. Do you understand me?"

"Walter—" she said, but he cut her off.

It wasn't like that time she volunteered Walter and his truck to take some church chairs out to Killearn Gardens for a picnic that Walter was no way in hell going to. He was aggravated then, but not pure spitting mad. Had to be at the church at six o'clock in the morning to load those chairs, on a Saturday, Walter's sleeping-late day. He was cussing. Mother had to hug and kiss on him all week to get him to go. She told him God would appreciate it, Walter helping with a church thing. It seemed to me and Roy like one more thing God couldn't get done without Mother's help. God was just some floating idea in the air, but Mother was the real thing, with two feet on the ground. So Walter carried those chairs for the church. He did it the way a chain-gang convict digs a ditch.

But all of that was nothing like now, Walter's voice rattling, ready to strike, just because Mother bought a bunch of shoes that would every one be lost or torn up inside a week. "I'm sick to death of this do-gooding mess, Sarah. You hear me? One more stunt like this and that's it. I swear. I'm through messing with it."

He walked through the living room, where me and Roy and Benny sat frozen, slapped his hat back on, and tugged hard on it, pulling it low over his eyes. "What you looking at?" he said. We could not get up enough sound to answer.

Hollow-headed, I watched Walter walk across the room and out the door. He didn't slam the screen door, he closed it slow. It had a screech to it. Walter got in his truck and peeled out of the driveway like a policeman on his way to a crime. Mother hurried over to the picture window and watched his highway department truck roar off down California Street.

I looked at little Benny sitting still as a rock. His face looked like somebody had erased part of it. Like his face was a piece of lined paper with all the words gone.

Walter didn't come back for supper, so we finally ate without him.

By our bedtime Walter still wasn't home. Like a robot,

Mother got Roy and Benny bathed and into their pajamas. She tucked them into bed—said their prayers for them because they were no good at it and took too long. She came in my room, kissed me, turned the lights off, and closed the door. Now she could go sit alone in the living room and wait until Walter came home. I knew she wasn't going to get into a lonely bed in the dark and worry herself into crying like she used to do with our real daddy. No. She was sitting up in the living room all night if she had to. Forever if she had to. Mother sitting on the sofa with her legs folded beneath her, hugging a pillow on her lap.

I couldn't get to sleep.

I'd always thought Walter was like a mountain the same as our real daddy was a valley. A valley is green and deep with streams twisting through, a valley could be very nice, but to some people it just seemed low down. Walter like a mountain the way mountains don't move around, just sit there and let people move around them. All this time me thinking Walter was a peaceful mountain, when really he was a volcano—a volcano looks like a mountain in every way except it's got boiling insides.

I wondered if Mother was doing something wrong when it came to men. And if Walter didn't come back, then what? We'd move back to the trailer court? Go live with Granddaddy on his farm in Alabama? Be some of those people that line up at the Salvation Army?

Melvina would say, "Lord, Mrs. Sheppard, you can't keep a husband, can you?" She would say that, it half her fault in the first place. Walter gave up on us because stupid Melvina couldn't get her own dumb kids any shoes. Had one hundred kids, then acted pitiful because she couldn't get enough shoes. I was tired to death of it too, like Walter. I was. I was tired of them next door never having one thing they needed, hardly had nothing, and us having to watch them do without until we got to hating what it is we had, because it was better and plenty and we ought to be enjoying it but we couldn't. Melvina wouldn't let us. Skippy wouldn't let us. No colored people anywhere would let us enjoy ourselves because they were always sitting around somewhere having nothing. Waiting for some check in the mail that never came. Waiting on nothing. Nothing. Nothing. I had a low opinion of God because of it.

Walter was still not home. I would hear his truck drive up in the yard, would hear old George scramble up out of the flower bed or scratch on the screen. I would hear the keys rattle in Walter's pocket, all those keys he kept on a chain, so when he walked it sounded like he had a hundred dollars' worth of spending change. It would be music, some here-comes-Walter-home-again song. But Walter didn't come.

I thought Walter understood Mother better. Like me and Roy do—and probably even Benny. We know she is not an ordinary mother. Not like Karol, Patricia, and Bubba got, a secretary mother who is always too worn-out for any kid foolishness, who stays at the beauty parlor all day Saturday and paints her long fingernails Romance Red. And not like Jimmy and Donald's mama, who is nice but don't do anything but clean up her house all the time and spray for roaches. And all those mothers that mostly minded their own business—and their own kids' business—and didn't worry that much about the entire world.

Sometimes me and Roy wished Mother would grow African violets in the windowsills and crochet toilet-paper covers. We wanted Mother to be regular, but she never would do it. Couldn't do it. We thought Walter knew that. I thought he understood. Some mothers, like Karol and Bubba's, would take the grocery money and buy their own selves fifty pairs of shoes, line them up in their closet like something to be proud of, which seemed like a thing that could make a husband mad. Mother never would do that. But Walter was mad anyway.

Keeping a man must be a hard thing. The hardest thing a woman had to do. Keeping a man satisfied, keeping him from running off because he's mad about something or nothing. It seemed like women had this natural stay in them, like Mother did, but men had a come-and-go quality. I didn't want to grow up and do it, belong to a daddy or a husband or be looking for one to belong to, live in a man's house, drive his car, buy food with his grocery money, cook what he liked to eat, iron his work shirts, hug him a bunch so he'd take some church chairs out to the picnic grounds. I was not going to do it.

When Mother was putting us to bed Benny said, "Why is Walter mad?"

"Just because," Mother said.

"Is he going to stay mad?"

"Maybe Walter is mad about me giving away the grocery money—for sure he is—but God is very happy about it. Walter is just a man," she said, "but God is God."

She made Benny cry saying it. We didn't like Mother to talk about God like he was something above what she was. We didn't believe it. We thought God would be nothing without Mother.

"I don't know what else a woman can do," she said. "God whispering a clear message in one ear—and Walter in the other ear saying, 'What's for supper?'"

I was glad God didn't talk to me like he did Mother. Give me tear-the-family-apart messages. I had tried talking to him, but he never answered me. It would not surprise me if he wrote Mother letters, or sent telegrams, or called her on the telephone. But I was glad he didn't do me like that.

Would Walter come back or not? Would he quit loving Mother since she do-gooded so much nobody could stand it? Would he go up to Melvina's and snatch those shoes off those kids' feet and throw them in a sack and take them back to the Sears store and demand his money back? Would he sell this green California Street house and move back to his peaceful blue trailer—alone? Would he just never be seen again, like Old Alfonso next door—then we'd hear he was off dancing with some good-looking woman at the Elks Club? What would Walter do?

I had no control over myself when I was worried like this. I prayed before I noticed I was doing it. I offered God deals he couldn't pass up, swearing to be perfect for the rest of my life if he would just make Walter come home. I talked God's ears off. Begged. And then I wondered how I was supposed to know for sure God was listening to me. I wanted a little proof—like a bolt of lightning out of my window or a voice in the darkness. Finally I settled on a plan where I would lie with my hand up in the air, like when you wanted to get called on to answer the question, except I was lying in bed, eyes closed, and just my hand straight up in the air. I wanted God to touch it. That was all. I wouldn't look. I wouldn't ask for more. Just wanted him to touch me so I knew he heard me. I knew he would do it if I waited long enough. He must have known who my mother was. He would touch me if I just didn't give up. So I reached. And kept on reaching. And with my eyes closed and a long time passing I got tired. And finally I fell asleep and my arm dropped down, and I forgot.

Walter was still not home.

Maybe that was God's idea of a miracle—letting you fall asleep and forget for a while—which was a miracle of sorts, I guess.

But the next morning I remembered instantly, because the air was not good to breathe, and every breath I took I was sucking in the bad. It was not like a morning when you were little and you jumped out of bed and ran through the house yelling, "Did Santa Claus come?" We didn't run through the house screaming, "Is Walter home?" We walked silently into the kitchen with our pajamas on. Mother already had our breakfast on the table. "Good morning," she said. "Sit down and eat while it's hot."

The living room was cleaned up, the magazines arranged neatly on the coffee table, the pillows arranged on the sofa, the furniture polished with that greasy lemon smell, no toys laying around. It was like company was coming. Me and Roy and Benny listened to Mother rattle dishes in the kitchen. The shower wasn't running, so Walter wasn't in it. The look on Mother's face said what we wanted to know.

It was the first day of school. Me and Roy got on our new school clothes, Mother saying cheerful stuff. Benny was practically crying about not going too and Mother told him she would get Melvina to bring Leroy and Nappy with her today, since the rest of her kids were supposed to be going to school now that they had new shoes to wear, and nobody was left to look after Leroy and Nappy. She said they could play outside with Benny on his pedal tractor, get Benny's little plastic army men and his toy cars and make towns with sand roads and shoe-box houses.

Benny, Leroy, and Nappy had spent all summer messing around in the dirt like that, turning on the water spigot and drinking out of the hose, squirting each other in the face. Now it kept Benny from worrying Mother to death about how long until Roy got home from school, and made it so Melvina could work at our house and look after her own kids at the same time. Make three peanut butter sandwiches for lunch instead of one. Yell out the screen door, "Hush that racket," and, "Stop that throwing sticks before I come out there and throw a stick myself—right on your behinds." It worked good, not much trouble to it.

Me and Roy trooped off to school. I had my hair long now. It would reach in a ponytail. I had a new school dress that didn't look so babyish—Patricia said where did I get that dress, because it was a sharp-looking dress—so I looked pretty good, but I didn't feel that good. I knew Mother was going to stew over Walter all day.

Then me and Roy saw Skippy and Orlando and them going up the dirt road the opposite way from us. Saw them in their shoes. I waved at them, since I didn't mind waving at somebody going off to school like they should be instead of doing a bunch of Huckleberry Finn fishing, but they didn't wave at me. Skippy just did this dance in the road, one them crazy-looking colored dances—him in his shoes, twirling around and jerking in the road, those feet going. It was nice. It was nothing to Skippy that his no-good daddy stayed gone. He probably liked it that way.

Roy didn't say a thing about Walter being gone. But I knew he was more mad at Mother for making Walter mad than he was at Walter for being mad.

I told myself when I got to school I was putting on some of Patricia's red lipstick.

You don't have to hurry up for bad news. Our real daddy taught us that. Bad news will wait for you. After school we couldn't wait to pull off our school clothes and get into shorts and bare feet. We saw Leroy and Nappy out underneath the picnic table, in the shade. Usually Benny came running when he saw Roy was home. Me and Roy banged on in the house to de-schoolify.

The house was clean. Mother was fixed up, had pin curls in her hair, but she was just-out-of-the-tub clean and wearing White Shoulders powder that smelled like magnolia trees. "Don't make a mess, you two. Me and Melvina have not cleaned this house all day for the two of you to run through it like a couple of hurricanes."

We could smell Melvina was making vegetable soup with a beef bone for flavor. It smelled like fall, when you started back to school, and you made homemade vegetable soup and cheese bread, saying summer was officially over, although it was every bit of ninety degrees, even with the fans going.

If Walter came home, then everything would be just right. He would smell that good soup cooking on the stove and see how pretty Mother could be when she wanted to, and he'd know that grocery money was nothing important. We could get along good without it, just this one time. Mother would probably say, "Never mind about that grocery money, because we are rich in the important things, Walter Sheppard." I could hear her say that because she said it to me and Roy and Benny when we begged for some fancy thing that cost too much. I didn't want her to say it to Walter, though. Thought if she had good sense she wouldn't.

Melvina sent me and Roy outside with peeled oranges. We sat up on the picnic table to eat them. "Where's Benny?" I said.

"Don't know," Leroy said. "He's gone."

"Gone where?"

"Don't know."

"Nappy, where's Benny?" Nappy only shrugged his shoulders.

"He's got to be somewhere," I said. Me and Roy started calling him, but he didn't come. "You guess he's hiding?" I asked Roy.

Melvina came outside yelling for him, but it was useless. Mother said for Roy to look in the woods and for me to look under the house and for Leroy to go ask Miss Margaret Ann. Then she started calling him.

It was not like Benny to go off this way. Mother said for Melvina to get Skippy to scout the woods. Her tone of voice said, Dear goodness, what if he wandered away and fell into the deep part of the stream or got bit by a poison snake. "Find him, Skippy. See if you can find him," she said. He and Orlando took off running, Skippy's feet blurring as he jumped over briers and wove through the trees, leaving specks of red imprinted in the air. His new shoes would get torn up.

Then Mother sent me and Roy down California Street, house to house, to see if anybody had seen Benny. We took off. We could hear Mother calling him, her voice floating through the neighborhood like a broken record. It sounded like a suppertime voice, with alarm in it. We were more than halfway down California Street, been to every house, and not a soul had seen Benny. The mothers hollered to their kids, "Any of y'all seen little Benny Sheppard?" "No, ma'am," they every one said. So me and Roy kept on.

Karol and Bubba came outside and went with us. It wasn't dark yet, but it was thinking about it. Me and Roy hoped Mother had found Benny by now, or Skippy had, so we left Karol and Bubba still going down the street looking for him, because they were enjoying having a good reason to ring doorbells. They kept at it with the vengeance of a posse and me and Roy started home, ran the whole way.

Benny was not found. Mother and Miss Margaret Ann and her husband, Jake, were in the yard with Melvina, Skippy, Leroy, and Nappy. They were gathered in a crooked circle. Skippy said, "Benny is not in the woods and it's wanting to get dark." We said nobody had seen a sign of him down California Street. Mother was thinking, What if somebody came by and picked him up—same as people came by and threw out puppies and cats, they could come by and snatch up a little boy. "Don't go imagining stuff," Jake said.

Melvina said to Leroy and Nappy again, "How come you didn't see that boy go off?" Their shoes were so scuffed I thought she would spank them when she got home. And Miss Margaret Ann was patting Mother's arm—Mother, all fixed up, planning on having things perfect.

"I'm going inside to call Walter, because Walter ought to

know," Jake said to Mother. "I'm calling him at the highway department."

Mother didn't say don't. She didn't tell about Walter being gone. She stood with her arms crossed, biting her bottom lip. If you looked in her eyes you could see all the things she imagined in there, where Benny was and what might happen to him. "We got to call the police," she said.

Melvina hated the way Mother would call the police at the drop of a hat. "No matter how bad things gets, the police can always make it worse," she said. "It's like when those little nasty mealy bugs get into a sack of flour, can't do nothing with it then, bugs crawling through it making it useless, can't do nothing but throw it out. It's the same with the police. Make a mess impossible to fix."

"Oh, Melvina," Mother said.

"I'm going home if you calling the police. I mean that thing."

"Yes," Miss Margaret Ann said. "Call the police. It will make everybody feel better. Let the police find Benny."

"We have to," Mother said. "It's been over two hours."

Jake came back outside and said, "Walter is not at the highway department." And there went Mother, her face, about of course Walter was not at the highway department, he was clear up in Valdosta with his brother, Hugh, or down at Panama City eating seafood in an oceanside restaurant, checked into a pink stucco hotel with cement flamingos stuck here and there in the courtyard. Walter was gone. No need for anybody to call Walter.

"I'm calling the police." She turned to go inside. The mosquitoes were out. Jake was shaking his head, saying, "Ain't like Benny to disappear this way." Melvina felt bad because when she looked out after the boys this afternoon just saw two and counted three.

Here came Karol and Bubba. And Donald's mama in the car. And one-half the neighborhood coming to gather in our yard. Wait with us because waiting was always better in a crowd. Gathering up is what neighborhoods do with something wrong. Annie came down with more of her brothers, her black shoes looking like she had shined them with Vaseline, and Melvina said, "She gone to call the police." Annie said, "That woman love the police." It looked like there was going to be a meeting. Melvina's kids chasing each other. Every child in the yard barefooted, but not Melvina's kids. They scrambled around after each other, big-footed in their new shoes. Skippy's feet looked like a set of taillights moving about the yard. Karol was sucking her thumb, and some kids we didn't hardly know or like were playing pitch with gumballs off our gumball tree. Miss Margaret Ann cut on the porch light. Me and Roy felt nervous. We were thinking how nice we'd be to Benny when he got home. Roy was going to let him sleep with him, both of them on the top bunk.

Then somebody hollered, "Here comes Walter." And everybody looked up California Street, up the dirt road past Melvina's, and we saw that highway department truck throwing up a little dust cloud, but not much of one because the truck went slow, had its lights on. Me and Roy ran to the edge of the yard by the street with everybody else. "Here comes Walter!" He saw the bunch of us standing out in his yard, and tooted his horn, flashed his headlights. He waved like he was in a parade. And we saw Benny. He had Benny.

"Thank the crazy Lord," Melvina said.

Benny was in the back of Walter's truck, not the cab. Mother's going to have a fit, I thought at first. Then I saw that he was sitting on his little orange tractor in the back of Walter's truck. That boy was smiling.

Mother saw them out the picture window and ran out to the truck, and as Jake lifted Benny out Mother grabbed him, hugged him, kissed all over his face, couldn't even talk, couldn't even fuss. Tears went down her face and Walter walked around to where she was and she just looked at him. Couldn't say a word. Carried Benny in the house.

People gathered around Walter and said, "Where was that boy?" They said, "Thank goodness he's safe, because there isn't no telling what might could happen."

"You ought to whip him," Melvina said. "I'd whip one of mine that run off that way."

Walter lifted the toy tractor out of the back of his truck and set it down. Leroy and Nappy both made a run for it.

"Take turns." Melvina yanked the tractor to the edge of the crowd. "Get out from under people's feet."

Walter leaned against the truck bed and answered questions. "I was driving home from work," he said. "I went by the Snack Shack like I always do, not paying any attention, and I see this little child driving his toy tractor up to one of the gas pumps out front. I laughed until I looked close and seen it was Benny—clear up in French Town. So I stop to get him, says, 'Benny, what in the world are you doing way up here?' and Benny says he come to get gas because he was about to pedal all the way out to the highway department." Walter laughed telling it, but he didn't tell it all—that Benny was coming after him, to bring him home to Mother. He only told that part later.

He bought Benny a candy bar, said he bet his mama was fit to be tied, a little boy in colored town by himself, so he loaded Benny in the truck and came home. He was not mad. Me and Roy certainly noticed that Benny was riding in the back of the truck, where we always wanted to ride, but Walter hardly ever let us.

So the people went home. Melvina and Annie lingered until last, then rounded up Leroy and Nappy, who ran through the woods home, whooping like two wild Indians. Skippy was standing at the edge of the yard, leaning up against a tree with his arms folded, his shoes glowing like two embers. Walter glanced at him. "Skippy," he said. "Too bad you couldn't get red shoes."

Me and Roy went inside with Walter, that soup smelling good. I don't know what got wrong with me. I spent almost the whole night praying for Walter to come home. Then there he was—home. I should have said, "Walter, I'm glad you're back. So glad." A simple thing like that.

I walked into the house with Walter in dead silence, so did Roy. We acted like we hadn't noticed Walter was gone all night. We acted like all we cared about was that soup cooking and how fast we could get to it. Ordinarily I would have fussed about Walter letting Benny do what he almost never let me and Roy do—and Benny younger than us. I would make a fuss out of it, say it's not fair, but because of how things were, I didn't. Walter could have let Benny drive the truck and I wouldn't have said a word.

Mother was quiet. She got Benny bathed and into his pajamas. If she got mad at him we didn't hear her. Then we sat down to eat. Walter was quiet too. He just ate. Mother hardly looked at him. Me and Roy didn't like how tears kept going down her face and she couldn't do one thing to stop them, just wipe them away with her napkin. And me and Roy ate our soup as fast as we could—wanted out of that quiet room.

After supper Walter sat in his chair and read the paper. Me and Roy and Benny watched some TV. Mother cleaned off the table and washed the dishes. We could hear them rattling. Walter cleared his throat and turned his newspaper page. It was a bad feeling, the tension in the house. Mother and Walter were ignoring each other, acting like they didn't even know each other, but they were two magnets and there was this pull between them. We could all feel it. If I stood between Walter in his chair and Mother in the kitchen it was like when the rains came and the ditches flooded and that strong water rushed downhill, pulled you with it. But it was not about water. It was in the air, that pull.

I don't think Walter knew one word he read in the *Tallahassee Democrat*. I don't think Mother knew what dishes were washed and not washed. She just opened a cabinet and put any dish anywhere. Because Mother was a magnet and Walter was one. And they didn't know what to do about it. That pull.

Mother should have been finished in the kitchen, but she didn't come out. We didn't know what she was doing, but suddenly we heard a crash like a dish breaking, shattering on the hard linoleum floor, and we heard Mother say, "Damn," which Mother never said. Walter got up and walked in the kitchen, where Mother was stooped down with a whisk broom.

"You okay?" Walter said. He stood there and looked at Mother picking up broken pieces. He looked at her shiny curled hair and those bare feet with that light pink polish on her toes. It was so much like Mother, squatted down in the middle of something broken. Dealing with a mess and blaming herself for it. Trying to clean up things that were not right. Like if that plate was a person, then Mother would save all those little splintered pieces and get out the glue. Everybody would say to her, "Forget it. You'll never get that fixed. It's ruined. Throw it out." And Mother would sit up half the night with the glue and a million pieces that didn't fit anymore and try to put that plate back together. If a person was a plate she would do that, because that's how Mother was. Maybe Walter knew that.

"Don't step on that glass," he said.

Mother stood up with a dustpan of glass bits and took a couple of steps to the trashcan, near where Walter stood. She dumped the broken pieces in the trash.

"Sarah," Walter said.

She looked at him, like it was a hard thing to do and it hurt to do it.

"It's only a plate." He smiled at her, not a smile with any teeth in it, his mouth stretching across his face as slow and easy as a snake in the sun. A smile Mother recognized. "It's not the end of the world," Walter said.

Mother laughed. She was a wreck, crying and laughing together. Walter reached out and put his hands on her. He pulled her close to him, and it was like she melted into a puddle in his arms. He held her the way you squeeze an orange—the more you squeeze, the more juice you get. Mother crying hard, those tears rolling down her face, and her arms went up around Walter's neck, her making sobs that were someplace between laughing and crying. Walter lifted Mother up, twirled her around the kitchen—her feet didn't touch the floor. His head was bent down and resting on Mother's wet neck. He was holding her like she couldn't get loose if she wanted to—and her, like she never did want to.

It made me cry to see them. I'm like Mother about crying over a happy thing just like it was something sad. To see Walter love Mother in the kitchen, hug her like that, her lifted off the floor, held up high the way she should be. Mother and Walter wrapped around each other, twirling, and they didn't care who saw them. Mother was happy-crying. My insides melted and I went to them, wrapped myself around them too. Then Roy came. And Benny. Me and Roy were crying just as hard as Mother. Crying so hard we were shaking, all of us, our crying coming in waves, all of us tangled together like a wad of paper clips on some magnets. That good pull.

Walter didn't cry, but he couldn't get us to stop. He said, "Ain't nobody died and y'all forgot to tell me, did they?" And we laughed in the middle of our crying. Walter said, "Who turned your spigots on?" but he knew who did. He knew everything was about him. We were all soaking wet—it a too hot night, and us in a too hot kitchen.

Mother said, "I love you, Walter." So then me and Roy and Benny said it too. And he hugged us all, put his face up

150

against Mother's and was quiet. In a minute he said, "You're all right yourselves." His arms were pressing me and Roy and Benny hard against Mother's legs and his, squeezing us together into one tangled thing.

That night after we were in bed, supposed to be asleep, I heard Mother and Walter in the living room talking quietly for a long time. I heard them like a humming motor, like machinery that's fixed again and working so good it purrs. They sounded as good as a window fan, drowning things out. I think Mother was promising Walter things. She was saying that she was wrong about shoes—that she had stopped believing in them. I bet she was asking him for forgiveness right that minute. I was glad I couldn't hear her.

In a little bit they went down the hall to bed. They put on the radio in their room. It played a love song, but I couldn't hear the words clearly. They closed the door. I heard it click. And they locked it.

*A*FTER the night the sheriff came and got Old Alfonso it was like he vanished from earth. Melvina never mentioned his name except when me and Roy said, "Tell us about the time Old Alfonso got after you with that knife, Melvina. Tell us about him busting the door down with the ax. Tell about when he tried to choke you with a piece of clothesline. Tell . . ."

"Men are past useless," Melvina said.

Mother said Melvina knows this because it's been proved to her over and over again. Now Alfonso Junior, her oldest boy, took over where his daddy left off—proving it.

Alfonso Junior was going through changes. More than wanting to be left alone—like he always did—but now going off who knows where and staying gone half the night. Then all the night. Wouldn't say a word about it. So Melvina started guessing, and she guessed good. Alfonso Junior had found a girl.

It was Skippy who told her which girl, and Melvina went crazy, acting like Alfonso Junior had picked out the worst girl that could be picked. Virginia somebody. We'd seen her before, because she used to come to Melvina's yard and hang around with Annie. They plaited each other's hair, or we'd see them hop-skipping up the dirt road, going to the Snack Shack with a quarter. That was then. But this was now, Melvina throwing a fit over Alfonso Junior getting friendly with Virginia. "That fast girl shaking herself around this neighborhood, shaking herself in a boy's face," Melvina said.

"I think it's sweet," Mother told Melvina, "Alfonso Junior's first love. It's puppy love."

"Puppy love my hind foot," Melvina fussed. "Ain't no puppy to it. It's pussy that boy's after. Ought to call it pussy love, because ain't no puppy to it."

"Guess it wasn't anything to do with love back when Old Alfonso got after you either, was it?" Mother said.

"I never was nothing like that fast girl. I didn't run up and down the street," Melvina said. "No sense in advertising— unless you got something to sell."

"Shoot," Mother said.

Skippy became Melvina's spy. It was his job to keep an eye on Alfonso Junior, trail him, report back to his mama, and Skippy was good at it. He made a joke of it, how lovesick Alfonso Junior was, carrying on over Virginia, the loudmouthed girl who used to hang upside down by her knees on a low limb, letting her panties show, and eating blackberries until her teeth were purple.

Since Melvina spent most of her life in our kitchen, me and Mother and Roy listened to the reports too. We knew everything about it. How Alfonso Junior scratched on Virginia's window and Virginia climbed out. Couldn't go far because Virginia had to listen for her brothers and sisters. Her mama off strutting and Virginia staying home being the other mama. Shouting distance was all. One holler away from the house.

Then it changed. Virginia climbed out the window, Alfonso Junior waited for her, his hat on his head, and they walked to the Snack Shack, that for-colored-only-because-everything-costs-twice-as-much and gather-up-here-and-do-nothing store. They got them a cold drink and each a pack of salted peanuts because some way Alfonso Junior had started to have spending money. Cigarettes in his shirt pocket.

"Alfonso Junior been telling lies," Skippy told Melvina, as he sat at our kitchen table eating a sandwich Melvina made him out of our leftover breakfast bacon. "He's talking about all the money he's got, and gon get more. Said before long he's gon have a car—take Virginia for a ride when he gets it, let her wave to people out the window."

"Ahhhhh." Mother smiled. "Alfonso Junior is dreaming big. Love makes you do that."

Melvina looked at Mother like she would like to slap her across the world.

Mostly Virginia ran around barefoot like everybody. Lots of nights we saw her walking up the sand-dirt roads late, stepping on sandspurs, flipping up the bottom of her foot so Alfonso Junior could pick the sandspurs out. Took him a long time to do it, standing there holding her naked foot. In the moonlight.

Once, late, when Walter drove by the Snack Shack we saw Virginia sitting out front when every nice girl was home in bed. Walter said, "What you guess she's up to—besides no good?" Virginia and Alfonso Junior on a bench in front of that closed store, Virginia drawing circles, X's, and swirls in the sand with her toe like it was a finger. Like her hands, sitting flat on the bench beside her, were gone to sleep so her feet took over, and she drew with her toes. Erased with the soles of her feet.

Walter slowed down at the corner, so me and Roy had time to yell out the window, "We see y'all lovebirds," but we knew it was useless. Walter could've driven the car right up to them with the lights and horn both blaring and they wouldn't have noticed.

But Alfonso Junior did notice Skippy, his mama's spy. "You better not follow me around. You might learn something you too young to know." Virginia would laugh and Alfonso Junior would throw a rock at Skippy to chase him off.

"I seen Alfonso Junior with a roll of money as big as his fist," Skippy told Melvina.

But when Melvina asked Alfonso Junior where he got it, he said, "Mama, you're crazy and your feet ain't mates." So Melvina quit asking. When Alfonso Junior slipped a five into her apron pocket, or left ten in an empty coffee cup, or twenty that time in her shoe, she didn't say, "Where in the world did you get this?" She just put the money to good use, didn't ask questions she might hate to hear the answer to.

Then Skippy tells Melvina that Alfonso Junior and Virginia quit bothering with the Snack Shack, which all it was was a gas station anyway. Now Virginia put on shoes and fixed herself up with red lips, and she and Alfonso Junior walked all the way up to the Blue Bird Cafe, smoking cigarettes, Alfonso Junior whispering, "Honey, you look good."

"Them two kids think because they're lovesick, it means they're grown," Melvina said.

I pictured them dancing in the Blue Bird Cafe, that dark

pumphouse, squirming, throbbing. Music pouring out of it, slow and easy—like something leaking, supposed to stay inside, but oozing out, easy. And the people all jittering, rumbling, and slow-bouncing on rubber legs.

It was Walter who found out Alfonso Junior was running whiskey. Taking some to somebody's house, some out to the car waiting in the street. Walter said he'd seen Alfonso Junior carry liquor so good a policeman with his dog walked right past him, nodded, and never knew for one second the boy was carrying liquor. "Y'all making something out of nothing," Walter said. "Myself, I like to see a enterprising nigger."

It worried Melvina sick. "Lord, Melvina, let the boy be," Walter said. But she kept sending Skippy out evening after evening and he kept bringing her reports, which Mother and us stayed in on the best we could.

One night he tiptoes around, looking at the Blue Bird people like they were in a picture show and he'd paid money to watch them. Skippy in the bushes. Skippy behind a car. Skippy peeping in the door the way a mouse peeps in a cathole. Alfonso Junior chased Skippy until he caught him, then beat what Walter called *the living hell* out of him.

It was the only time I ever saw Skippy cry. He hobbled down to our house looking for Melvina. Nine o'clock that night, and Mother and Melvina in the kitchen trying to Rit-dye a bedspread in the sink, heating pots of hot blue water on the stove. Melvina was beside herself at the sight of Skippy, his mouth pouring blood. "Merciful God," she said, grabbing a rag, dipping it in the dye water, pressing it to his lip.

"Walter!" Mother yelled. "Walter!"

He hurried to the kitchen. "Boy, you look like you walked into an airplane propeller," he said.

.

The next day Alfonso Junior was crazy enough to come straggling home. Melvina tore out of our kitchen after him, so did I, and Mother came. We gathered up, all of us, at the edge of Melvina's yard and she started right in with laying-down-the-law, thou-shalt-thou-shalt-not, too-big-for-your-britches, waving her arms like she did when Nappy got into the poison roach pellets that time or when one of her little boys tore the screen out of the door by laying on the floor banging his feet up against it until he had it all the way ripped out, just did it for no reason. Throwing a fit now like she did then, saying, "Beat your brother like that, like a dog."

Alfonso Junior was mad too. Wanted Melvina to quit yelling, and she wouldn't do it. "You gon run me off like you run off your own husband if you don't shut up," he said.

"Don't be saying run-off-your-husband to me."

"Run Daddy right out of here into another lady's house. Just stayed on his back until he's gone."

"You crazy-talking."

"Daddy ain't gone. He's up in French Town, at the Blue Bird every night. Ain't dead or in jail or nothing else. Just gone from your mouth flapping breeze."

"Don't lie to me," Melvina screamed.

"I ain't lying," Alfonso Junior said. "I seen him myself. He's staying up in French Town with his new woman. Name's Rose Lee."

Now even though Alfonso Junior is a liar, we believed him anyway, because it was such hateful news and he was enjoying it like it was the truth. Me and Roy and Mother believed everything colored people said, because they shocked us into it, but Walter was the kind that didn't believe none of it. If he'd been listening to Alfonso Junior he'd have said "Hogwash" and gone back in the house, where the fan was going. But us, everything sounded like the truth to us, so we believed it. The news went over us like a bucket of water.

Melvina was like Walter, not quick to believe. Her way was to never believe anything—at first. She stood with hands on her hips, elbows jutted out like flaps on a boat, for balance, or like brakes. She was a woman who dared the truth to get itself believed.

Melvina took the news of Old Alfonso being alive the way people usually take the news of somebody being dead. "He's no such a thing," she said.

"Is too, Mama."

"Then say you swear and hope to die."

"I ain't saying hope to die. I'm saying I seen Daddy."

"And him with a woman? What kind of woman?"

"A woman woman. Some woman probably don't boss him day to night."

"Named Rose?"

"Rose Lee."

"How do you know her name?"

"Somebody said, 'Here come Old Alfonso and Rose Lee.' And here they come, so I know it."

"Your daddy's back?"

"Been back."

Melvina got a look, like her face was a tire going flat, a retread losing its patch. The rest of us stood staring at her, our own memories of Old Alfonso leaping up like ghosts from a grave. Old Alfonso was not dead. Not gone forever. It was like if they told you the war was over and then later you found out it was a trick—you looked up and saw bombs falling out of the sky and you knew it was a trick. Maybe Old Alfonso would come back and take up where he left off—trying to kill Melvina every day of her life.

"You ought to be ashamed," Mother said.

"Can't apologize for the truth," Alfonso Junior said.

"Of course you can," Mother said.

Me and Roy and Mother circled around Melvina like sticks propping up a leaning thing and watched Alfonso Junior walk away until he was completely out of sight.

"Don't worry, Melvina," Mother said. "If Old Alfonso comes back, Walter will be waiting with his gun."

Melvina was stone quiet.

Afterwards the rest of us tried not to think too much about Old Alfonso being back. We kept our fears private. I only thought about him when it got dark. I knew he could hide in the dark, blended right in, and so it seemed he was everywhere at night, watching me, getting ready to climb in the window, slit my throat, and set the house on fire. But I only thought about it when I was in bed with the door closed. I didn't dwell on it.

But Melvina did. Sometimes she looked out the window like she was expecting him to come home carrying his clothes in a cardboard suitcase.

"Melvina, it's a blessing him having some other woman to make miserable instead of you," Mother said.

"Maybe he's a useless man," she said, "but he's *my* useless man."

It was a colored-people thing—the way they counted people same as other people counted acres or money in the bank. If Walter said, "I got a Ford pickup and a used Chevrolet needs work," Melvina'd say, "I got all them boys, Annie, and a no-count husband somewhere." If Granddaddy said, "I got eighty-eight acres out in Macon County, Alabama," Melvina'd say, "So what? I got a house full of kids and one husband too, belongs to me legal."

She acted like she forgot that time Old Alfonso knocked her tooth out, or when he sliced her across the chest where she's got that pink scar. So I said, "Melvina, what you want with a man like Old Alfonso? He nearly killed you once a week."

"He didn't start out that way, baby," Melvina said. "Used to be he wouldn't hurt nothing or nobody."

She thinks I'm crazy enough to believe it.

Melvina was sitting on the sofa with a sack of pecans in her lap and a nutcracker in her hand. The pecans reminded me of little skulls, Melvina popping them open with a loud cracking noise, sometimes pausing to eat the brains out of one of them.

Mother was lining up the *Life* magazines in a fan shape on the coffee table, arranging them by date. "One thing I know, and I learned it hard," she said, "is you can't change a man, Melvina." She began making a second fan out of the *Time* magazines, arranging them the same way.

"I'm going to pray about it," Melvina said.

"You might as well," Mother said, "because it takes God in heaven to change a man."

A couple of weeks later, as Melvina stepped out our kitchen door to go home after work, screaming and shouting erupted up at her house. Roy and me heard it and tore outside past Mother, who hollered, "You two stay in this house!" Then she ran after us, but stopped beside Melvina on the back steps. "What in the world is wrong?" she said.

Next door we saw Annie dash out of Melvina's house carrying Nappy with her. "Alfonso Junior, stop!" Her voice was a knife slashing into a perfectly harmless afternoon.

Skippy ran to Melvina's yard just as Alfonso Junior chased Virginia out of the house onto the porch. Alfonso Junior grabbed her, and before she could get loose, he swung at her, trying to slap her face. But he missed and she crumpled down on the porch, screaming. When he let go of her, she fell sideways and hit her head against a metal chair. She let out a bloody-murder wail.

Annie and Skippy could not get to her, because if they

came close Alfonso Junior would kick at them. "Let her alone," he hollered. "I'm just making her understand something."

"Her nose is bleeding. Looks like her nose is broke," Annie hollered.

Virginia was howling like a cat. Every time she tried to get up Alfonso Junior shoved her back down. Annie screamed for him to stop. Melvina's dogs were barking.

"Do something, Melvina," Mother said. "You got to make him quit it."

"You the one calls it puppy love," Melvina said. "You the one says it's *sweet*."

"Go back in the house!" Mother hollered to me and Roy, but we didn't do it.

Virginia was crying loud, but she didn't slap back or tear into Alfonso Junior like she ought to have. She didn't claw his eyes out, scratch his face, or call him filthy names. She only cried. Alfonso Junior couldn't make her stop for the longest time. The more he yelled the more she cried. The more he shoved her the less she resisted, until she was lying flat and still on the porch and there was nothing else Alfonso Junior could do but stop. There was no farther down he could push her, so he just stood on the porch looking stupid and hitting his fist against the door frame.

"I hate your guts, Alfonso Junior," I yelled.

"Shut up." Roy slapped his hand over my mouth.

Then, slowly, Virginia began to sit up straight-backed and stiff, making herself available to all the hitting Alfonso Junior could ever come up with, like if he was looking for a target, she would see to it he got a bull's-eye. But he didn't come up with any more hitting. He just looked at her with her hands over her face, her bloody nose, that shake-crying she was doing, and he started this "Baby, you okay?" mess and, "Honey, I ain't meant to do it."

Virginia was rock quiet, not moving except to try and

wipe the blood away with the back of her hand. She stood up, slow, Alfonso Junior helping her, but her like she didn't see Alfonso Junior whatsoever. As far as she was concerned, the boy was invisible. When she began to walk, he bunched himself like a clumsy crutch beside her and leaned against her. But it was useless and he quit, because, to Virginia, Alfonso Junior was as good as not there.

Annie was still fussing at Alfonso Junior. "Look what you done."

Me and Roy stood at the edge of our yard, our toes on the line, pretending we were deaf, when Mother said, "Did you hear me? I said come back here."

Virginia didn't say a word, not to Annie or anybody. She walked across the yard like a queen, with her head held back, pinching the tip of her nose closed. The regal slant of her head, her eyes looking directly into the sun as she walked—the black inner tube of my heart, overpumped, was ready to burst with love and fury.

Alfonso Junior was like a puppy yapping at Virginia's heels. "Talk to me, baby," he said, circling her like a dog about to be fed. Because he didn't have a tail to wag he wagged his arms. He stood in front of her like a roadblock, walked backwards, his arms waving up and down. "Ain't no sense to get mad. I ain't meant nothing by it. Come on, baby, now."

Alfonso Junior was so ashamed that any minute I thought he would lay himself down flat across the road and let Virginia walk right over him if she wanted to, or he'd grab one of her feet, hold on, let her drag him all the way up California Street or all the way to Georgia. He wanted to kiss her but she wouldn't stop walking long enough. He was begging and prancing in circles like a dog after his own tail. He said, "I'm going to buy you something nice. You too sweet to be acting like this, baby."

It was a pitiful thing to watch. Anybody loving somebody

that much. I could hardly stand to watch it. Alfonso Junior was all over the girl with sweet words. I wondered if Virginia was going to love him again tomorrow—or next year, or ever. I wondered if she would be like Melvina and keep on loving a man whose favorite thing was to almost kill her, over and over, and then be sorry afterwards. Maybe being sorry for something was the best feeling in the world and that's why Alfonso Junior liked it so much.

Run, Virginia! I wanted to scream. But I stood like the cat had got my tongue. I wanted to scream for Virginia to pull out seven guns and shoot Alfonso Junior for every day of the week, shoot him in all the places where his heart should be. Don't love him, Virginia, don't spend a minute of your life loving him. Me and Roy and Mother will help Melvina hold him down—the whole world will hold him down— and let you get even. Let you slap his face a thousand times, until he cries and says he's sorry.

As soon as Alfonso Junior and Virginia were out of sight up the road, Melvina walked home, with Mother on the steps yelling, "It scares me, Melvina, the way your boys take after their daddy."

Melvina passed me and Roy. She looked at us with eyes as sharp as pins. "Scat," she said, waving her hand, shooing us off, disgusted. "Get away from my yard."

She thought we didn't feel things. I wanted to tear my skin open and show Melvina my beating heart. This world tied love into hateful knots, and our lifetimes were too short to unravel them. She thought someone needed to slap some love into us so we could understand that. I think she wanted to do it herself—right then. "Go home," she ordered.

"We don't have to," Roy said. "It's a free country."

We ran home terrified by Melvina's laughter. It was louder than screaming. She slapped her hands together. Her closed eyes set loose a flood.

*T*wo or three times a day Melvina looked at herself in the bathroom mirror. I'd see her shake her head no. She was so down in the dumps there was nothing we could do to cheer her up.

"God wastes a lot of time on young women," Melvina said. "If I didn't know better, I'd say he was partial to them hisself."

"Now Melvina," Mother said. "You're a handsome-looking woman and you know it. You think we don't notice all those colored men over at the Winn Dixie running their eyes up and down you. They act like their eyes are raking leaves off a fertile piece of ground."

"It ain't true," Melvina said. "When mens look at me they think, Lord, wonder what-all that woman could do for me. I bet she sure could simplify my life. Don't none of them ever think, Wonder what I could do for a good woman like that. My trouble is, I didn't bargain hard enough when my equipment was top of the line."

"You're talking foolish," Mother said.

"Lucy, you listen to what I tell you. Bargain hard when your equipment is top of the line. If there's anything men like, it's a bunch of fancy equipment. They rather have a fast woman than a fast car. I know it for a fact."

"Melvina, you don't sound Christian," Mother said.

"Christian is what happens to a woman once her equipment stops being top of the line. Religion is her only hope then."

Melvina started going to church three times a week. She and God had come up with a plan. It had to do with a man cleaving unto his wife. It was about ask and you shall receive, knock and the door shall be opened, *Won't you come home, Bill Bailey?*—a song Pearl Bailey sang on the radio that made Melvina say, "Thank you, Jesus!"

Walter says Melvina has got a bad case of religion, like religion is something a person comes down with, same as the earache or hives. "She's crazy if she thinks all her churchgoing will bring Old Alfonso home. Most likely it will do just the opposite. Melvina ought to know nothing scares a man more than a woman with a bad case of religion." Walter talks like religion is catching. It seems like it scares him for sure—same as the mumps do, which he has also escaped getting.

Since Walter is not a churchgoer, he doesn't worry about anything religious—which worries Mother. "Walter, it sure would set a nice example for Roy and Benny if you would come to church with the rest of us sometime," she said to him once.

Walter acted like she was suggesting he wear a dress or bake an angel food cake. "Lord, Sarah, everybody knows church is for women." He said that in front of Roy, who had dedicated his life to never doing any sissy things whatsoever. When Roy heard Walter say this he looked at Mother like she had been telling him some awful lie all these years and he'd always thought better of her than that. Mother was furious with Walter—so he tried to make up for it.

"Look, buddy," Walter said to Roy, "when I was a boy I had to do my time. Now you got to do your time. As long as you got a woman in charge of you, then you pretty well got to go to church if you want her to be fit to live with—but it's not forever, son. Just try to remember that."

This was not what Mother had in mind. She snatched Roy by the arm and yanked him away. I remember this plain because it was the first time it dawned on me that what Walter said was the truth. I should have noticed it for myself. *Church is the place where God and women get together to try and do something about the men in this world*. It's where women go to get talked into loving men for spiritual reasons, since after a while they run out of any other reasons to do it. God is there to keep women hoping for miracles.

Last summer Mother let me go to Vacation Bible School with Karol and Patricia, even though they're Baptist. We learned all these terrific Christian cheers for Parents' Night. Our mothers made us cheerleader suits and we made our own pom-poms out of crepe paper. We sashayed around in organized circles, shouting, *"Jesus, Jesus, he's our man. If he can't do it, nobody can!"* We ended the cheer with a spread-eagle leap. A couple of mothers took pictures, with tears in their eyes.

Then, I didn't see the truth in it, like I do now. I can look at Mother or Melvina and see it. If a woman wants a dependable man in her life she has to let Jesus be it. Then real men don't have that pressure on them. Like I bet Old Alfonso thinks he's something because he's got Rose Lee for a side woman, but the truth is she is just a drop in the bucket compared to Melvina's side man—Jesus himself. So see, in a way Melvina is outdoing Old Alfonso with keeping something going on the side. She loves Jesus, and it's a lucky thing for Old Alfonso, because he gets the spillover from it. Just like Granddaddy used to get the spillover from my churchgoing grandmother. Just like Walter gets it now from Mother. You'd think men could see the practical side of religion. As far as I can see, everything about church works to their advantage.

Besides, church men never seem like regular men. The preacher wears a robe to the floor, like a long, hot dress, and the choir director wears one too, and all the men in the choir do. Where else can men get away with dressing like women that way? They seem like men who don't know how to fix things, you know, build sheds, keep cars running, hunt deer, fry fish in the yard. I don't think they throw their kids up in the air and catch them either. They talk softly to them, saying, "Be good. Be quiet. Be still." Maybe I shouldn't say so, but I like regular men better than church men. And I guess whether Mother knows it or not she does too—since she's married two of them.

*G*RANDDADDY came to Talla-hassee on Walter's forty-second birthday with the back of his pickup loaded with manure. Walter shook Grand-daddy's hand and thanked him five or six times. Then Walter and Skippy spread the manure all over the yard, front and back, and set the sprinkler on it. It was terrible-looking and -smelling both, and drew a world's record number of flies to the yard. Mother said it was an embarrassment, and wouldn't let us go around barefooted for the longest time. She stood in the yard that afternoon, arms folded, and watched Walter and Skippy shoveling and sweating. Walter was a happy man.

"I don't know where men get themselves," Mother said.

After she went in the house Walter said to Skippy, "You know what's the trouble with women, Skippy?"

"Naw, sir, not all of it."

"They only see what they want to. They look at manure and all they can see is manure."

The truth was we didn't need that load of manure, because we already had the best grass on California Street. Anybody would say so. Mother said our grass was so green it was blue. In the evening it was. Always mowed and trimmed. Our house looked like a decent face right in the middle of an outstanding haircut.

·

One day Patricia, Karol, and I were lying out in the sun on a quilt. We had coated ourselves with a thin layer of Crisco like *Movie Star* magazine suggested, saying it was Sandra Dee's beauty secret. Now no-see-'ems, those tiny gnats, were stuck to us, but we were willing to make sacrifices for beauty. Roy, Bubba, and Benny were all over the place fighting or playing—the two things looked the same. Walter and Skippy were working on the lawn mower, changing the spark plugs, when Bubba's Daddy walked into the yard.

He hem-hawed, shifting from foot to foot until Walter hollered for Roy and Bubba to drag the picnic bench over for Bubba's Daddy to sit on. He sat with his elbows on his knees, held his hat by the brim, turning it around and around.

Patricia and Karol hurried over and sat down in the grass beside him, and so did I, the Crisco on our legs gluing us to the earth.

I guess nobody ever told Bubba's Daddy that Walter didn't know a thing about visiting and didn't do any of it. He might listen, but he wouldn't quit work he was doing and join in the conversation like other people did. "Hold that down with the pliers," he said to Skippy.

"That's what I wanted to see you about," Bubba's Daddy said, coughing. "I've got work needs done and I was thinking maybe you'd let me borrow your colored boy here."

Skippy flexed his chest muscles.

"What kind of work?" Walter said.

"I need a fence put up, one thing. My wife's after me to pen up my dogs. Thought you might loan me your boy here."

"He's no good at putting up a fence," Walter said.

"I'm going to supervise every step."

It sounded like a hailstorm on a tin roof—Skippy pound-

167

ing the lawn mower with the hammer. I put my hands over my ears. Walter looked startled. "It's rusted on," Skippy said. "Gon take hammering to get it." Walter braced the mower and Skippy pounded at it like you do a snake with a stick.

"So, what you say?" Bubba's Daddy asked.

"You'd be wasting your time," Walter said. "If he could build a fence I'd have him build me one."

"Niggers beats all," Bubba's Daddy said. He shook his head in a way as good as a hundred more words said, like what he wanted to say didn't need said, since he had shook it loose from his face, his eyes, the hair on his head.

"Lucy," Walter said, "go inside and ask your mama to get us something cold to drink. We're parched out here."

I took off into the house, slapping at the grass and dirt pasted to my Criscoed body. I told Mother that Walter was thirsty, then ran back out as fast as I could so I didn't miss anything. Bubba's Daddy was a man I couldn't turn my back on for a minute, for fear what he'd say when I wasn't listening was twice as awful as what he'd say when I was. He acted like he didn't see Skippy sitting not five feet in front of him, dark as night, and listening to every word said. Bubba's Daddy should hush in front of Skippy, but he was loose-tongued, and now Skippy would know certain things—about white people. I was a white person. I hurried back to my spot in the grass beside Patricia and Karol just as Bubba's Daddy was getting a second wind. "Mother's making iced tea," I told Walter.

Bubba's Daddy took out his pack of Lucky Strikes. He held the pack out to Walter. "No," Walter said. Bubba's Daddy lit a cigarette and sucked, making his belly swell. "See that bird?" Bubba's Daddy directed his voice at Skippy, pointing with his cigarette tip.

"Here goes Daddy's bird speech," Patricia whispered.

Skippy glanced at the fat man. His eyes were blind as knobs on a radio face.

"Birds stay with their own kind. Black birds with black birds. Blue birds with blue birds. Red birds with red birds." Patricia rolled her eyes and mouthed her daddy's words along with him, making me and Karol bust up. I laughed because I was nervous. "You see what I'm saying, boy?"

Skippy scratched the side of his face like he hadn't heard the question.

"If people don't stick with their own kind, then someday we'll all look like those cats with scrambled fur, one green eye and one brown one. Mongrels."

I knew the cats he meant. Their fur didn't know what color to be so it tried to be every color at once.

"God made us different for a reason." Bubba's Daddy flicked his ashes in the grass.

Walter coughed. He hated religious discussions.

"How about some iced tea?" Mother sang out. She carried a cookie sheet with rattling glasses on it, the ice tinkling back and forth, a sound that cooled me just to hear it.

"It sure is hot, isn't it?" Mother handed Bubba's Daddy a glass of tea. She lowered the tray where Walter and Skippy were squatted. "Why don't you rest a minute?" Walter took a glass and ran it across his forehead.

"Here, Skippy," Mother said.

"No, ma'am." Skippy kept his eyes on his work.

"Skippy, I made a glass for you and I want you to drink it. It's too hot to be working in the bald sun."

"You trying to tell her you're not thirsty?" Walter said. "She's not liable to believe it."

Skippy lifted a glass from the cookie sheet. His hand shook when he put it up to his mouth to drink.

Mother gave Karol and Patricia and me our tea and called Roy, Benny, and Bubba to come get some too. They took it and ran to the rabbit pen across the yard, spilling most of the tea on their feet. Benny's rabbit, Mopsy, had had babies again, seven of them. Roy, Benny, and Bubba were naming them—even though Mother would give them all away as soon as they were old enough. They held the babies up in the air and looked between their legs trying to decide whether a boy's name or a girl's name was in order.

Mother sat down on the picnic bench and crossed her legs. Bubba's Daddy drank his glass of tea in one gulp. "I was just saying how people are like birds." Bubba's Daddy was not even halfway back into his bird story when Mother said, "People are nothing at all like birds."

Walter cleared his throat.

"If we were birds I'd have to lay eggs. And you"— Mother laughed—"you'd have to lift off the ground and fly."

Skippy spit a mouthful of iced tea, spraying everybody. His snicker broke into a whoop. He was half choking himself laughing.

Bubba's Daddy crushed his cigarette on the bench where he sat. Suddenly it felt like it was about to rain, but it was nothing about the sky, it was the feeling we made ourselves—the people in the yard.

"I was talking about integration," he said. "We're getting an organization started in the neighborhood. The colored are just about finished tearing up their own school, so now they want to come to the white school and tear it up. So we're getting organized. . . ."

"Excuse me." Mother picked up the cookie sheet and for a second I almost expected her to snatch the iced tea out of all our hands, sling it in our faces, leaving us sitting stupid and startled. Instead, she walked in the house as upright and solid as a wooden column.

Walter and Skippy didn't look up from their pliers and screwdrivers. Karol and Patricia and I sat in a row in the grass like three hear-no-evil, see-no-evil, speak-no-evil monkeys. We sat cross-legged, our coats of Crisco gleaming. Roy and Bubba and Benny were spitting ice and sticking baby rabbits into their glasses trying to make them drink.

Their shrieking voices reached the rest of us in the awkward span of silence.

"Is your wife talking for you too?"

"I can talk for myself," Walter said. "When I got something to say."

"She's your second wife, isn't she?"

"She's my wife. Period."

"I didn't mean nothing by it. Just figured she was your second go-around."

"Hand me those screws," Walter said to Skippy, who dug through the tool box looking for them.

"So you saying you can't spare the boy?"

"I guess I am."

"I intended to pay him."

"Save your money." Walter turned back to the lawn mower.

Bubba's Daddy put his hat on his head. "Let's go," he barked at Karol and Patricia. "Get Bubba and let's go." His ears were fire red and he walked away fast for a fat man.

Sometimes Walter acted like he didn't have to participate in life if he didn't want to. Nobody could make him. He kept doing what needed doing on the lawn mower, melting himself in the hot sun, clanking around with his tools, saying nothing and thinking thoughts no one would ever know. I felt desperate for him to say some vague certain thing. I was paralyzed and unable to move until he said it—so I sat still and waited for it, a sentence like a dose of medicine I would die without. But the sentence never came.

I watched Walter and Skippy for a long time after everybody else left. Walter finally finished and went inside to cool off, but I stayed on while Skippy put the tools in the box and wiped the lawn mower with a rag. I couldn't take my eyes off him. Sweat dripped down the sides of his face, his chest glistened, but his face was like a door slammed shut. *Let me in, Skippy. Don't you see me sitting here? Don't you know my heart is pounding?* "Do you want me to help you put that away?"

He acted like he hadn't heard me. I picked tufts of grass, tore them into tiny pieces, blew them out of my hand so they'd fly for a second, like green confetti. "Skippy, don't pay Bubba's Daddy any attention."

He ignored me.

"He doesn't mean any of it," I lied. "Even if he does, Mother says he's the most ignorant man she ever saw."

Skippy still ignored me.

"Are you mad at Walter?"

No answer.

"He doesn't mean what he said either. He knows you can build a fence. You're the only one he'll let touch his lawn mower—you know that, don't you? Have you ever seen Roy mowing? Walter says you have a natural sense of machinery."

I was trying to give Skippy a lie for a present, but he wouldn't take it. I wanted to give him something practical he could use, something nice to take home with him. So I lied. This lie, that lie, like going through a ring of keys, trying this one, trying that one—but none of them would work.

"Even if Walter does mean what he said, the rest of us don't." I tugged at a handful of grass. It came up by the root this time. Clumps of dirt fell on my feet. I rubbed them into mud. Now my hands were dirty too. Skippy closed the lid on the tool box and snapped the latch down. "At least I know Mother and me don't mean it. We don't think colored people will tear up the white school." I tried to press the clump of grass back into place, but it wouldn't stand up anymore; it fell sideways as soon as I let go. "We are in favor of integration, Skippy, I swear." I thought about it a minute. "I know for sure Mother is."

Skippy leaned against the closed tool box and wiped his forehead with the same rag he had used on the lawn mower. "Lucy," he said, "why don't you go on in the house, where you belong."

*I*T was not daybreak yet when Skippy came banging on our back door. "Daddy's back home," Skippy said. "He's sick."

"What in hell?" Walter's hair stood up that crazy way it does when he first wakes up in the morning.

Mother came into the kitchen with her housecoat wrapped around her. "What's the matter, Skippy?"

"Mama said come tell you they brought Daddy home last night. He's beat up bad."

"He's drunk," Walter said.

"No, sir, worse than that."

"Let me get some clothes on. Wait right there." Mother hurried to her room to get dressed.

"What do you think you're going to do when you get up there?" Walter yelled at Mother. "Melvina think you're a nurse or something? Shoot." He turned to look at Skippy standing in the door. "Your mama think she's a nurse or something?"

"Naw, sir."

"Shoot," Walter said.

In a minute Mother came back dressed in shorts, scrambling around looking for her flip-flops. "We might need to get him to a doctor," she said to Walter.

"You and who else?"

"If he's sick enough, Walter."

"He's no sicker than he wants to be."

"He's bad sick," Skippy said. "Got the hell beat out of him."

"See." Mother hardly looked at Walter as she started out the door. "Melvina and I can get him to the emergency room, I guess."

"Sarah, you're no Florence Nightingale, or what the hell ever her name was."

"This is the answer to Melvina's prayer, Walter. I guess you're too blind to see it. Come on, Skippy," Mother said.

"Wait right there." Walter went and got his flashlight and handed it to Skippy. "I don't want to have to come up there after this thing. You bring it back when you're done." Skippy took the flashlight, triggered it on, slapping Walter's face with yellow.

Mother and Skippy started through the woods. Roy and me could hear Mother's flip-flops flapping as she hurried along, because we were awake good and up now too. "Get dressed, Lucy," Walter said, "and look after Benny if he wakes up before your mama gets back."

"What's wrong with Old Alfonso?"

"Been in a fight," Walter said. "What else?"

Before we knew it Walter was dressed too and slamming out the back door on his way up to Melvina's. "If your mama thinks she's a nurse, then I guess that makes me a doctor, don't it?" He pulled his gray hat down low on his head, the words "Sweet's Concrete" stitched above the bill in black letters. "I'm making a house call. I know just the medicine for Old Alfonso."

"Who was Old Alfonso fighting with?" Roy asked.

"I don't know"—Walter opened the kitchen door and started down the steps—"but I'm on their side."

Pretty soon the sun came up. Roy and I sat in the kitchen eating a second bowl of Cheerios and watching out the window. We knew Old Alfonso must be desperate sick—or dead—when we saw Walter drive our car into Melvina's yard. Skippy ran down to our house to get some newspaper to lay over the backseat. I gave him yesterday's *Tallahassee Democrat*.

"Is Old Alfonso okay?" I asked.

"Would they be taking him to the hospital if he was okay, girl?"

Melvina and Mother wrapped Old Alfonso in quilts so he could be carried out to the car easy. But there was no easy to it. Walter had his head and Skippy got his feet, still kicking. Old Alfonso was a patchwork caterpillar, jerking, hard to keep hold of. Walter and Skippy shoved him into the car like it was the too little cocoon he had finally squeezed out of and was being forced back into before he had the chance to burst into a butterfly.

"He looks like one of those mummies," Roy said.

Mother and Melvina got in the car with Walter, all three of them in the front seat, and off they went. Skippy stood in the yard and watched them leave. "I'll go up there and get the details. You listen for Benny," I told Roy. But when I started towards Melvina's house Skippy saw me and turned his back to go inside.

"What happened?" I yelled, running, trying to catch him before he got away. "Skippy. Wait. Why did somebody beat up Old Alfonso? Who did it? "

But he never turned around.

"I know you hear me, Skippy. I know you're not deaf." He went inside the house and closed the door.

Mother said when they got to the hospital Walter lied. He told the doctor Old Alfonso was one of his workers at the highway department, and the doctor believed him. Mother said it beat all she ever heard.

"I never knew Walter could lie like that," Mother said.

She said Melvina turned to wood listening. She was like a tree planted in the terrazzo of the waiting room with Mother crouched in her shade. The more Walter talked, the woodier Melvina became, until she was leafless, her greenness giving way to something darker. She was as stiff and lifeless as a totem pole with a hard face carved in the top, Mother said.

In a little bit the doctor came out into the waiting room where Walter and Mother and Melvina were sitting, and said Old Alfonso had broken ribs, a bruised lung, and some inside bleeding. "He ought to stay in the hospital and be looked after. Can he afford to do it?"

"No. No, he can't," Walter and Melvina chimed in.

"If he needs to stay, then he ought to stay," Mother said, but she told us later that Walter and Melvina shot her a look that said don't-get-started-on-this-now-we-mean-it.

"I don't have all day to fool with this," Walter told the doctor. "I'm a working man."

Mother said two colored men in white suits rolled Old Alfonso out on a hospital bed and loaded him into the backseat by lifting the sheets up like a hammock and swinging him into the car easy. The whole way home Melvina didn't say a word. "What's wrong, Melvina?" Mother kept asking. "Is something wrong? We're trying to help you. That's all. You're the one that called us to come up there."

"If we'd really wanted to help her we'd dump him out somewhere on the side of the road and be done with it," Walter said. "I know a stretch of highway where it'd take them twenty years to find his bones."

"Walter, for heaven's sake." Mother looked at Melvina's stone face. "He's just talking to hear himself talk."

When they got Old Alfonso home, me and Roy and Benny were waiting in the yard. "Who done it?" Roy said.

"Hush, Roy," Mother said. "It's no time for questions."

When Melvina saw that Annie and the boys had gone back to sleep and had not hit a lick at cleaning up, she fired up at them. "Every sheet and quilt I own is nasty dirty and you all laying up in the bed." Her voice blasted through the house like a gunshot signaling the beginning of a race. "Get that floor mopped up. Annie, you heat some wash water for your daddy's clothes. Shoo that dog out of here. Skippy, go get a chicken from the people up the road so I can fix some broth. You all get out of that bed before I snatch you out. Get some clothes on." All her kids jumping like lit fire-crackers, popping up, shooting across the room, clearing out of the way. "Yellow-haired Jesus," Melvina said. "If I didn't stand here and tell you to breathe, I guess the lot of you would smother to death from lack of instructions."

Skippy and Walter carried Old Alfonso inside. "Is he gon die?" Roy said. Twice Old Alfonso opened his eyes and looked up to see Walter's pink face.

"I've done some stupid things in my life," Walter said. "If you all are lucky he won't last through the night. If he does, I guess this time next week we'll be carrying Melvina to the hospital."

Melvina flashed her eyes at Skippy, who welcomed the chance to get out of the house and take off up the road.

"I got a living to make," Walter said. "You all let me know when the funeral is." He walked out on the porch, where Orlando was sitting, Nappy on his lap, his legs wrapped around Leroy to keep him from falling off the edge of the porch. "You ever considered building a pen to keep them in?" Walter said. The three boys stared at him. "What y'all looking at? Hadn't you ever seen a white man with less sense than God give a goose?"

He stomped down the steps shaking his Sweet's Concrete head. Once on the ground he looked the boys right in the eye. He fished in his pocket and pulled out an assortment of change. "Here"—he handed Orlando the coins—"take them up to the store and buy them a Milky Way. You're going to play hell getting any breakfast out of Melvina."

Orlando pulled back and would not take the money. He

cut his eyes away from Walter. Leroy stepped forward and took it, and when he did Orlando leaped up and grabbed it out of his hand, nearly dropping Nappy on the floor.

Roy, Benny, and I got down off the porch. We were starting home with Walter when Orlando yelled, "Mister." Walter turned around. "We don't like you."

"Good," Walter said. "Let's keep it that way."

Who beat up Old Alfonso? That's what everybody wanted to know. By the time he was well enough to answer questions, that piece of his memory was gone. All he knew was he'd gotten in a fuss with Rose Lee and left her house to walk back to the Blue Bird. Next thing he knew, some men stumbled over him lying half dead in a ditch. They tried to take him to Rose Lee, but she was too mad to have him. So they brought him home to Melvina. He couldn't remember a thing.

Bubba's Daddy would not let Patricia, Karol, or Bubba come down to our house anymore. When we went to their house he stood blocking the door and said, "They can't come out." As we left to walk home he yelled, "Is it true what I heard? Did your daddy drive that nigger to the hospital?"

We turned to face him and saw Karol's face peeking out from behind the curtain, staring at us with a solemn look.

"Did your daddy do that?" Bubba's Daddy said. "Answer me."

"He's not our daddy," I said. "He's our stepfather."

Afterwards, whenever they saw me, Patricia and Karol would go the other way, pretend they couldn't hear me calling their names. It was like I had gone invisible. Karol had a spend-the-night on her thirteenth birthday—but did not invite me. Whenever I called her and Patricia on the telephone to come down to my house and lay in the sun, they said they couldn't because they had to go someplace. Then later I would see them dancing on a quilt in their own yard.

W̶E met Julie, our daddy's new girlfriend. He called Mother and asked if he could bring her by to meet us—his only children, the ones he hadn't seen in all this time—even though last we knew, he still lived less than three miles from us. Mother pretended it was a perfectly normal request. She has taught us to pretend equally well. You would never catch any of us rudely distinguishing normal from abnormal. We operate on the basis that everything is fine if Mother says it is.

We were scattered around the yard when they drove up in their white car, packed to the gills, clothes hung on a rod in the back. They got out holding hands, walked across the yard like it was a trampoline, something between a bounce and a leap in each step they took to the picnic table. The drama of their entrance reduced the rest of us to audience.

For a minute I thought maybe the whole bunch of us might just stand in our tracks and stare at them—at Julie especially, this woman who floated across the yard leading Daddy. She looked golden—not like a woman who wrote poems—like an ex-cheerleader, like any minute she would do a cartwheel, show her underpants, and say, "Two bits, four bits, six bits, a dollar!"

"Hey there, Lucy," Daddy said. He hugged me, and for a minute I thought he was even going to twirl me around in the air. But he couldn't—not with only one free hand. I settled for his pressing my head hard against his shirt, nearly poking me in the eye with the ballpoint pen clipped to his pocket.

Benny ran across the yard and jumped on Daddy, which loosened things up. "Benny boy! How you been?" So of course, Roy came over too, but he didn't want any kissing mess. Daddy shook his hand and pounded him on the back.

"I sure have missed you," he said. "I want you to meet Julie here. I've been telling her about you."

"Hello, Lucy, Roy, and Benny. Very nice to meet you."

"Hello," we said with artificial politeness that would make Mother proud.

"Lucy," Julie said, touching my hair lightly, "you look just like your daddy. Your hair is as blond as his. And as soft." Julie and Daddy looked at each other with eyes that I recognized from movies. Starry eyes. I don't know if Roy noticed or not, Daddy and Julie rubbing their gaze all up and down each other.

"Johnny, your children are beautiful," Julie said.

"I told you so." His gaze engulfed us like transparent wrap, the non-cling kind.

"Is that your car?" Roy asked.

"Sure is," Daddy said. "Got it about six months ago. Bought it used, but you'd never know it. You like it?"

Obviously Roy did. It was a car that made us think things must be looking up for Daddy. At last.

Mother and Walter walked over from where they were sitting in a couple of low-slung metal chairs in the yard. They walked slow, like they had the rest of their lives to get there—Walter saying something under his breath to Mother, his hands in his pockets.

It had been a long time since we last saw Daddy. Whenever he came around he brought this same feeling with him—that our world was too small since there was no room for him in it. Like we only had five chairs to our name so he would have to stand up, or we only had five chicken breasts so he would have to eat a wing, or we only had five sweaters so he would just have to freeze to death. Daddy stuck his hand out and Walter shook it—which was almost more than you could ask for.

"I want you to meet Julie Meyers, from Miami. Julie was a graduate student in English this semester."

I didn't know whether or not to believe him. Julie looked too blonde, too cheerful to be smart. Where were her sensible shoes? She didn't even wear glasses.

Mother smiled. "Hello, Julie."

"Hello, Mrs. Sheppard."

"Call me Sarah."

"Okay. Sarah."

Walter excused himself, said he had to go check on something about tomorrow's road crew. He got in the truck and drove off. Benny wanted to go with him, but Walter said, "Not this time."

"Well," Mother said. "Well." She watched Walter go around the bend in the road and head for French Town. "Why don't you come sit down at the picnic table," she said. "I'll get everybody some iced tea. How does that sound?" She went in the house smiling, as friendly as the day is long. Outdid herself with decency.

Daddy and Julie walked over to the picnic table and sat down. Roy and Benny and I did too. Daddy said, "How's school?" We told him school was out. Then he talked about how much we'd grown. Benny told everything he knew, and Roy was pretty polite. I mostly stared at Julie. She was not one bit like Mother. She had curly honey-blond hair which she had fixed in a page boy, but it was frizzing in the humidity and I was glad. She was fair-skinned, had powder on and rosy cheeks and bigger breasts than Mother. She wore a sundress with tiny flowers on it and her sandals were pink to match the dress, and she had painted toenails and smelled like honeysuckle perfume.

Julie let Daddy do most of the talking. She had her hand

on his hand one minute, her arm through his arm the next. She didn't watch to see what she was doing, her hands just knew. She ran her hand gently up and down Daddy's back when he talked. Every chance he got, Daddy looked over at her, raised his eyebrows as if to elicit some unspoken yes. I should've told Roy to get the hose and put out the fire.

I looked at Julie's breasts. Every smart girl I'd ever known pretended not to have breasts—or else really *didn't* have them, which was why she decided to be smart instead. When Julie leaned against Daddy's arm, her breasts threatened to escape her rosebud sundress.

Mother came back carrying a tray of iced tea and some sliced cake on a plate, just like she'd do if the preacher came. "Here we go," she said. "Julie, I hope you like your tea sweet."

"That's fine," Julie said.

Mother wasn't fixed up like she could have been. When she wanted to, Mother could be drop-dead good-looking. She never did look totally bad—like on this day she had on clean shorts and a white blouse and flip-flops. Her hair was not in a ponytail but brushed out. Not curled, though. She already had a good tan, so her face had that summer shine to it. She was pretty but was just not drop-dead fixed up like I said. Like Julie was.

If I'd been Mother, I'd have made a beeline for the bathroom and put on her ruby red lipstick and a big dose of My Sin. But Mother didn't think like that. No, she just let Julie sit there golden, fit to kill.

Mother was black-haired. Sometimes when the sun hit her right you could see the blue in her black hair. By the end of the summer she would be so brown that people would ask if she was part Indian, and she'd say, "No, my grandmother was a black Scot." People hated this answer. They immediately lost interest in her looks, disappointed in her lack of savage blood. Even though I am a blonde myself,

I thought Mother must find it unforgivable for Daddy, who used to call her Pocahontas, his Indian princess, to suddenly strut into the yard with about the yellowest, pinkest woman he could find. I knew Mother must have wanted to get Walter's gun off his closet shelf and shoot Daddy in his tiny heart. I felt like doing it myself.

"Well, Julie, tell me about yourself." Mother handed her a sweating glass of tea.

But before Julie could answer, Daddy did. "Julie and I met in a poetry seminar."

"Oh," Mother said. "Do you write poetry, Julie?"

"Does she write poetry?" Daddy said. "She's on fellowship, Sarah. Julie's one of the smartest women I've ever met." Julie must have felt satisfied. Like a contented cat. I swear I could hear her motor going.

"That's nice," Mother said.

Daddy reached over and took Julie's hand. "I wish you could get to know her, Sarah. You'd like her. She's been a real help to me too."

"Really?"

"She looks at me and sees somebody, Sarah. Somebody good. I can't tell you how much that means." Daddy's voice trembled slightly. Mother seemed startled, paused mid-sip, squinting, tea glass stuck to her lips. Is that where Mother went wrong? Did she forget how to look at Daddy and see somebody good? She swallowed the cold tea, but it went down the wrong pipe and strangled her a second.

Julie was watching Mother. "It's nice of you to let us come today, Sarah," she said quietly. "I know it's not easy—"

"Julie understands me—what I write—which keeps me on track," Daddy continued.

"How nice," Mother said, stabbing a piece of cake with her fork. "Julie, you must inspire Johnny."

"We inspire each other." Julie looked Mother in the eye.

"Johnny has one of the gentlest hearts I've ever known in a man. But then, I guess you know that."

Mother had a look on her face like if she had ever known it, she had since forgotten. She looked at Daddy, a matter of seconds, like he was new.

"Were you ever a cheerleader?" I asked.

"No, Lucy. But she could have been." Daddy grinned. "She's pretty enough."

"Johnny!" He was embarrassing her. I could tell by the sweet whine of her voice. If I talked that way Walter sent me to my room until I stopped pouting. But Daddy liked it.

"Don't be fooled by this pretty face, Lucy. There's more to Julie than that."

Julie blushed. "We're happy together, that's all. Put us together and we're both—whole."

"Have some more cake," Mother said, "won't you?"

If Mother had been any nicer to Julie it would have killed us all. We sat around and visited like Daddy was the preacher and Julie was the preacher's wife and Mother was the chairman of the Methodist women. So this was the salvation Daddy had been waiting for all his life?

If it was brains Daddy wanted, why hadn't he stuck with Mother? Everybody that knew Mother thought she was smart. Sometimes Walter said she was too smart for her own good. Was it poetry Daddy wanted? Mother could've been a poet if she'd wanted to.

Daddy did most of the talking, Julie punctuating with quiet remarks, but I stopped listening. Finally Daddy and Julie got ready to leave. They were like two people who had stepped out of a dream into the unnaturalness of daylight, and now it was time for them to return to the imaginary world they came from.

Daddy put his arm around me. "Lucy, you take care of yourself now, and I'll see you this fall. See if you can't slow down all this growing up you're doing." He smiled and looked at my face, but I could tell his eyes were focused on something in the back of his own head. He was operating on automatic father. "Speaking of growing, I know I missed your birthday again this year. Seems like when I think of it it's passed by. I'm going to get better about it, I swear."

I wanted to tell Daddy I had had a fine birthday without him. Walter got me a transistor radio almost exactly like the one Patricia's got. It was the best present I ever had—Walter surprising me. He came walking in with a small cardboard box, not wrapped with a bow, but still the best present in the world. He had a paper sack with batteries too. It surprised Mother as much as it did me. I kissed Walter's face fifty times.

Almost from the minute I got that radio it's been turned on. I go to sleep at night with it under my pillow, sweet Elvis Presley turning me into a woman while I sleep.

"Missing my birthday was nothing important," I said, but Daddy wasn't listening.

After the hugging and the sugar good-byes we said to Julie, and Daddy looking at Mother like he always does, they left. Julie floating by his side, those hands that had probably touched every inch of my daddy waving good-bye. Daddy revved the motor, then jerked the car into the street, making it squeal and fishtail. As they sped down California Street he sounded the horn. Mother didn't even look up. I waved good-bye—not to them, but to myself, the invisible daughter, always riding silently, unnoticed, in the backseat of my daddy's fast car.

Mother cleared off the picnic table and hummed. She stopped in the middle of her tune, smiled, shook her head, then kept on. I think she was relieved to see Daddy and Julie go around the first curve and disappear on their long trip south. I think she liked being the woman in Daddy's rearview mirror, waving good-bye. It was one of those nice moods she gets in, where, if Walter was home, she'd stop everything, sit in his lap, and wrap her arms around his neck.

Later, when Walter did come home, Mother said, "Julie is a smart woman, Walter. She writes poetry."

"Is that right?"

"What did you think of her, Walter?"

Walter shrugged his shoulders like he didn't have an opinion on the woman, but Mother wouldn't let that do. She kept on with it. "Did you think she was pretty? Did you like her hair? Did you see those sandals she had on?"

Finally Walter said, "Well, she was put together. I didn't notice much, but I noticed that. She's built to last." He winked at me.

Mother saw him wink, threw her glass of half-melted ice cubes at him, pretending to be mad. It was like the times Walter caught a frog, held it gently, petting it like it was a baby bird, saying, "Sarah, come kiss this frog and see if it turns into a prince."

"Get away from me with that thing," Mother always said, and started running.

Then Walter would say to Roy and Benny and me, "I bet you didn't know I was a frog when your mama met me, did you? I bet you thought I'd been a prince all my life."

"Walter Sheppard, I mean it," Mother'd say. "Put that thing down." But she didn't mean it. Walter chased her around the yard with the frog—me hollering, "Run, Mother! Hurry!" and Roy and Benny hollering, "Catch her, Walter! Catch her!" She only acted mad because it made the chase more fun that way.

But on this particular afternoon Walter didn't have a frog, so he ran and grabbed Mother, lifted her up over his shoulder, her bottom in the air, his arms clasped around her bare legs.

"Put me down right now." She pounded her fists on his back and shouted his name, "Walter Sheppard. Walter Sheppard, let go of me, you crazy man!"

"Not until you say 'Pretty please.' " Walter ran, bouncing Mother on his shoulder, gently knocking the breath out of her.

"Pretty please!" she screamed.

"Not until you say 'Pretty please with sugar on it.' "

"With sugar on it!" She screamed again, dissolving in a fit of laughter. Walter and Mother both collapsed on the ground, two felled giants rolling in the green grass.

I thought of Daddy burying his face in Julie's curly hair—I imagined him saying *IloveyouIloveyouIloveyou.* I looked at Mother and Walter lying in the grass, shot in the heart by a couple of Cupid's arrows.

*S*KIPPY was keeping the grass mowed good. It seemed like he'd grown a foot taller this summer and wasn't skinny like he used to be. His voice had dropped so low it sounded like a man's. When he spoke I had to look to be sure the words were coming out of him. There was a warm, heavy sound to his voice now. It made me listen better.

One evening he was finishing up in the yard and I was out there too, in a lawn chair, listening to my portable radio, which he noticed. "Where'd you get that?"

"My birthday."

He fiddled with the lawn mower quietly, like he was shining the thing, like a lawn mower was something you polished. Sam Cooke was singing "You Send Me," and I couldn't tell where the song stopped and the air began . . . *honest you do, honest you do, honest you do.* Skippy kneeled beside the mower, going over it, the rag wrapped around the tip of his finger, touching the rag to his tongue, then hard-rubbing some particular spot, the muscles in his arms knotting.

The evening was deep blue, sticky and warm and full of bugs. But the smell was wild and green, everything growing, growing—little explosions of leaves. If you were quiet enough you could hear vines tangling in the woods, and the ripe, forgotten blackberries hidden in lush stickers begging. When the world was blue like this—and warm and green—you could hear yourself think. Good rock and roll filled the yard, and the lightning bugs came out, flashed to the music like tiny stars—private fireworks, small secrets flashing. But then mosquitoes claimed the yard like they always do. They loved my ankles and wrists too much—so they chased me inside. I took my portable radio and walked barefoot across the sweet-smelling grass to the house. Skippy never looked up.

That night when I was asleep, my legs tangled in the sheets, my radio under my pillow, I heard my name in a loud whisper. "Wake up, Lucy." Someone was in the flower bed. I rolled over and sat up in bed. "Who is it?"

"It's me."

"Skippy? What are you doing?" I couldn't see him at first, his dark self out my dark window. I kicked the sheets off, got out of bed, and felt my way to the window like a blind girl. When my eyes adjusted to the dark I looked at him. He had on long pants and an ironed shirt, not his usual shorts and bare chest. "What are you doing out here this time of night? Walter would have a fit."

"Mr. Sheppard likes me."

"Well, he doesn't like you sneaking around looking in the windows in the middle of the night. I know that."

"Where's your radio?"

"What?"

"Your radio. Where is it?"

So that was it. Waking me up because he wanted my radio. "You can't have it," I said.

"I'll bring it back in a little bit. I won't let nothing happen to it."

"I'm listening to it, Skippy."

"I don't hear nothing."

"It's under my pillow. I listen while I sleep."

"Get it."

Like a sleepwalker I went over to the bed and got the radio from under my pillow. It was playing a slow song. The Everly Brothers. I walked back to the window, sat on the windowsill, and held up the radio so Skippy could hear it. Then I unlatched the screen and pushed it open, and he stuck his head and shoulders inside. He smelled like soap and toothpaste. He took the radio in his hands. "That's nice, girl." First thing, he switched the station to some low-shouting colored music. He bobbed his head and danced so you could barely tell it, like the muscles under his skin were dancing, but his skin was being still. He held the radio to his ear and closed his eyes, like the radio was a pitcher of music and he was pouring it into himself, and I could watch it running all down inside him. In a minute he looked me right in the face. His eyes were so nice I couldn't look at him more than a split second.

"Let me take this for just a little bit, Lucy."

I knew I should say no, but I couldn't when he was nice like this, handsome, with long pants and a clean shirt on. "Skippy?" I said it like just speaking his name was dragging something out of me. But he didn't say a mean thing. He was asking for the radio like I was a person and he was a person. It was different from usual.

"One hour," I said. "Don't break it—or lose it."

He ducked his head under the screen and closed it. "I bet you let in a swarm of mosquitoes," I said.

I couldn't fall back to sleep without radio music. I pictured Skippy walking up the dirt road to the Snack Shack, dancing his way up there in his long pants. Why was he dressed like that? It was the way Alfonso Junior acted when he first got after Virginia. Was that it—a girl? Skippy going to the Snack Shack, looking sort of good, wanting the radio to show off with.

It was nearly two hours later when Skippy came back. I heard him coming and got out of bed to meet him at the window. "I told you I'd be back. Lift the screen."

So I did. He set the radio inside on the ledge, then stuck his head and shoulders inside like before. "Here." He reached into his shirt pocket. "I brought you these." He handed me a fistful of little silver-wrapped chocolates.

I unwrapped one, slowly peeling off the silver paper. The chocolate was soft. It unwrapped melted, so I had to lick it off. "So, do you have a girlfriend up at the Snack Shack?"

Skippy grinned. "Zat what you think?"

"Maybe," I said. "It's possible."

"Why don't you come out this window and I'll take you up there and show you. Ain't no girl up there worth the notice."

"Wouldn't Walter love it?" I laughed. "Me going to French Town in the middle of the night in my nightgown." I handed him a piece of chocolate candy and he took it.

Skippy picked up the radio and changed the dial to a white station, Dion singing, *I hop right into that car of mine and drive around the world.* "I told you I'd bring it right back, wouldn't nothing happen to it," Skippy said. He put the radio in my hand. His fingernails were so clean. He must have soaked them to get the motor oil out from under them. "I got to go." He closed the screen and walked away.

I took the radio and got back in bed. I was glad Mother and Walter had the window fan in their room, how loud it was, how it hummed them off to sleep and kept them that way like a never-ending truck roaring down some highway in their heads. Because if they had come in my room and seen me in my nightgown at the window talking to Skippy I don't think they would have liked it. In fact, I think they would have had a fit.

*B*Y now Old Alfonso was sitting up, and eating pretty good too. Melvina spent the day running back and forth between our house and hers. She acted like she had to come down and work for us or else Mother would not pay her and she needed the money bad. But I think Melvina knew better. That Mother would pay Melvina no matter what. She'd pay Melvina just for being colored, like being colored was one hard job and Mother knew it and paid Melvina because she was so uncommonly good at it.

While Melvina was down at our house, who walks over to her house, in broad daylight, dressed to die in a tight-fitting yellow dress with shoes to match—but Rose Lee. "I've got to talk to Old Alfonso," she says, handing out banana Popsicles she's brought in a paper sack. "These are for y'all. Eat them fast. Don't let them drip."

Annie slips out the back door and tears down to our house to get Melvina, who is unsuspecting. She has got her shoes off and is eating a meatloaf sandwich, watching *Queen for a Day* with Mother. Annie bangs in the house, yelling, "Mama, that Rose Lee's up there with Daddy." Before you could blink, Melvina was out the door, storming through the woods, Annie right behind her, and Mother on guard at our kitchen window, yelling, "Melvina, now don't do anything you'll regret."

Rose Lee had brought Old Alfonso a bottle of whiskey. It was in a sack, and he had just taken hold of it when Melvina came inside the door like a fierce gust of wind, grabbed that bottle out of his hand, and waved it above her head like a furious Statue of Liberty.

"What does she think she's doing here?" Melvina asked Old Alfonso, as if it was his job to speak for Rose Lee, his other woman, dressed up like a daffodil—and as fragile as one, her thin legs in pointy-toed high heels that had cost God knows how much.

"It ain't what you think." Old Alfonso sat up in bed. "I'm a sick man. She's here to see about me."

"So, you an angel of mercy?" Melvina looked for the first time, hard, at the woman. Later she wouldn't be able to remember a thing about Rose Lee's face, but she could describe every stitch of clothes she had on, plus her watch, plus the color of her fingernails.

Rose Lee began to back towards the door.

"Look, Mama." Leroy waved his Popsicle. "She brung these."

"Get outside with those drippy things," Melvina said. The children pressed themselves against the wall and didn't move. They licked fast and furious, Popsicle sticks protruding from their mouths like wooden cigarettes. Melvina pointed the whiskey bottle at Rose Lee. "You better get your face out of this house unless you want changes made in it."

"The whole bunch of you isn't nothing but fighting crazy," Rose Lee answered. She got down the steps, moving backwards. As soon as she hit dirt she broke into a run.

"Let me see you run," Melvina yelled. "Is that all the fast you can run?" Melvina's dogs came bounding out from under the house and took off after Rose Lee, who stumbled out of her high-heeled shoes, stopped to retrieve them, then kept running.

"You're crazier than he is," Rose Lee yelled. "You can have him with icing on his butt." Even Rose Lee's screams were thin, yellow, and delicate.

"You can't give me nothing that already belongs to me," Melvina yelled. "Them dogs bite!"

When Melvina was clearheaded she told Skippy to take the bottle of liquor up to the Blue Bird and sell it for what he could get and bring her home the money.

Then Melvina came back to our house and told Mother the story and they drank a cup of coffee over it. I listened to every word. They talked about what a trashy woman Rose Lee was and how funny she looked running up California Street with her shoes in her hand, how undignified and foolish she was. "What you guess she paid for that dress?" they said.

Melvina takes some pride in the hardness of her life—how much more is required of her, and how she always measures up to that requirement. It is like she feels bad for Mother and us, comfortable white people, who don't make the most of ourselves. Not like Melvina, who since she has that hard life is gon take pride in it, and show it off, and live it like she was handpicked by God to do it.

*T*HEY were having a Bible-reading contest at Trinity Methodist Church. When Mother saw that I didn't sign up for the contest, she said, "Lucy, if you'll read the Bible—every word of it—I'll give you ten dollars." Since then I'd been working on it. Ten dollars would be enough to buy myself a two-piece bathing suit for next summer. I wanted one like Patricia's got.

The deal was to read the Bible—not necessarily to understand it. I kept at it, trying to read at least ten pages a day no matter what. I have to say the Bible was a disappointment. Mother had no idea it was backfiring on me. It became clear to me how impossible it would be to ever please God. I felt sorry for the people who tried so hard—and I decided not to be one of them. You can never tell whose side God will be on. He keeps you guessing. It's like playing checkers with Walter—it's better just to make your move and not try to figure out what his plan is. You can't beat Walter at checkers. Once you know that, it makes playing much more fun because you can take every kind of risk.

When God had Noah build the ark for his family and then drowned everybody else on earth, saying Noah was the only good person he could find in all the world, that did it for me. It just shows how little God understands people if he thinks there is only one good person in the world at any given time. I don't trust that kind of thinking. God looks down on people and sees nothing but their sin, the same way Walter looks at people and sees nothing but their skin. God can't see past sin any better than Walter can see past skin.

I even picture God looking like Walter, only old, with a long beard—but he is all head. A big head swollen like a tick after it has sucked blood long enough. I love God, though, the same way I love Walter—because I need him, and there is something in me that makes me love him even without a good reason. Mother is the only person I know who is good enough to be loved by God. Me, I've lost interest in it. I try to keep my two-piece bathing suit in mind instead.

I imagined myself at Wakulla Springs standing on the

high dive—all eyes on me from below—anticipating my leap into the air and the long and terrifying fall into the cold liquid glass below. It would be like diving into a mirror. So far I had been afraid to do it. This would be the third summer I'd climbed the high dive just to contemplate jumping off, just to look out over the beach dotted with bright towels and the bent shapes of pink people, the glass-bottom boats cruising the shimmering aqua, stopping over the huge fake alligator cemented to the bottom of the springs. You could hear Yankee tourists shriek with delight when they saw it. "Is it real?" they'd ask. "Yes," the guide would lie. "He sleeps there." Cameras would click and snap.

Florida is based on lying to Yankees. First, they wouldn't believe the truth of things even if they knew it, and second, they weren't any more interested in the truth than anybody else. They wanted to believe particular things. Florida tried to help them do that. Besides, Yankees were entertaining to have around. When they came down here to gawk at us, we gawked right back at them. The truth was, southerners felt sorry for Yankees. Usually when I saw them I was overcome with sympathy. I tried to be as nice as I could for that very reason. They were so crazy about equipment too. Regular cameras, movie cameras, tape recorders. They didn't seem to go around just natural. They were inclined towards apparatus. Southerners hate apparatus and wish people would quit thinking it up.

Standing on the high dive, I could see the jungle boats traveling at the edge of the spring, the guide pointing to sleeping snakes draped on tree limbs, herons and hawks navigating the sky, alligators with their noses protruding floating in the transparent liquid, rows of sunning turtles, orange-finned fish in the shallow water. The guide carried a fake gun and pretended to shoot bears and wildcats stalking the shore. The imaginations of the listeners formed a cloud above their heads, which floated upward in the blue, blue.

At Wakulla Springs people sunned on one side of the water, alligators sunned on the other. The water was so clear you didn't have to worry about alligators sneaking up on you. They mostly slept in the sand. It was almost as if they understood the line of red bubble floats that marked the swimming area. On those rare occasions when a misguided alligator swam towards people, the lifeguard blew his whistle and shouted, "Everybody out of the water!" and in a frenzy of shrieks and splashes people scrambled out of the water and stood dripping wet along the shore, wrapped in striped towels. If a lifeguard went out in a rowboat to chase the alligator away, people said, "Frieda. Quick. Where's my camera?"

The water at Wakulla Springs was cold no matter how hot the world was. That's what made me respect it—along with the fact that it was exceedingly beautiful. I thought this upcoming summer might be the one. I might finally be brave enough to jump into the mirror of ice water. Whether I did or didn't, though, I planned to be wearing a two-piece bathing suit when I stood on the high dive thinking it over. At the very least I would be looking good.

"You reading your Bible again?"

I was laying on my back in Walter's truck with my legs hung out the window, fighting my way through Deuteronomy. "It's not my Bible. It's Mother's." I sat up and showed Skippy her name printed in gold letters across the cover.

He leaned against the door of the truck and made a clanking sound.

"You've got something under your shirt," I said. "What is it?" I reached to see, but he backed away, and when he did a bottle of whiskey slid out and landed at his feet. He snatched it up, glancing around to be sure nobody else saw it. "Where'd you get that?" I said.

"That's my business."

"You stole it."

"It happens a woman gave it to me."

"You're lying."

"That's what I do when I'm not stealing, I lie."

"Does Melvina know you've got it?"

"Mama doesn't know everything I do."

"You're not going to drink it, are you?"

"Drink it? No, I'm going to dab it behind my ears. What else would anybody do with whiskey?" Skippy unscrewed the lid and took a sip. I could see it was not his first.

"Get in." I opened the truck door. "Let me taste it."

"I'm not wasting good whiskey on you."

"One swallow?"

"No."

"If you don't let me taste it I'm going to tell Melvina you're out here drinking."

"Go tell her, then." Skippy started towards the woods, the bottle beneath his shirt. "You the kind would enjoy tattletaling a lot more than you would a drink of whiskey."

"Skippy, wait. I was kidding."

"You're childish," he yelled. "I don't care what you tell or don't tell."

"You're going to turn out the same as Old Alfonso. You're going to end up a drunk like your daddy." Skippy ignored me and weaved into the tangle of woods.

I hate myself sometimes.

You have to be in the right mood to read the Bible, and I wasn't anymore. Moses was trying to get his people to the Promised Land, but they fought him every step of the way because he was so full of new ideas he scared them. They had the same trouble believing that I did. God certainly had a temper. I snapped the Bible closed and thought about my two-piece bathing suit. I wished Skippy could see me in it, standing on the high dive, the wind blowing my hair, my posture good, shoulders back, legs tan. He wouldn't say I was childish if he saw me leap from the high dive. People on the shore who didn't even know me would applaud and scream, yes. He would be impressed, I knew it. But it could never happen because they don't have colored people at Wakulla Springs except in the kitchen at the restaurant.

The summer before last a family from Michigan saw the colored cooks fixing food for white tourists, and the father walked into the kitchen and said he was from up North—as if they couldn't figure that out. "Saginaw," he said. He wanted them to know he sympathized. "I'm on your side," he said.

The cooks stared at him like he was a crazy man. They stood like deer in the road caught in a headlight beam. "You're not allowed back here," they said. He took their picture, four colored women and two colored men dressed in white aprons. "No picture-taking in the kitchen," one of the women said. "You can't just come walking in here. I don't care if you come from up on the moon."

When his food came, the man was like Jesus at the Last Supper—barely able to eat a bite. Mother wanted to go over and explain things to him, but Walter said, "Sarah, sit back down and mind your own business." The colored cook stood with her hands on her hips, scowling at him from behind a glass partition. "He don't own this kitchen," she said.

I liked to imagine Skippy at Wakulla Springs anyway. I would take him on the glass-bottom-boat ride and the jungle cruise. People would stare at us. One person would say, "That's the most handsome colored boy I ever saw," and others would nod agreement. We would get Melvina to make us a picnic lunch, and we'd eat it on a blanket in the sand. If any white boys tried to bother Skippy, I would make them stop. Maybe they would say, "Lucy, you are

pretty in that bathing suit." And I would say thank you and
turn away from them, grab Skippy by the hand and pull him
into the water. Maybe I would climb on his shoulders and
hold on to his head, while he gripped my legs, and we would
make a live totem pole, walking around in the not-too-deep.
He'd sling me off and I'd scream, fall backwards, and come
up with my hair soaking wet. We would practice holding
our breath underwater and opening our eyes and looking at
things. Later we'd rent a float, lay on our bellies, and paddle
all over the place in the ice-cold water. We would talk about
ourselves and neither one of us would be afraid. I would
say, "Skippy, do you believe in God?"

I hated being such a coward. I hated the way the world
bent me into shape. It was not the shape I wanted. It was not
the shape my heart designed. I wanted to be like Moses, not
like that herd of people wandering around lost. I turned the
radio up, *Kiss me and maybe . . . happiness is waiting for
you and me, if you'll . . .* If, I thought. If. If. If. I felt like I
would bust out of my skin, my heart explode like a cherry
bomb if I didn't do something with myself.

I opened the glove compartment and saw Walter's
half-full bottle of whiskey underneath maps of Georgia,
Florida, and Alabama. Maps of the entire world as far as
any of us knew. I don't know who ever told Mother and
Walter this was the promised land—but they believed it. I
bet there was a chamber of commerce sign at the Florida
state line saying: *Welcome to the Promised Land.* I took the
bottle of whiskey, unscrewed the lid, and smelled it. It made
me think of paint thinner. I stuck the bottle in the elastic of
my pants, grabbed Mother's Bible, and headed for the
woods and the torn-up fort Roy and I had built out of pine
logs two summers ago.

The fort was deep in the woods. The ground was padded
with red pine straw and clumps of starfish-shaped gum
leaves. The creek was reduced to a trickle. I crossed it in two

places, no jumping required. I had gotten almost to the clearing when, like a covey of startled birds, sticks and pine cones came flying at me.

"Get out of here," a voice yelled from behind our log fort. "Go home!" My heart hammered hard a second, but Skippy couldn't disguise himself.

"You scared me," I said.

Skippy stood up. "Everything scares you, girl."

"It does not. Most especially you don't. I knew you'd be out here."

"What do you want, then?"

I walked around the edge of the log wall where Skippy was standing none too steadily. "Look." I pulled Walter's whiskey from the waist of my pants.

"You stole that?" Skippy was molasses-mouthed.

"Yes."

"What for?"

"Just to try it."

"You better go back."

"You can't make me," I said. Then Skippy's legs gave way and he swayed too far, stumbled and fell, grabbing my arm as he went down. "Look out," I said. "Don't yank me down." I crashed to the ground with him. We were both sprawled in the pine straw, Skippy cushioning his bottle like he was a soldier and the bottle was a grenade that he had to be careful with or it would blow us both to kingdom come.

He thrashed in the pine straw, giggling, trying to roll himself up to sitting position, but he couldn't because the whiskey had put some of his parts to sleep and he was ordering his arms and legs to do things but they wouldn't. I started laughing too, because there wasn't any way to help it. I pulled Skippy up to a sitting position and he slid back and leaned against a pine tree. He smiled at me and shook his head. "Miss Lucy white girl."

I liked the way he said it. He took a big swallow of whiskey. His bottle was half empty. He wiped his lips with his finger. Skippy had the nicest face, it was square and his eyelashes were curly. I couldn't hardly look him in the eye.

"It's not your fault, is it?" Skippy held up his bottle and pretended to look at me through the brown liquid. "God ran out of color in a hurry when he started making people, so there wasn't nothing to do but make up a bunch of whites with the little scrap of color he had left. Do your Bible say that? Lucy-white-girl?"

"What have you got against white people?"

He laughed. "Lucy, Lucy, Lucy."

"Really, Skippy. I've always wanted to know. Tell me."

"What are you doing out here? You come to read your Bible some more?"

"It's not mine. It's Mother's. I already told you that. She's making me read it. Besides, she's paying me money so I can buy . . ."

"Buy what?"

"A two-piece bathing suit. With spaghetti straps. It comes to about here." I held my hand below my waist.

Skippy waved the bottle in the air. "I'm going to drink a swallow of whiskey out of respect for you and your new bathing suit," he said.

"You hate me, don't you?" I unscrewed the lid on Walter's whiskey bottle and put it to my lips. The smell took my breath.

"You're scared to taste it?" he said.

"No."

"What are you scared of?"

"Nothing," I lied. I put the bottle to my lips and let the tiniest bit of whiskey into my mouth. The warmness slid down my throat like a swig of Clorox.

"A piss ant would swallow more than that."

The taste of the whiskey softened my tongue. I knew the

201

smell of whiskey and the hot feel of it, but not the real taste. So I took a second sip.

"Take a real swallow this time," he said, which I proceeded to do, acting as if it was nothing but co-cola, how big a gulp I took. I drank the way I thought Virginia-most-famous-colored-girl-in-French-Town would do if she were me—but when I tried to swallow, I couldn't. It felt like swallowing a lighted match. My cheeks puffed, sneeze sprayed out my nose, my eyes watered. I wanted to spit the whole mouthful out, but I held it in and little by little twisted it down. I had to with Skippy watching. Afterwards I laid myself out on the pine straw like somebody shot.

Skippy slapped his hands on his legs, laughing at my contortions. "Shoot. I didn't expect that out of you."

The feeling I had that afternoon didn't have anything to do with whiskey. It was a way I had felt lately, where sometimes I was not myself. Sometimes I was everybody. Sometimes I was nobody at all. It changed. I could be Mother if I wanted to, or I could be Patricia, or I could be a beautiful girl in the bright sunshine standing tall and straight on the high diving board. It was strange and exciting, and for a few minutes made me brave and free. "Let's drink it all, Skippy. Let's drink the whole bottle."

"You're carrying a Bible out here and talking about let's drink this whole bottle of whiskey."

"It's almost half gone now," I said. "Let's finish it."

"What about your mama?"

"Are you going to tell her?"

"What about Mr. Sheppard when he finds out?"

"Walter doesn't have anything against drinking whiskey. He'll know his whiskey is missing, but he'll never find out who took it." I picked up Mother's Bible, moved it behind a tree so we wouldn't be looking at it and it wouldn't be looking at us. I placed a handful of straw over it like I was tucking the book into bed for the night. "Now."

"You act crazy."

"Just don't think about the Bible right now."

"I'm not thinking about any Bible."

"It says love thy neighbor, Skippy. I'm your neighbor, so you should try to be nice to me."

"I'm nice enough." He upended his bottle, took the last drink, and leaned back against the tree. I sat down next to him and took a drink out of Walter's bottle. Then he did. Then I did. We kept on, taking our time, taking turns. It took us a half-hour or more to drink it all. My mouth was getting used to it. My throat was finally willing to swallow. Then the bottle was empty. Skippy slung his empty bottle through the woods, where it hit a tree, shattered, and fell to the ground jingling like a Christmas bell.

"You probably shouldn't be messing with whiskey," I said. "You'll turn out the same as your daddy." I laid down in the pine straw with my eyes closed.

"No need for you to worry about how I turn out."

"I'm not worrying about it."

"You're talking about it. That's the same thing."

"Believe it or not, I've got more to worry about than how you turn out, Skippy Williams."

"Yeah, I see you got more worries than the law allows."

"I'm nothing like you think."

"How you know what I think?" Skippy picked up a pine twig and pitched it up in the air. It hit low branches and banged its way back to the ground not a foot from where I was laying. "You don't have any idea what I think."

I picked up the stick, propped my head on my elbow, and began to tap on the pine straw. Pretty soon I was tapping out songs, keeping at it until Skippy caught on, sang a lyric that fit the tune. *Lord, I want to be in that number.* If he couldn't think of the real song, if my tapping was off, he made up something crazy. *I tried to tell you one hundred times, I need a dollar but you just got dimes.* Get-in-that-kitchen-and-rattle-those-pots-and-pans stuff. He was quick. *First you say yes, then you say no, stay if you want to, but I got to go.* He picked up a stick too and together we beat out songs, pounding the quiet straw-covered earth for a long, happy time. I liked hearing Skippy sing, *I know I done you wrong,* the line from the Bill Bailey song. He closed his eyes, his head bounced. The music that came from him chilled me and warmed me. At the end of each song he opened his eyes to see if I was really listening. I was. My voice shook when it was my turn to sing, *Lipstick on your collar gonna tell on you.*

The world was full of boys. Why was Skippy the only one who seemed necessary to me? I stayed ready to argue with him, ready to fight if I had to, but inside our mistrust was this other, unnamed thing. Skippy could sing like somebody on the radio. He knew it too.

We probably would have kept singing into the late afternoon except that my stomach growled so loud it stopped me mid-song, *He walks with me and talks with me*— My stomach made a disgusting noise. I rolled over on my side and threw up everywhere.

"Damn." Vomit splashed on Skippy's foot. "You sick?" The next minute Skippy wasn't looking so good himself. He threw up too, worse than me. He made a horrible noise in his throat and waved me away with his hand. If vomiting was a contest, he'd have won. "Look what you made me do," he said. Beads of sweat popped out on his face. He laid down, said he couldn't open his eyes because looking at the swaying treetops scrambling together made his head explode. We closed our eyes and laid perfectly still.

Throwing up made me feel better, but Skippy was bad off. He hunched over and vomited three short, terrible times, with just minutes to groan in between. Every time he laid his head down it made him want to vomit again. He made noises that go with dying. He had tears in his eyes.

"I'll get Melvina." I began to stand up. "Wait here."
Skippy grabbed my arm to keep me from going. He was
too sick to talk.

"You don't want me to get Melvina? Then who?"
He nodded no. His fingers pinched my skin so tight it
hurt.

"You're too sick, Skippy. Let me get somebody."
He refused, laid back down in slow motion, and released
his handcuff grip on me. I pushed up a pile of pine straw to
make a pillow under his head. He laid one arm over his
forehead, the other across his stomach. He was trembling.

"You need a quilt," I said.

"Lucy," he barked in a hoarse whisper.

"I'm not telling anybody. I swear." I tore through the
woods. When I got to our yard I saw that Melvina had the
wash hung on the line. I hurried, unpinned two towels and
the blue spread from Roy's bed, which was not quite dry. I
tried not to let myself think what Melvina would say when
she saw half the wash missing. I flew back to Skippy—the
spread trailing behind me, snagging on briers as I pulled it
along.

Skippy looked asleep—or dead. "Here," I whispered,
"put this over you." He lay still, not moving a muscle, so I
did it for him, covered his feet with the spread, tucked it
around the edges of him the best I could.

I tried to think what Mother did when a person was sick.
It's what I automatically resorted to in bad situations, trying
to be like Mother. I was trying now, but because of drinking
whiskey, something she would never do in her life—
swallowing what I knew was a sin as well as she did, but I
did it anyway—this was different. I thought, *I am not my
mother, not her arm or leg or a place in the back of her
head*. It was the first time the thought had come to me. I
could taste whiskey even if she never did, waste money on
movie magazines, smoke cigarettes, wrap a stolen quilt

around a colored boy in the woods—anything. A split oc-
curred, of Mother and me into two people instead of just the
one her that we had both always been. *I am not my mother.*
What would she think when she found out?

I took a towel and ran to the stream, a ditch really, that
straggled through the woods. I dipped the towel in the
trickle of water, ran back to Skippy. "Here." He opened his
eyes. They were fire red. He took the towel, stuffed a wad
of it into his mouth, and sucked some water out. Then he
wrung the towel over his head, dripping water on his face.

I flashed to Wakulla Springs. Skippy had just come out of
the cold water and was drying himself off. The day was a
glorious yellow. Roy's bedspread was laid out in the sand,
and Skippy and I sat on it together. Skippy was beautiful. I
watched him dry himself with slow, deliberate swipes, his
muscles tight and dark, his body like it had been carved
from hard, polished wood. Beads of water sparkled in his
hair, the sun ricocheting off them in prisms of color and
light around his face. I was glowing in the sheen of baby oil,
pinkening on my way to a tan, my heart clean and strong
and true—nearly bursting because I had just leaped from
the high dive, made a brave if not graceful fall into the deep
waters, with Skippy watching me. He had changed his mind
about me now. He said, "Lucy, that was a beautiful sight."
The sun was aimed at the two of us. We glowed.

Skippy moaned and pulled the towel away from his face.
He folded his hands over his chest and became perfectly
still, like a soldier who had been ordered to sleep. I sat a
short distance away, head on my knees, arms around my
shins, picking up brittle pine twigs and breaking them into
pieces like snap beans.

We stayed that way most of the afternoon. It began to get
dark. Twice I went to sleep and woke up with a jolt. I
moved near Skippy to see if he was still breathing, imagined
what I would do if he died. I would cry as hard as Melvina.

At his funeral she would yank me by the arm and say, "Lucy, straighten up. You don't have any cause to carry on this way." My family would be the only white people at the funeral. Even Walter would come, in the suit he bought to marry Mother in and hasn't worn since. He would carry his hat in his hands. The colored people would be mad that we came and would make us stand in the very back. They would point to me and say, "This girl was the last one to see him alive." I'd be looking up in the air, trying to see Skippy's spirit when it came loose. I'd beg Melvina to bury him at Wakulla Springs underneath a live oak tree or some palms. "Are you crazy?" she'd say. "That place is crawling with snakes. The alligators would sleep on his grave." She would bury him in the weed-patch graveyard behind the colored church, where she could keep an eye on things. But his spirit would hover at Wakulla Springs—not in the kitchen either—higher than the high diving board, high up in the yellow sunlight above this cold blue world.

I pulled bits of pine straw from Skippy's hair, watched him sleep, wanted to touch his face but was afraid he would open his eyes. I looked at his mouth and imagined kissing him. If I did it right now God would see me—but that was less frightening than the thought that Skippy would wake up and catch me at it. What would he do? Laugh? Humiliate me? Say, "Lucy, you're so stupid, that's not the way you kiss." I put my fingers to my own lips and kissed them, a slow and noiseless kiss, then I laid the kissed fingers softly on Skippy's lips—so that he would be kissed and never know it. Yes. Yes. He didn't even open his eyes.

When Skippy finally woke up he said he felt better, but he didn't look much better. He rubbed the wet towel across his lips. We both knew it wouldn't do for anybody to have to come looking for us. "You better get home," he said.

"You sure you're okay? I can stay."

"No need," Skippy said.

"They'll look for me if I don't get home."

"Nobody's keeping you. Go."

I snatched up the spread where it lay wadded beside him, thought of whipping it across his face like a soft slap. As I yanked, Skippy yanked too. He tugged on one side, I tugged on the other—stuck like that. I glared at him. He smiled with his eyes and I felt like the bolts holding my bones together were all unscrewing at once. "Wait a minute, before you go." He began to stand, put his hands on his head, cussed, and sank back down. "We got to do one thing. Get me some of that broken whiskey bottle I slung over there. A sharp piece."

"What for?"

"Just get it."

Since he was sick, I walked to the spot where the bottle had shattered against the tree, picked up a piece of sharp glass, brought it back, and handed it to him.

"This is the best way to keep a secret." He took the piece of glass in one hand and jabbed it into the soft part of his thumb, suddenly, for no reason. Blood started. He squeezed his thumb to make it bleed more.

I knew about this. Crossing blood. Roy called it blood brothers. Roy loved it. He did it with Bubba. He did it with Donald too. He would do it with anybody, I guess, because he liked the idea of the cuts so much by themselves, never mind if it really meant anything or not. I had never done it before. It seemed something for boys. Skippy handed me the glass. "You do it."

"I don't like blood—seeing it." Skippy was silent, so to keep from thinking it over too long, I just did it—jabbed. First time was too easy and—nothing. I did it again, fast, sucked air, made a crying sound, and saw my blood. I milked my thumb like Skippy was doing his.

He held his hand out towards me. "We're supposed to put . . ."

"I know about this," I said solemnly, pressing my thumb against his, hard at first, then just a gentle pressing. We were careful not to touch our other fingers. "How long?"

"Until the bleeding stops." We pressed hard again to be sure. It was probably half a minute, the whole thing, but it was an entire-lifetime half-minute. I was trembling. At one point Skippy held my wrist, to steady it. My muscles tensed. We kept our eyes focused on our thumbs, away from the other person's face. I was happy.

"Okay." Skippy gently pulled his thumb away. We both put our thumbs to our mouths to suck our wounds.

Roy's hard voice floated through the woods calling my name. "I better go," I said, thumb still in my mouth. I picked up the spread and towels. "They'll come looking for me if I don't go."

Skippy nodded.

"You sure you're going to be okay?"

"I am if I don't die." He grinned.

I stumbled home. The thing that had happened was too much to think about until I got far from it, all the way to the next town, or to Georgia, or someplace in the tomorrow. Some things you have to think about lying down. I was hurrying to line things up in my head, first, second, third. Tasting whiskey was nothing, I thought. Nothing. But I had at least one drop of colored blood in me now. Skippy's blood. I flung Roy's spread and the nasty towels on the empty clothesline—I'd think up a good excuse later. Couldn't even imagine Melvina's mad face right then.

"You're late," Roy hollered. I hadn't seen him, standing still as a tree in the yard, with his suspicious eyes shooting at me. "Where've you been? Mother's mad."

"So?" I defiantly tossed my head as I swung by on the way to the house. "Who cares if she is?"

"Walter's mad too."

I stopped. Walter's anger fell into a more dangerous category than Mother's. "Why?" I said.

"Old Alfonso stole the whiskey out of Walter's truck."

"He did not. What makes him think Old Alfonso took it?"

"Because it's missing. That's why."

"He can't prove it was Old Alfonso."

"Funny nothing ever turned up missing before Old Alfonso came back. Walter's been up at Melvina's house threatening to call the police. Old Alfonso swears he doesn't know a thing about it. A nigger will lie as soon as look at you."

"Roy, you're too stupid to live."

"You missed supper. Mother's cleared the table."

Things worsen at night. They draw up in the daylight and bloom full at night. Worrisome things. Old Alfonso wasn't guilty. Was it the first time in his life? I swore to God I would make it up to him. I imagined inviting Melvina and Old Alfonso to Wakulla Springs. Melvina hated snakes too much to ride the jungle boat, its fake guns shooting everything—no, just the glass-bottom boats. We could all look right through that blue water to the very bottom of things. Sometimes I thought the water at Wakulla Springs was the only clear thing God ever made.

I kept picturing crossing blood with Skippy. His cautious eyes. The pink underside of his warm hand. Every friend I had would quit me if they knew. Patricia would think it was nastier than anything a white girl could do, and she knew every nasty thing. Karol would think I'd ruined myself all the way, those times Skippy came into our yard she held her nose acting like something smelled bad—meaning him. She didn't know how easy it would have been for me to kill her then. I'd punished her a million times in my imagination,

210

put her on the chain gang, given her polio, made her a blind girl selling peanuts in front of the State Theatre on Saturdays. If she knew I had Skippy's blood in me—that I was glad about it—she would quit me forever. And Walter would, quit Skippy and me both. But not Mother, since a woman can't quit her own kids. Not Roy either—he'd be eaten up with jealousy, Skippy crossing blood with me and not him.

People would say kissing Skippy didn't count, if I told how I did it. They'd say it wasn't a kiss unless both people knew. Skippy would swear it never happened. But it did. He was kissed and had no idea. He couldn't undo it either.

It wasn't until I got in bed and wanted to read myself to sleep that I realized Mother's Bible was left out in the damp, buggy Tallahassee woods, where it would most likely ruin overnight. It was borrowed from Mother too—and not mine to lose.

*L*AMAR Forehand could go longer and farther on no encouragement at all than any boy I ever saw. "May be a lot of things that boy don't have," Melvina said, "but he do have determination."

He had started getting his big brother, Sherrill, to drive him over to my house just for no reason. They'd stay maybe fifteen minutes, never get out of the car, sometimes bring me french fries. Then they'd screech up the road like greased lightning.

Sherrill was more interesting than Lamar, because he was older, and when Lamar got stuck on something to say,

Sherrill would help him out, which I thought was mature. Four or five times Sherrill asked me if I wanted to go to the shopping center or something, but Mother never would let me. "You are not old enough for boys with cars," she said.

Soon, if Sherrill's car drove by, Roy and Benny and even Walter were conditioned to shout, "Lucy, it's the Forehand boys again," and I'd come outside to talk to them. Sometimes my hair was rolled up, but I didn't care. It is so much easier to be natural with boys you don't like too much.

Every time Skippy saw their car he cussed. If I came outside he glared like I'd sunk to rock bottom. "I don't see why you hate them so much," I said.

"Hate who?"

"If looks could kill, they'd be dead in that car."

"I don't know what you think you're talking about."

"They've never done anything to you," I said. "You don't have to stand around and growl at them." I pretend I don't notice the way Skippy looks at that car. I pretend I don't see how much he wishes it was his.

"You're overcomplimenting yourself, girl. All I'm looking at is a car that needs the alternator set before they burn the engine out."

Then there was a switch in things and Sherrill started coming by my house without Lamar.

"Where's Lamar?" I said.

"Don't know. Somewhere. You want to take a ride?"

"You know Mother won't let me."

So Sherrill got out of the car and sat on the picnic table or once on the screened porch, and he stayed longer than fifteen minutes. Every time he said, "Let's go for a ride, Lucy. Come on."

"Sherrill, my mother thinks you're too old."

"Ask her anyway." I stared at him like he was asking me to fly. "That is, if you want to go."

"I do," I blurted out.

"Then ask."

I asked. Mother said no. Sherrill drove off in his clean, washed car, probably to ask some other girl that very minute, whose mother would say, "Yes, princess, of course you can go." Tallahassee was full of those kinds of mothers. Sometimes I just didn't have the energy it took to be Sarah Wilcox Sheppard's daughter twenty-four hours a day. "You've got plenty of time for boys with cars," she said.

I locked myself in my room the rest of the afternoon and pouted more elaborately than I ever had in my life. I kept thinking of me with a boy almost seventeen, who drove a clean car, and was pretty cute, and could have asked any popular girl in Tallahassee but asked me instead. I pictured my fingernails painted, my hair fixed perfect and sprayed to stay perfect.

When Walter came home and wanted to know what I was pouting about, I told him. "Sherrill Forehand asked me to go for a ride and Mother wouldn't let me."

Walter looked at Mother. "If you ever saw him on the football field there wouldn't even be such a discussion as this, Sarah. Let those other punks ask Lucy and I'd say hell no, but Sherrill Forehand is the exception."

After supper Walter showed Mother two articles he'd clipped out of the *Tallahassee Democrat* about Sherrill making touchdowns.

That night Mother changed her mind. For Walter, not me. "You can go, Lucy. Walter's more excited than you are."

Skippy was unloading manure out of the back of Walter's truck, spreading it in the flower beds. I had my hair rolled, and I sat on my windowsill and watched Skippy in his bare feet, no shirt, just shorts that were one wearing from gone. Skippy not more than sixteen, but in a grown man's body. His reward for doing like a man too early was looking like a man early. I watched the smooth way his shoulders tightened and loosened. His shorts were wet with perspiration. Skippy in his body the way some folks are in a house, comfortable and proud of the place.

"Hey, Skippy. Over here." I waved.

He stopped and looked. "What you want?"

"Just saying hello."

"I got work to do."

Skippy was handsome to watch, so handsome.

That evening when I was dressing to go riding with Sherrill, Skippy was sitting at the woodpile. We never had a woodpile until this very day, just because Walter said he'd like to take out a couple of those pines in the back to let in a little light. So Skippy decided today was the day, all on his own, which impressed Walter out of his mind. Now Skippy sat, ax beside him, resting before he finished the job. The chopping that didn't actually have to be done but wouldn't hurt if it was.

That night Sherrill Forehand drove into the yard, got out with his clean shirt, wet hair, and polished shoes. He didn't see Skippy sitting on the stack of logs. Didn't notice Skippy noticing him. He came to the door and said all the right things to Walter and Mother. Then Mother took a bunch of pictures, including one with Walter and Sherrill together, and one with Roy and Benny and Sherrill together. She tried to take one of Melvina and Sherrill too, but Melvina said, "God, no."

Then we came out, with me hung on Sherrill's arm the way couples do on shows. He had a big white-boy smile on his face, opened the car door for me, whispered, "Shoot, girl, you look good enough to eat." Mother and Walter stood on the porch watching, so did Roy and Benny. Melvina's face was plain at the kitchen window. But Skippy never looked. Didn't watch that part about us getting in the car. Couldn't watch because he was too busy chopping firewood. I looked at Skippy hard as I walked out to the car, hard, because I wanted him to see that I can be pretty. I wanted him to believe it. I wanted to wave at him and say, Yes, Skippy, this is really me in this dress, with my hair curled, please God, look at me and see. But Skippy was too busy splitting logs—going to need that firewood, the only house in north Florida with firewood and no fireplace.

It was only nine o'clock when Sherrill's car pulled up in front of the house bringing me home that night. I had been shy, but Sherrill said he liked shy girls. He got out and opened the door for me. He was holding my hand and whispering to me, saying things that made me feel sort of excited about myself. So far he had said he liked my eyes, my hair, my skin, my smile, and he was still at it as we walked up to the porch. I knew he couldn't mean all of it, but just the idea that he could think to say it thrilled me enough. A boy who can talk, a boy good with words, well, it's nice. I started to think there was hope for Lamar too, as soon as he learned the art of conversation.

Up on the porch, sitting in the dark like they had never done before in their lives, were Walter and Skippy, both of them smoking cigarettes. All you could see were the orange ashes when one of them sucked in. I saw them before Sherrill did, sprawled in porch chairs. "There's Walter," I said, letting go of Sherrill's hand.

"Damn," he said very quietly.

"What are you doing smoking, Skippy?" I walked onto the porch. Skippy didn't say a word.

"You two have fun?" Walter asked.

"It was fine, sir," Sherrill said.

"What's Skippy doing here this time of night?" I asked.

"Well," Sherrill said, putting his hands in his pockets, "guess I better be going. Had a real nice time, Lucy."

"Me too."

"So, I'll be seeing you." Sherrill backed down the steps to the ground. "Night, Mr. Sheppard. Night, Lucy."

"Night, Sherrill," I said.

He walked out to his car, got in, and drove off, his headlights flashing around the darkness as he turned the car back onto California Street.

I glared at Walter and Skippy. "What do you two think you're up to?"

"I'm seeing to it you get home okay," Walter said. "Your mama's orders."

"What is Skippy doing smoking cigarettes? Melvina is going to have a fit, you giving him cigarettes."

"Skippy is keeping me company. No law against that."

I walked inside and let the screen door slam behind me. I bet they felt smart. I saw that smile on Skippy's face. Bet Walter thought he'd keep Sherrill from kissing me good night at the front door like people are supposed to. Maybe Walter thought he and his sidekick, Skippy, had ruined Sherrill's chance—with the two of them sitting there watching. But Sherrill is no stupid boy. The truth was, Sherrill had stopped the car twice on the way home. Kissed me before we ever got to the house, so Walter hadn't spoiled what he thought he spoiled. I had half a mind to go back outside and say, "Sherrill kissed me two times already, so there." But I closed the door to my room and went to bed instead.

That night I fell asleep remembering the kissing. It was not what I had hoped kissing would be. It was slow and easy and very warm, but it didn't make my heart jump or sling my imagination off to the sorts of exciting places it wants to go. Only Skippy does that to my imagination, and he does it without touching me at all. Just seeing him sitting on the porch smoking cigarettes with Walter, I started to sweat and get confused. But I am going to have to stop it, because this is America. Skippy is not one of my choices.

*J*T was Saturday. Nobody was home but me. I was halfway to the Snack Shack looking for Skippy when I spotted him in a lady's yard, patching a water hose.

"What are you doing up here?" he said.

"Looking for you. Do you want to come to my house for lunch? I made tunafish." He looked like he was waiting for the punch line. "Nobody's home. Just me."

He dropped the electrical tape and wiped his hands on his shorts. "Is this a trick?"

"No, I swear to God."

"It better not be."

We walked home. Half the people in French Town probably saw us. We passed in front of Melvina's house. All she had to do was look out the window. We came in my front door right into the living room. It was Skippy's first time in our living room. Skippy looked at the dining room table, where I had set two places on plastic mats. I used plates from the good china Mother got when she married our real daddy. I folded the napkins like I had seen in a magazine. Those napkins had never been used before. Mother was saving them in case the president of the United States ever came to supper, I guess.

While Skippy washed his hands I went to the kitchen and got the tunafish sandwiches I'd made earlier and wrapped in wax paper. I poured potato chips in a bowl and opened two Dr Peppers. When Skippy came to the dining room everything was ready. "Sit down right here," I said.

"What would Mr. and Mrs. Sheppard say if they knew I was in here with you?"

"I'll clean the dishes and they'll never know. Besides, this is my house too, isn't it? Don't I live here too?"

"You do unless they find this out."

Skippy ate slow and neat. I gobbled. "We have to talk while we eat, Skippy. It's impolite if we don't."

"What'd you invite me over here for?"

"So you could come in this house and see everything. So you won't think we're hiding anything."

"And what else?"

"And because I'm sorry about the way things are. I got in Sherrill's car and thought to myself, I wish Skippy had a car like this. I'd give anything if you could. . . ."

"I'm going to have a car one day. I'm not going to live in Tallahassee all my life."

"Where will you go?"

"Memphis. Save some money there, then New York, maybe."

"New York! My God, Skippy, if you go to New York . . ."

"What if I do?"

"I'm coming to see you. I swear. Make you take me on the elevator to the top of the Empire State Building. I bet we could see all the way to Tallahassee from there."

"Well, come on, then." Skippy laughed.

We talked about the things we would do if we lived far from Tallahassee. Skippy would open a machine shop. He'd have a crew working for him, some of them white. He'd get an apartment at least twenty stories up. At night he'd go to clubs and dance with Yankee girls.

I got us each a second Dr Pepper. Poured the rest of the potato chips into the bowl. "I'd ride the train if I came to see you. I wouldn't care if it took a month."

"Why you want to go to New York so bad?"

"I just want to see what all the fuss is about. Plus I want to ride in a taxi."

"When you get off the train from Tallahassee I'll pick you up in a taxi," Skippy said. "White and colored can go around together in New York if they want to. Nobody bothers them."

"How do you know?"

"Everybody knows that."

Neither one of us heard the kitchen door open. *"I ain't believing what I'm seeing!"* It was like we were caught stealing. Melvina stood in the doorway, fire in her eyes.

"I was fixing to go," Skippy said.

"Boy, have I got to tell you what would happen if Mr. Sheppard found you in here?"

"I ain't worried about what would happen."

"No, you just put me in the grave worrying for you."

"I invited him, Melvina. It was all my idea."

"I don't care if it was God's idea—it's still Mr. Sheppard's house. You just inviting trouble in. I ain't raised neither one of you to do like this."

"We're not doing anything wrong, Melvina. There's no harm in it."

"Let's go, Mama." Skippy took Melvina's arm and led her to the door. He smiled and lifted his finger to signal me good-bye on his way out.

I watched Melvina and Skippy walk through the woods to their house. She was chewing his ears off. They weren't gone ten minutes when Walter drove up, got out with a string of probably twenty decent-sized fish. Roy and Benny were sunburned. I knew they would come inside, get a cold drink, and then spend the next hour out by the rabbit pen helping Walter clean the fish. I'd rather die than participate.

I went to my room, locked the door, and pretended I was asleep. I had things to think about—like whether imagining a thing was anything like having it really happen. Probably not. It takes guts to make things happen. I went to bed and dreamed of guts.

*B*Y summer Old Alfonso was back to his real self. Men started coming around to Melvina's in a green car that played the radio full blast. We saw them rolling up there, loud and laughing at every single thing, dragging across the yard where Old Alfonso sat in a straw-seat ladder-back chair. They carried on right there where we could watch them. They outlaughed everything in the world. "They must be joke maniacs," Roy said.

Loud-talking men under Melvina's shade tree—sometimes they brought food with them and sat around licking their fingers and having a high time, getting Old Alfonso drunker than drunk, just like he used to be. Twice they brought messes of fish, cleaned them, fried them in a pot in the yard. Late in the night we heard them, the kids too, feasting. Melvina made slaw and hush puppies. We knew because she yelled, "Who needs more slaw? More hush puppies?" I bet it was midnight.

The men usually went off in one big swarm, and since Melvina wouldn't let Old Alfonso go with them, they left him in a crazy state, his meanness juiced up. It was Skippy's job to carry his fall-down daddy into the house at night, or to see to it he didn't get into the house. All depending.

Walter didn't like drunk niggers sprawled out next door. Loud music going day and night. "What you guess they're heehawing about up there?" he said. "I'd hate to know."

"How is Melvina supposed to keep a yard full of men from laughing if they feel like it?" Mother said.

"These the people you write letters to the newspaper on behalf of, Sarah?" The drunker Old Alfonso got, the louder the ruckus at Melvina's house, the more Walter said to Mother, "Yeah, I can see why you want your kids going to school with a bunch like that. Any decent mother would."

It was like Old Alfonso and his friends were on Walter's

side without knowing it, like they had taken it upon themselves to prove how wrong Mother was. When Mother talks about colored people she thinks of Melvina, Annie, and Skippy—all people she knows and likes. When Walter thinks of colored people he forgets the ones he knows best and thinks of Old Alfonso and the wild-Indian colored people up at the Blue Bird—people he never met in his life.

One Sunday afternoon, late, Melvina was at church, her kids were home, and Old Alfonso and his friends were in the yard cleaning fish. It was twilight. Skippy had just put the lawn mower away. Our yard smelled clean and sharp, of wild onions and honeysuckle. The cut grass felt cool against our bare legs. The sprinkler was arcing back and forth in the far corner of the yard, making a good imitation-rain sound. Roy, Benny, and I sat with our white rabbits on leashes made out of old neckties. We were teaching them to eat M&M's. Benny was devoted to Mopsy. If Mother sent him out after supper to feed the rabbits, he'd stay gone an hour. Walter had to go get him. Pitch-dark, and Benny sitting in the grass with Mopsy asleep in his lap. She'd turned out to be the prettiest rabbit of all.

Walter poured charcoal into the grill. He doused the charcoal with lighter fluid, struck a match, and tossed it in. The grill burst into a volcano of flames. Walter stood back with his hands in his pockets and watched.

Mother came out of the kitchen carrying a plate of red hamburgers, with a sack of buns clenched between her teeth. She had already put a cloth over the picnic table and set out plates and silverware. She was barefoot, and she smiled at Walter as she handed him the meat. When Mother cooked hamburgers in the house she ruined them with bread crumbs and onions, trying to make the meat go further, so in the end they tasted like little meatloafs. But Walter wouldn't allow her to tamper with the ground beef when he cooked on the grill.

Next door, Old Alfonso and the men were getting ready to fry fish. Skippy brought out the fish-frying pot and hung it on a hook contraption he'd rigged up. Annie scooped Crisco into the pot while the men watched. She was dressed in a blue dress I had never seen. Her hair was pulled straight back and she had a clip in it. Old Alfonso lit the fire beneath the pot and fanned it to get it going.

Walter laid the hamburgers carefully on the grill. They were the same color as the underside of his hands. He hollered to Roy, "How many can you eat, Roy? Six? Seven?"

Mother was sitting at the picnic table glancing at *Ladies' Home Journal*, an article about a woman whose husband died and left her with four kids to raise. From time to time Mother read a passage out loud. "Listen to this, Walter."

Roy and Benny were lying on their backs staring at the sky, talking about what kind of Chevys they were going to drive when they grew up. I was watching Annie glide around her yard in her new dress. She was straight-backed and surefooted. Our rabbits nibbled grass.

"Roy"—Walter carefully flipped a burger with his tongs—"how about go move that sprinkler over about ten feet this way." Roy jumped up and ran to do it.

Just then one of the men at Melvina's flicked his cigarette into the trash barrel and it poofed up like a flame when you turn on a gas stove. Walter said later it was those gasoline rags Skippy used on the lawn mower that caused the fire to shoot up that way. The flames licked out like they were going to devour the clothes hanging on the line. The flames were hot fingers after those clean shirts and underpants. "Don't let those clothes catch fire!" Annie yelled.

One man hurried over and kicked at the trash barrel to scoot it sideways. He kicked until he got it rocking and bouncing, but not scooting. Leroy shrieked. The trash barrel wobbled—slow, exaggerated wobbling—then tipped over and poured out in the yard. Like spilling a bucket of fire. Every burning thing out of the trash rolled into the yard, caught the weeds on fire. "Get the children out of the yard! Nappy, get away from the fire!" Annie yelled. The men went crazy trying to stamp out patches of fire, hopping and stomping their shoes at it—yelling like all get-out.

As soon as Walter saw the fire he took off towards it and yelled for Roy to bring the hose. But Roy was one step ahead of Walter, already halfway to the fire, dragging the hose behind him, unscrewing the sprinkler as he ran, soaking himself. "Wait!" Walter screamed to Roy. "Stop!" Mother yelled. "Roy! Roy!" But Roy was like a wild boy dragging that hose to the fire, and he didn't notice that the hose was looped around the legs of Walter's grill until he tugged so hard the grill crashed over on its side, slinging our hamburgers into the grass, spilling hot coals all the way to the patch of woods between our house and Melvina's. The way the fire leaped up, it looked like the weeds had been lying there just longing for a hot coal. Fire was slapping everywhere. It crackled and spit, sounded like something huge frying on an unwatched kitchen stove. Black smoke twisted around like a fluff of witch's hair.

Melvina had a spigot at her house, but no hose. Skippy was filling a bucket of water to throw on the fire, and people yelled, "Hurry up." Walter broke into a run. "Get back," he shouted at Roy. "Get back." He grabbed the hose out of Roy's hands and pointed the nozzle at the blaze. The water shot out, sizzling when it hit the fire, thickening the smoke. Roy was barefoot, couldn't stomp on the fire, so he kicked at it, furiously. He looked like a boy doing the hully-gully, his arms swinging, all that leg action. As soon as Walter killed a spot of fire, Roy jumped on the wet place and pounded up and down on it. Walter kept it up, hosing down first our fire, then the fire in Melvina's yard. Meanwhile, Skippy was running with bucketful after bucketful. "Over here!" a man would shout, and Walter turned, nozzle first, wetting anybody in his path. "Right here! This way! Over there!"

Eventually the smell was all that was left of the fire. The men got sticks and the hoe and the broom and stirred the wet places to make sure the fire was out good. They worked together at it until they were satisfied.

Old George sniffed around our grill because he smelled our felled hamburgers. Benny ran to put Mopsy and the other rabbits in their pen. Annie was trying to guard the pot of frying fish. The smoke had turned the evening a strange purple. Everyone had gone gray from smoke.

Walter, wet and smoky like Old Alfonso and the rest of them, said, "Y'all gon burn up the damn woods and the houses too. And your fool selves. Next time I'm going to let you do it." His neck swelled like a frog throat.

Instantly, Old Alfonso got that brick-wall look on his face. The one when colored people hate white people so bad and cannot do one thing about it but just stand there.

"If you want to cause trouble, do it someplace away from here!" Walter shouted. He was covered with soot, looked as black as they were—but nobody was forgetting for one minute that Walter was red-faced. And white.

Every person in both yards stood dead still, waiting. Silence fell like an ax and nearly chopped the world in two. We all looked at our feet. Some of us held our breath, waiting. "You hear me?" Walter said.

A couple of the men nodded. "Say?" Walter looked right at Old Alfonso, who stood silent as a stone wall. "You understand what I'm saying?"

Old Alfonso didn't look at Walter with his eyes. His face looked in Walter's direction, but his eyes slid past him, over his head, or through the middle of him, same as if he was invisible. He focused on some far-off thing.

The other colored men did their eyes the same way. They

would not look direct at Old Alfonso when he answered Walter. It was like they wanted to spare him, so they fixed their eyes on something next to him, like a charred tree limb, or something behind him, like the line where the treetops crossed over into the sky. Or maybe they just looked down at their own shoes and wondered whether or not they were ruined now.

"Yessir," Old Alfonso said.

He had to say it. It might as well be a law written down somewhere. Probably couldn't have said it if he wasn't at least partly drunk. "Yessir" was the answer when Walter told him what he could and could not do in his own yard.

"Nobody was hurt, Walter." Mother turned towards the house.

"This time!" Walter said. "Goddammit, Sarah," he snarled, half slinging the hose at her. "Roy, come put this hose away." Roy gave the task elaborate effort.

"If you all come around here disturbing the peace again, I'll call the law," Walter shouted as the colored men walked away. "You can count on that."

I looked at Skippy, but nothing could make him look at me. I knew he felt my eyes, because he turned his back so deliberately.

Walter walked to his knocked-over grill and his wasted hamburgers. He mumbled and yanked the grill right side up with one hand.

The men loaded into the green car and went tearing up California Street, probably to the Blue Bird. They took Old Alfonso with them. Skippy finished frying the fish and Annie called all Melvina's kids inside to eat. It was quiet up there except for the screen door squeaking open and slamming closed. At our house Mother made fried Spam sandwiches and we ate in total silence.

It was the start of Old Alfonso running up and down the road again. It was the start of him drinking himself insane and sleeping in the yard. But Walter didn't care. "One drunk nigger is better than a handful of them," he said. That's how it was, back to normal.

If Old Alfonso was sitting in his yard when Walter came home from work, he went inside ceremoniously. If he stayed outside he made a show of scooting his chair around, officially turning his back on us.

"Good," Walter said. "The man's back is his best side."

I know this can't be true. And I'm not saying it is. But it seemed like Melvina had more regard for Old Alfonso when he fell into his niggerish style again, running around, coming home drunk, causing nothing but trouble. Like she wanted her man alive and kicking, even kicking up a fuss, just kicking. I don't think Melvina thought much of Old Alfonso when he turned into a slow-moving kind of man. She didn't think much of him when he was sober and laid up in the bed all day, or sitting like a granddaddy rocking in that ladder-back chair in the yard. Now, back on the prowl and into trouble again—that suited her better. I think Melvina likes some nigger in her man. I really do.

Mother says the colored act out their feelings more. Like if they dance they wear themselves out, if they sing they make a show of it, if they cry—like at a funeral—it's like a dam broke, with all those tears flowing and pouring, people carrying on in a flood of grief same as they would in a flood of water, screaming and shouting. And when the colored get mad, it means fight or pull a knife or something. And drunk on them is more acted out too, shows up more, because they put more into it. Don't hold nothing back. They're not afraid to show their feelings when the time comes. It can scare a white person.

Then there is Walter. He's white about everything. Like he only dances if he has to—if Mother makes him—and all he will do is slow-dance, and he don't like it. Walter doesn't

sing, he whistles. Maybe snaps his fingers. And he doesn't
cry, not that I ever saw. He closes up over things. When he's
mad he tries to keep calm and only act half as mad as he
really is. He doesn't carry a knife or a razor just in case. He
slings words, but that's all.

And drunk—never knew Walter to be drunk, unless you
count that New Year's Eve when he came home from the
Elks Club and Mother was trying to get him down the hall
quietly, but he stumbled up against my door and I woke up
and saw them. Beating up Mother did not cross Walter's
mind. No. Just the other. All he wanted to do was love her
to death.

The burned place in the woods between our houses was
like a scar. Even when Walter and Old Alfonso weren't
home, their anger was like something they'd left out in the
yard, something of theirs they forgot to take with them, and
now when the rest of us went outside it got all over us too.

"Blue-eyed Jesus," Melvina said when she came home
from church that night and saw the woods half burned
down and heard what happened, and heard that Old
Alfonso had gone off in that car. Mother saw her come and
started out the door to talk to her, but Walter hollered,
"Sarah, stay in the house."

The next morning Melvina came down after Walter left
for work, poured herself a cup of coffee, and sat across the
kitchen table from Mother. "Them two mens living next
door to each other is like two rocks rubbing," she said.
"Bound to be a spark sooner or later."

III

Last Chance

*I*T was the hottest summer ever. I was in my bed, but not asleep. I sat cross-legged in my new shorty pajamas Mother had bought me. I felt just short of a movie star—pretty, in the most surprising way. I looked in the mirror, rubbed Jergens lotion all over myself, then brushed my hair and looked at my face and my eyes and talked to myself as quietly as I could. The night was too hot for even a sheet over me. My transistor radio was playing, good songs coming and going like friendly, quiet people floating through my room. Music the nearest thing to a breeze I know of on a hot Tallahassee summer night.

Mother and Walter were in the living room watching TV. Mother was laying across the sofa with her shirttail out and a row of pin curls in her hair, and Walter was sitting in his favorite chair with his shoes off. They had the oscillating fan going, grinding out air as thick as cotton.

The usual loud cars roared up and down California Street past our house. Jimmy, for one, barreled his daddy's car up the road. "Like a bat out of hell," Walter said. Jimmy drove around the neighborhood half the night, went by our house twenty times. Sometimes Patricia was with him, sitting close beside him with her hand on his leg. Sometimes Patricia was with some other boy in some other car, the radio going, riding up and down the street in a hurry to get nowhere. It was a way to cool off, in somebody's daddy's car, all the windows down and that warm night air blowing on you in its wet way. The car making what breeze it can because nothing else will.

231

Alfonso Junior was delivering whiskey by car now too. It wasn't his car, but he had use of it which was almost as good. When he drove down California Street he tooted the horn in front of Melvina's house a certain way that we all came to recognize. "There goes Alfonso Junior, bet he's running liquor." So cars were up and down our street a lot. We didn't pay much attention because it was summertime, when it's natural for cars to be racing up and down the road.

But this night a car full of yelling people roared by our house a time or two. Walter noticed it. I heard him get up and look out the picture window. "What the hell?" About the time he settled back in his chair, here it came again. When the car got exactly in front of our house there was a bang, like when a car backfires—except the picture window shattered and glass flew all over the living room. Walter dove for the floor. "Walter!" Mother shrieked. "Are you hurt?" The car screeched up California Street like somebody else screaming with Mother, "Walter, oh my God!"

I heard the broken glass clinking like a silverware drawer when you shove it closed. I ran into the living room. Walter was lying on his side under a blanket of shattered glass. Mother was scrambling to him on her knees.

"Get down, Lucy," Walter said.

I squatted in the doorway.

"Are you all right, Walter? Please, God."

"The glass," Walter said, "look out, Sarah." But Mother was all the way over to him now, reaching for him, brushing glass bits off him like it was beach sand.

"Thought I was dead," he said, feeling himself with his hands. "Shit." He touched his face, where half a dozen glass cuts were reddening into blood drops—and on his arms too. The lamp was knocked over, the shade crushed on one side.

"What happened?" I said.

"Why?" Mother said. "Why is somebody shooting at us?"

232

Fear ricocheted through my body.

"Who was it, Walter?" Mother said.

"Damned if I know." Walter looked at his hands, studying the backs first, then the palms, his lips pressed together, almost white. He shook. I didn't know if it was fear or anger. It frightened me, because Walter doesn't shake over anything. I never saw the man shake before.

He took deliberate steps over to the window, stood right in front of it, looking out. There was nothing. There was not a sound except the TV laughing and the crickets shrieking. Mother and I watched him in silence. Without saying a word to us, he walked onto the screened porch and just stood there, looking out at all the darkness. Then onto the porch steps. Standing there. Out into the yard. All the way out to the street. He just stood in the middle of the road, looking first in one direction and then in the other.

Mother, who was barefoot, tiptoed out of the broken glass. She put her arm around me. Old George was up on the porch scratching at the screen, wanting to go with Walter.

"Do you think they'll come back?" I asked.

Mother shook her head. It was not yes or no, either one.

When Walter came back inside, saw us huddled together, he said, "Y'all go on to bed." We didn't make a move. "They're gone," he said.

"What are you going to do, Walter?" Mother said.

"I'm gon make sure don't nobody come by here again. If they do, they'll be sorry this time around. Y'all go on to bed. Now."

Mother tried to get close enough to hug him, but he wouldn't let her. "I'm all right, Sarah." He stepped away. "I want you to go on to bed now. I mean it." He spoke in a brittle voice, just as sharp as a sliver of that broken glass. "Do what I say."

We went to bed like he said. He would not even let Mother put peroxide on the cuts on his face and arms. He wouldn't let her sweep up any of the broken glass either. We were afraid to cross Walter, so we just did what he said and went to bed.

Mother checked on Roy and Benny, sound asleep back in their room. Then she came into my room and said don't worry. "I bet it's just a carload of boys out drinking. It wasn't anybody that wanted to shoot us, I know that." But she didn't know it. She was saying Band-Aid words. Words that are supposed to make you feel better even though they really don't.

In a while the sheriff's car pulled into the yard and Walter walked outside and talked to him. I sat up in bed and looked out the window, and it gave me the creeps. A sheriff's car at our house in the pitch-dark. That radio of his mumbling out into the night and nobody paying any attention. Walter talking, using his hands to talk, which I took as a bad sign—Walter having so much to say.

The sheriff got back in his car and drove up California Street towards French Town. I think Walter stayed up most of the night in his chair by the window. He had his own gun laid out beside him. I heard him get it. I heard Mother say, "Be careful." Walter told her to go to sleep. But I doubt she could do it. I couldn't.

The next morning Roy and Benny thought it was the greatest thing that had ever happened, a gunshot blasted into our house, shattering glass from here to there over the living room so it looked like a bunch of splattered ice cubes spilled out of a drink cooler like the one we took co-colas in when we went to the beach. Roy and Benny loved it, same as they did firecrackers on the Fourth of July. Saw Walter's loaded gun and him sitting beside it. "Why didn't you wake me up?" Roy said. "Next time wake me up." He picked up Walter's gun and aimed it out the busted window. "I'll blow their heads off."

"Roy!" Mother shrieked. "Don't touch that gun. Put it down." Roy looked at Walter to see if he needed to mind Mother or not. Walter nodded set the gun back on the table if you don't want your mama to throw a fit. So Roy put it down. "I don't want you boys to come near that gun, do you understand me?" Mother said. "Tell them, Walter. I don't want either one of them laying a finger on that gun."

"You heard your mama," Walter said.

Melvina came down like usual, saw that busted window and wanted to know everything about it. Walter asked her if she had heard anything last night—the loud car, the gunshot? She said no. But he said he didn't see how she could help but hear it. "You sure you didn't hear nothing?" he said.

"I done told you ten times, I'm sure," she said.

"Was Old Alfonso home last night?"

"He was," Melvina said. "Laid up in the bed."

"You sure he didn't slip out at no time and go off to the Blue Bird or someplace?"

"He ain't left the house."

"You sure?"

"I'm as sure of it as I am my own name," Melvina said. They went back and forth like that. Melvina didn't like his questions. Neither did we.

Roy wanted to tear off down the street first thing and get Bubba and Donald and just about anybody else to come see our shot-out window. Come see the broken glass and Walter's gun, loaded, ready to blow off the head of anybody that was fool enough to try such a thing again. Shooting at Walter Sheppard's house. Roy was ready to tell it good, all of it. There was hardly any blood to show for it, just Walter's handkerchief he had dabbed on the tiny cuts on his face, which I think disappointed Roy a little. Roy would have preferred a flesh wound where maybe Mother had to remove the bullet with a pair of eyebrow tweezers. "Can I have this bloody handkerchief?" Roy asked Walter. "I want to show Bubba."

But Mother made Roy stay home. She said she didn't want the neighbors, like Bubba's Daddy especially, to hear more than was necessary about it, because, awful as it sounded, it could be something that maybe Bubba's Daddy already knew plenty about. Me and Roy and Benny couldn't believe our ears. Our mouths hung open when she said that. Bubba's Daddy didn't seem all that crazy.

"Nobody knows what course hate will take in a person," Mother said.

"You saying Bubba's Daddy did it?" Roy asked.

"There are plenty of people down on California Street that would like to take hold of a situation and deal with it in their own way," she said.

It was like me and Roy and Benny were paralyzed over talk like this. And Mother was funeral serious about it.

Meanwhile word passed up and down California Street to all the neighbors, and different ones came down to discuss it with Walter out in the yard, to say what they would do if it was them that got shot at. People called Mother on the phone, women with questions and ideas of their own. When colored women from up in French Town, some we knew and didn't know, walked by our house to get to their jobs as maids on the white end of California Street or to catch the city bus to a downtown kitchen where they fried food all day, they stopped in the road to discuss our shattered window among themselves. Sometimes they said to Walter in the yard, "Who bust out your window like that?" He yelled back, "You tell me and we'll both know." Sometimes they walked up to our door two at a time. When Mother came out they said, "We seen your busted window. How it happened? Who done it?"

"Believe me," Mother said, "I wish I knew."

Some of Melvina's friends came down and stood in our kitchen and said, "What's the world coming to?" I stood in the hall and listened to them.

"He thinks Old Alfonso done it," Melvina announced.

"What give him that idea?" they said.

"He's the most convenient choice," Melvina said.

"I guess he'd be guilty if wanting to was enough," one of the women said. "Half of French Town'd be guilty if wanting to was enough."

"White people don't have no stretch of the imagination when it comes to trouble," another woman said. "It kills me the way they do."

"Hush," Melvina said. "You can't talk about white people when you're standing in a white man's house. They're all ears over here."

"Who you think shot that gun?"

"I couldn't tell you," Melvina said. "I'm liable to come to work one day and they'll be thinking I done it. The honest truth is don't nobody know."

Since nobody did know, every person made up his own personal version of what most likely happened. Miss Margaret Ann said somebody did not like that letter Mother wrote to the *Tallahassee Democrat*. "Now, it was an easy letter to misunderstand, Sarah. I'm sure you know that." Jake said he bet it was a released convict off one of Walter's road crews. The sheriff said, "No, it was a carload of troublemaking niggers," especially with us living so close to French Town. "Niggers getting bolder every day that passes," he said. Walter was even more specific. He thought that if Old Alfonso didn't pull the trigger himself then he was at least glad somebody else did. That bothered Walter. A gunshot into his house and Old Alfonso probably glad about it, probably laughing over it, probably did it himself or knew who did. Mother said, "What if it was the Klan or somebody? What if they thought they were shooting at a colored house and they shot at our house instead, because we're so close—right on the dividing line?"

Me and Roy listened to all this talk until we had ourselves scared to death. We thought about somebody almost killing Walter. Then we thought, What if they shot Mother too? What if they went around the house shooting bullets in every window until they killed us all? When we thought of a killer he was a stranger that we didn't recognize. He was shadowy and foggy, and he floated. He was somebody that didn't know us, and we didn't know him, and he mostly went around at night with guns in all his pockets. Roy said he kept snakes on the floorboard of his car, tangled up in the springs of the car seat. They licked his heels with their forked tongues while he drove down California Street in the dark. We imagined him, were curious about him and afraid, but he wasn't real to us. No more than a thing in a dream.

Mother and Walter what-iffed so much. And the sheriff did. And Melvina got guessing too. Pretty soon, instead of narrowing it down any, it got to where it could have been any living soul in Tallahassee that shot that gun.

If the picture window was the house's eye, that bullet blinded it, lodged deep in our living room—and the wound festered. Now our house was clumsy and confused, like a sudden blind man—still alive, but with a bullet stuck in his head.

Walter had to order replacement glass to be shipped from Jacksonville. It took three weeks. Meanwhile Walter taped flattened cardboard boxes over the window. Two of them said "Kotex" in bold letters and Mother asked him twice to take them down, but he wouldn't. He insisted nobody would read the words—he hadn't noticed them himself until she pointed them out. It looked like our house was sitting with a big flesh-colored Band-Aid over its eye.

The day after the picture window was replaced, looking about as good as new, but we all knew it wasn't—just like a glass eye, it might look okay but you never could see out of it the same—that very next morning, Mother sent Benny out to get the Sunday newspaper. She was fixing breakfast, and me and Roy were getting dressed for church. Walter was still asleep like he always did on Sunday. The house smelled like bacon, the kitchen putting off a sizzle sound. I was thinking about whether or not Mother would let me wear stockings to church, when Benny began to scream. It sounded like playing at first. I had to stand still and listen carefully to know it wasn't.

Before I knew it for sure, yes, Benny is crying, I heard Walter run down the hall, saw him go by my bedroom door in his plaid pajama bottoms, with Roy right behind him. Benny was screaming like he couldn't get his breath. I ran to him too. It was the loudest screaming I ever heard. Mother was calling his name and hurrying for him with the greasy spatula in her hand. We poured out of the house like it was on fire, running to Benny's screams. As soon as we were out the door and down the steps we stopped dead.

Benny was standing in the yard holding Mopsy, her head sliced off and hanging by a bloody strip of fur. He was holding her tight, close to his face, and patting her as he cried. Mother screamed when she saw him. His own face covered with blood where he had kissed Mopsy's fur and laid his wet face against her; the rabbit's head had dropped back over his arm, and it dangled from side to side as Benny rocked her back and forth like a baby. He was gasping. His pajamas were drenched with blood.

"Oh, sweet Benny, sweet Benny," Mother said. He buried his face in Mopsy's belly.

Roy stood horror-struck. I did too. Little Benny, his red, broken face. His eyes slits, puncture wounds in his head. His mouth stretched sharp and white, he cried like the sound was coming from his own head cut off. It twisted something inside me hard and tight. I raised my hand to my mouth, bit my fingers to make it stop.

Mother was kissing and patting him. "Don't cry, Benny."
Roy kept staring at that bloody rabbit, her mouth open, her eyes open. "Who killed Mopsy?" he said. "Who did it?"
For a minute we forgot Walter. He was standing on the steps holding the screen door open and watching us—like he was stuck. Like he had come as far as he could towards such a sight but could not come any closer. Watching Benny, who could not be comforted. Now Mother was saying, "Let me have Mopsy, Benny. You have to let go of her." But Benny only held tighter. Mother began to cry and to tug gently at Mopsy. "She's dead, Benny. You have to let go." Her voice was coming in splashes.
The screen door slammed shut behind Walter. He was standing bare-chested with his wild morning hair. We all looked at him, Walter Sheppard, with his eyes fixed hard on Benny. His jaw flexed. He ran his hands through his hair, just standing there staring at Benny and his dead rabbit.
"Why did somebody kill her?" Roy said. "Mopsy never hurt nothing."
When Benny lifted Mopsy, trying to show Walter what had happened, Walter couldn't stand it. He took two giant steps across the yard and grabbed Benny, picked him up, the rabbit still in his arms, and hugged them both. "Leave him alone. Y'all leave him alone." Benny put one arm around Walter's neck, the other one tight around Mopsy.
"Who did it, Walter?" Roy said.
"Why in the world?" Mother kept saying.
Walter carried Benny across the yard. When they got to the side of the house Walter turned to the rest of us. "Y'all get ready for church," he said. "Me and Benny are going to bury Mopsy."
"I'll help you." Roy started after them.
"No," Walter said, "you go with your mother and Lucy. We don't need help."
Roy stopped cold, the most disappointed look on his face.

He called out in a quiet voice, "You can have Trigger, Benny. Trigger can be your rabbit now."

"Elvis too," I said.

"Walter," Mother yelled as he disappeared around the house, "we're not going to church today."

He stopped and backed up. "Yes you are."

"But we don't want . . ."

"Don't argue with me, Sarah." Walter's tone was something we all understood.

Mother, Roy, and I went inside, dressed for church, and didn't say a word to each other. We got in the car, and as we backed out of the driveway we saw Walter and Benny at the edge of the yard, Benny sitting in the grass with Mopsy in his lap, partly wrapped in a croaker sack, and Walter with the shovel in his hands, stabbing the ground. Mother honked the horn as a way of saying, We're going now. See? but neither of them turned to look at us.

We rode silently, headfirst into the heat of midday. Then Mother turned to me and said, "Lucy, what in the world did you do to my Bible?" She held it up for me to see. The battered edges were curled, the pages stuck together in clumps, the red ink where Jesus spoke had bled, giving the Bible a bloody look. "It looks like it's been through the washing machine."

"I left it outside. It got rained on. I'm sorry." This was the first time Mother had mentioned the sorry condition of her Bible. She slapped it down on the seat beside her, aggravated. But under the circumstances it was a minor aggravation.

We did not go to church. We just rode up California Street so it looked like we were going to church. We rode past Melvina's church, Good Shepherd, and listened to them singing their heads off, the church roof banging up and down like a lid on a pot. Then Mother circled around and drove us out to the country, down old Bainbridge Road, where the trees hang over the road so blue and cool that it seems you are riding through evening at midday, then out past Lake Jackson, way out there like you're going to Georgia. We hardly talked at all, rode along, looking out the windows. Mother stopped once at a bait store and we got grape drinks and cheese crackers, at least Mother and I did. Roy wouldn't eat anything. He wouldn't even get out of the car.

As we rode, heading no place in particular, Mother said, "It is so beautiful out in the country. Don't you think it's beautiful out here?" We had the windows down and the warm wind across our faces, looking out at the pastures and cornfields and woods, and at the little fall-down houses up in the shade where the poor people lived.

"What kind of person would kill a rabbit like that?" I said. "Cut its throat and lay it in the yard like that?"

"If I find out who did it," Roy said, "I'm gon cut their throat the same way."

"Roy," Mother said.

"I am. I'm gon kill whoever done it."

"Hush," Mother said. "Look out the window."

There are only three colors on hot summer mornings. There is just green and yellow and blue. There is just sky, and grass and trees—with the sun soaking through so it glows and you can see the little waves of heat shimmying, sort of blurring it all together. The grass starts to look like water, like something moving, flowing up over the edge of the road like ocean waves on the sand.

"Walter used to bring us out here to dig grass," I said. "Remember that, Roy?"

Roy shook his head like he couldn't remember.

When we got home Benny was asleep and Mopsy was buried. Walter had broken a yardstick in two and made a cross to mark the grave. He was painting it bright yellow with a can of paint for highway dividing lines.

𝒯HE next Saturday morning
we were watching cartoons, the three of us sleep-haired,
sprawled on the sofa. Mother was in the kitchen plugging in
the coffeepot, when we heard hammering outside. Mother
looked out at Walter nailing something to a pine tree in the
front yard. She put on her flip-flops and hurried outside. We
followed, Benny still in his pajamas.

"What are you doing?" Mother said.

"We're moving," Walter said. "I decided it was time."
He walked towards the tool box in his truck, swinging the
hammer in his hand. Sometimes Walter is like a king who
can do things any way he wants to, don't have to take a vote
on nothing, don't have to answer questions. He got in his
truck and backed out of the yard, pausing long enough to
say to Mother, "Be home in a couple of hours."

We stared as he drove off. Then we turned to stare at the
"For Sale" sign nailed to the biggest pine tree in the yard.
We stood there so long, letting the shock of it soak in, that
Melvina came down to see what was wrong.

"What's he nailing on that tree?" she said.

"We're moving, Melvina," I said.

A cloud came over Melvina's face, her eyebrows knitted
together. "Where?"

"He didn't tell us."

Melvina looked at Mother, who was as quiet as she had
ever been in her life. "Why?"

Mother waved her hand at us like it was a magic wand
that could make children disappear. "Go play," she said.
Roy and Benny left, but I walked inside behind Melvina and
Mother.

"Mr. Sheppard think Old Alfonso shot y'all's window?"

"You know he does."

"He don't think Old Alfonso had nothing to do with
killing that rabbit, does he?"

Mother sat down in Walter's chair. "He just doesn't want any more trouble, Melvina."

"He think California Street the only place got trouble? What do he want? Old Alfonso to swear on the Bible he ain't done none of it?"

Mother closed her eyes and didn't answer.

"Mr. Sheppard sent the police around to Virginia's house looking for Alfonso Junior, said what did he know about a gun shooting your window. The police took Alfonso Junior's name down. You know that boy don't know nothing about it."

"He's up and down the road, Melvina. Maybe Walter thinks he saw something. That's all."

"That ain't all. Send the police around up there. And Mr. Sheppard been knowing us."

"Walter could've been killed. You know that, don't you?"

"None my mens trying to kill nobody. Just trying not to get their own selves kilt."

"Everything's a mess," Mother said.

"You ain't got to tell me about no mess."

Mother went back to her bedroom and closed the door and slept all day. The next day she got up to fix our breakfast, then went back to bed for the rest of the day, so we didn't have to go to church. Walter fixed us tomato soup for lunch and tomato soup for supper. On Monday Melvina said, "What happened to this kitchen?" She fixed our lunch and supper, but Mother didn't even get up to eat. That evening Walter fixed his plate and ate his supper in front of the TV, but he made us eat at the table. Roy and Benny slept in their clothes that night because there was nobody but me to tell them not to. If you knocked on Mother's door she would not answer. She didn't come out of her room until Tuesday morning after Walter left for work. She kept her bathrobe on until after lunch.

"Are you mad at Walter?" I asked.

She poured herself coffee, her cup rattling in its saucer. "If it wasn't for Walter Sheppard I'd be the old woman in the shoe. I wouldn't have anyplace better than a shoe to live. So if my husband wants to buy me and my kids a new house, the least I can do is be grateful." She blew into her coffee. It made ripples across the cup.

Once Walter decided we were moving and told us, it was like our heads went on and did it, immediately, moved over to Holly Hills, to that nice, clean brick house Walter picked out. It was a little house and the yard was small, but it was brand-new, had never been lived in before. I changed my mind on my room, from blue to pink and back to blue.

Mother made me clean out my closet and dresser drawers and under my bed. She made me wash the pencil marks off my closet door where she'd marked my height year after year and put the date beside it. The new people would not be interested in how tall I was at any time in my life. "Nobody wants a marked-up house," she said. I used Ajax to scrub it.

Mother stayed busy from morning to night digging through cabinets and closets. She made piles of stuff to throw away. Then Melvina went through them and got out anything she wanted—which was practically everything in the pile. They filled grocery sacks and set them by the back door.

Mother acted strange. We all noticed it. She sounded like a chirping songbird, her voice too high, and she sang her sentences. She talked about things she was grateful for. She counted her blessings out loud. She wanted everybody to smile. "It doesn't cost you anything to smile," she said to Roy when she made him carry out sacks of trash. He frowned at her even worse. "Smile, Benny," she said, "someday you're going to know how lucky you are." He fixed a half-moon smile on his face to please her. To me she said, "Lucy, a smile is better than a new dress if you want to look pretty."

"I don't," I said. I tried to have no look on my face at all, not a smile or a frown, just a medium face that would not draw comment.

Mother didn't try to make Walter count his blessings. She smiled if he looked straight at her, but she didn't say anything except, "I went through every cabinet in the kitchen today. Got rid of the most junk you ever saw. Come look."

Last time I saw Karol and Patricia they asked me where we were moving. "Holly Hills," I said. I started to say Holly Hills is about as far from French Town as you can get and still live in Tallahassee. But they were jealous enough without me saying it.

The third week the "For Sale" sign was up we showed the house to the McCluskys, an old couple from Michigan, or Minnesota, or Maine. One of those up-North places that start with an M, and which are all the same to us since we never have been to any of them and don't want to go because if we are going someplace we want it to be Miami, Panama City, Daytona Beach, or some good place like that. The McCluskys had retired and moved to Florida for their golden years.

The first time they came to look at the house they stayed more than an hour. When they left I knew the house was sold. The next time they came Walter and Mr. McClusky took the "For Sale" sign down. Word passed up and down California Street.

Walter told the McCluskys he had recently replaced the picture window, but he didn't tell them why he had to do it. He never mentioned that people shot at this house, and slit rabbits' throats in this yard.

When Mother told Melvina the McCluskys bought the

house, she tried to act happy. She danced in the kitchen, hugging Melvina, trying to twirl her around. But Melvina wouldn't twirl. "What's the matter with you?" Melvina said.

Mother put her hands over her face and broke into a million pieces right there in the kitchen.

"I feel good about the McCluskys as neighbors for you, Melvina," Mother said a couple of days later. "They're from up North. They don't have any wrong ideas about colored people. They haven't had a chance to get any wrong ideas."

"People is born with wrong ideas," Melvina said. "All the ideas anybody's got is wrong ideas. I lived long enough to see that."

Walter felt good about the McCluskys on behalf of his yard and nice grass. "They're thinking about putting in a garden out back," Walter told Mother. "I always wanted to do that myself."

"What stopped you?" Mother said.

"You won't have no trouble with the colored next door," Walter told the McCluskys. He went so far as to say, "Melvina is a good woman." Then he added, "Her boy Skippy is a good worker too. You can count on him." Walter didn't mention anybody else up there.

"I never had trouble with anybody colored," Mr. McClusky said. "Don't expect to now."

"Good," Walter said.

"There was a colored boy worked at the same factory as me, different crew, I saw him regular—every other day. We never had trouble. I didn't bother him. He didn't bother me."

"That's nice," Mother said.

"His name was Joe." Mr. McClusky thought a minute.

"No, his name was John. People called him John. Me and John never had no trouble whatsoever, and John was colored."

Walter took off his hat and scratched his head. He didn't say anything.

"Melvina is the best cook in the world," Mother said. "She makes good lemon pies and good anything you can name."

"Really?" Mrs. McClusky opened each kitchen cabinet.

"If you put in a garden and need help canning, Melvina could do a good job of it."

Mrs. McClusky listened politely. I don't know why southern people always act like no northern people know how to cook good food. Mother embarrassed me, going on about Melvina, her lemon icebox pie, her chicken gravy, her turnip greens and pepper sauce.

Mother made everybody come inside and sit down and have some of Melvina's peach cobbler. It was a good year for peaches, and Mother was trying to see to it that it would be a good year for Melvina too. We all sat down. Melvina scooped up the cobbler. Mother put clumps of ice cream on it.

The McCluskys were nice old people. Since they were Yankees I couldn't help but wonder who was going to be friends with them. I thought they talked funnier than we did, but every other thing we said made them laugh. They showed us their kids' pictures and their grandchildren's. They had a little curly dog in the car, named Snowball. After that day everybody seemed satisfied with each other. All Melvina did was sit on a stool in the kitchen and watch the whole thing, listen to every word.

Mother was doing overtime on how good Melvina was, same as if Melvina was for sale and Mother was fast-talking Mrs. McClusky into buying her. Mother acted like Melvina was something that came with the house—same as the stove did. The more Melvina listened, the more her face shut down, like putting a "Closed" sign in a store window. Somebody needed to slap Mother to make her stop.

"I've always kept my own house," Mrs. McClusky said. "I've never had any need for a maid."

The McCluskys were buying our whole lives right out from under us. Like we were selling our lives at no extra cost. Mother was letting Walter sell the house, and Melvina with it, and the pencil marks on my door, and my childhood itself, which nobody but me would even want.

Later, when Melvina was alone in the kitchen, I went in and stood awkwardly near her as she busied herself at the sink, opened and shut the refrigerator, stirred a smoking pot on the stove. I stood too close—in the way—like a shadow that had got mixed up on what to do.

"You in the way," she said, stopping what she was doing and looking at me with the paring knife in one hand and a half-peeled blood-red tomato in the other.

I meant to say everything, but my words went limp.

*S*KIPPY came to my window again. He said he wanted the radio, and I gave it to him with no argument. While he was gone I brushed my hair, because when I wake up it's all crazy-looking and it sticks out everywhere. He never laughed at me, though, which was part of the change in him, passing up a chance to make fun of me. I sat in the window and waited for him to come back. This time he wasn't gone long.

When he returned I unlatched the screen, and he propped it up with a stick, set the radio in the window, and switched it to the white station that I always listened to. The moment was hot with embarrassment because we didn't know the right things to say. He reached into his shirt pocket.

"Skippy, you got cigarettes."

He pulled a cellophane string, tapped a cigarette out with his finger, and put it in his mouth. I sat in the window watching him, just the way he liked it—the Skippy Williams I'd been watching all my California Street years. He lit the cigarette, closed his eyes, shook out the match. He was casual. Got that tobacco smell. Got that white smoke around his face. The tip of his cigarette like the hot yellow flashing in the darkest part of my heart. I don't like to say it, but Skippy looked close to wonderful smoking that cigarette.

"Does Melvina know you smoke?"

"Nope."

The radio music was good and I was thankful for it. Skippy sort of bounced yet mostly stood still. He hardly looked at me. Just listened to the music, stared into the black yard. "Why y'all moving?" He blew smoke in my face. The smoke cushioned the soft crash of our eyes.

"Walter sold the house. You know that."

"Why'd he sell it?" I liked the way Skippy flicked ashes right to the beat of the music, same as people snap their fingers. He looked twenty-five.

"You know why. You know somebody shot at this house—and you know Walter hasn't been right about it since. And then Benny's rabbit."

"Mr. Sheppard think Daddy done it?"

"Maybe."

Skippy sucked hard on his cigarette. "Don't lie."

"Okay. Yes. Walter thinks Old Alfonso did it. He thinks he shot the gun and killed Mopsy both. There. Does that make you happy?"

"The truth ain't designed to make nobody happy. But I like knowing you can tell a little of it."

Skippy turned away from me, shook his head, and looked out into the dark. I didn't like the way he did it, having some thought of his own he wouldn't say, then shaking his head like he wanted to erase it, turning his face so his eyes didn't tell me anything, not a clue. He smoked that fool cigarette like it was the only thing that mattered, that tip glowing like a caution light, on and off. "Daddy ain't shot y'all's house. The man don't even have a gun."

"I'm not saying he did it, Skippy. It's Walter that thinks so. Mother swears it was Bubba's Daddy. I don't know who did it. So don't get mad at me."

"I ain't mad."

"I can't help what goes on between Walter and Old Alfonso. But Walter sold the house. We don't have a say in it. Mother says we might as well try to act glad about it. You ought to be glad too—getting rid of us. That ought to make you happy."

"Always trying to tell me what to do, ain't you, girl?"

"My name's not 'girl.' Why can't you call me my name?"

"Okay, *Lucy,*" he said. "Don't tell me what to be glad about. I'll be glad about what I want to be glad about."

"Do we always have to fight?" Skippy could make me mad so fast—could get my insides boiling—then laugh in my face. I didn't want him to do it anymore. I sprang up from the windowsill. He grabbed my arm. I was afraid to look at him.

"Climb out that window and let's dance."

I laughed. Skippy at my window, that cigarette hanging out of his mouth, those dancing shoulders and feet and arms. "You're crazy, Skippy Williams."

"That's what all the girls say. They say, 'Skippy, you so crazy—and you can dance like a son of a bitch.' Come on, girl." He reached for my hand. "Whoops, I mean, come on here, Lucy. Come on out that window and let's dance."

"I can't dance like colored people. You'll laugh."

"I seen you and them girls dancing out in the yard. Didn't laugh, did I?"

"Probably did. Probably called us crackers and laughed."

"Shoot." He held his cigarette in his hand, easy, did some fancy stepping to the music, his eyes sort of closed. The music was getting inside me and squirming. "So, you going to climb out and dance with me or not?"

"I can't climb outside in my nightgown."

"Anybody ever tell you you're too sensible?"

It was good that we had the radio—strong music to fill places where we stared at each other and nothing else.

"It ain't gon seem right when y'all are gone. We was about to get used to you," Skippy said.

"I've wanted you to like me for the longest time, Skippy. But you wouldn't do it. Now we're going to move away before I can . . ." I felt Skippy's eyes on me. Why did I say that?

"You sorry you're moving?"

"I hate it." It was the first time I had said so, even to myself. "I don't want to move. I like it here."

We listened to "Soldier Boy," and "My Boyfriend's Back," and "Put Your Head on My Shoulder." Listened long enough for Skippy to smoke another cigarette. He took his time doing it. When he finished he dropped the cigarette butt to the ground and watched it die out.

"Skippy, you still want to dance?"

"With who?"

"Me, silly. You could climb in the window. We have to slow-dance because we can't wake up Mother and Walter."

He lifted himself up on the window ledge and put his legs through the window. The minute he stood on my bedroom floor I was nervous. He seemed so—real. "Come stand on the rug," I said, and pulled my pink throw rug into a clear space on the floor. "It's quieter."

Skippy stepped onto the rug and set the radio on my

dresser. I stood only inches away from him. "Wait for a good song," he said. I must have brushed my hair out of my eyes twenty times, waiting. Skippy smelled like cigarettes. "You scared?" he said.

"A little."

"You scared to dance with me—or you scared we'll get caught?"

"Both."

"Me too." He stepped towards me. "Here's a song. Listen." He put one hand on my waist, held my hand with the other. I was too stiff. My hands were sweating.

Skippy pulled me closer. Our faces touched. I can't remember the music. I only remember Skippy singing with it. I closed my eyes to listen. You could hardly call it dancing. We moved from side to side—that's all. His fingers on the hot part of my back. I was light-headed. Skippy's hands were warm, his fingers folded over mine. He didn't have any push in him when he danced, like some boys do. *This way. This way. Follow me.* None of that. Skippy moved easy, his touch hot and soft. I was trembling.

When the song was over he held my hand maybe one extra second. I looked to be sure. Yes.

"Let's do it again," I said. "One more song?"

"Better not. Better go."

I was so relieved. And so disappointed.

He ran his hand slowly down the side of my face, touching my hair, feeling it like he used to a long time ago—but this was different. I don't know if it happened fast or slow. He whispered my name. After he moved his hand his touch stayed. Before I could speak, he walked back to the window, quietly swung his legs out, and jumped to the ground. I watched as he walked across the yard quickly, then broke into a run like somebody was calling him and he had to hurry. In a few seconds the blackness swallowed him up.

I got into bed but couldn't sleep. Not even the radio

helped. Skippy Williams had danced with me, touched my hair. It made me happy and nervous. Even after he left I was nervous.

My room smelled like cigarette smoke. Some of it got in my head and clouded things, like steam that comes off hot pavement when it rains. I was alone in the dark a few minutes when the door to my room opened. I lay as still as sleep. It was Walter. He walked in without turning on the light. I opened my eyes to watch him. Bare-chested, barefooted, wearing only his work pants, he walked across the floor quietly, glanced at me long enough to be sure I was there, a lump in the bed, then made his way to the window, to look out into the yard. "Lucy," he whispered, sleep still in his voice. "Did you hear anything?"

I leaned up on my elbows to look at him. "No."

He fingered the window latch. "Somebody's been out there. Seen somebody run across the backyard. A man. I seen one, but it could have been two."

The sight of Walter was terrifying, pale-faced in the darkness, his hair clumped into points on his head, forming wisps of horns in the silhouette against the window. He was tiptoeing in his own house, acting afraid, and fear looked devilish on him. His white flesh, the arrow of hair running down his chest, his voice eerie because it wasn't designed for whispering, sounding coarse like an animal growl. His movements were so cautious I didn't recognize them as his. He usually moved as if he held deed to everything around him. I felt like a total stranger had entered my room half naked in the night.

"Somebody's been out there. Keep your windows latched, you hear?"

"Yessir."

"Go back to sleep." He reached up then, with both hands, to test the latch—and that's when I saw it. The gun in Walter's hand.

"*I*T's amazing what you can live without," Mother said. The bird had gone from her voice. Now what she said jumped from her mouth, suddenly, like frogs do when you try to hold them in your hands—jump loose and sometimes get away, and sometimes splatter themselves on the ground and die.

She kept losing things too. *Where in the world did I put those scissors? Who got that list I wrote? I put it down right here. Did somebody pick it up? Lucy, have you seen my scissors? You know they didn't walk off by themselves.* She thought we spent the day moving her things around, hiding them, trying to confuse her. *Whoever has that list has got 'til I count to ten to give it back.* Roy and Benny stayed outside because Mother was like that. It was mostly Melvina and me that had to listen to it all day.

Cardboard boxes overtook the house. Mother was fiendish, overseeing the packing of every box, repacking anything anybody else packed, stacking the boxes herself, so that all the edges were flush and the boxes piled together formed a neat rectangle the size of a casket in every room.

We had to watch her close to keep her from throwing away everything—especially something we really wanted. It became all the same to her, worthless and worthwhile. She threw away plenty of perfectly good stuff that we would probably come up needing someday. Melvina carried most of it home with her. "Ain't nothing wrong with this. If you crazy enough to throw it away, I'm crazy enough to take it." When Mother lost the next thing and searched the house, calling for it, asking Melvina and me what we did with it, we just looked at her and said, "Shoot, you probably threw it out."

She packed up Walter's chewing tobacco, his flashlight, his loose change, and everything else he kept in his top dresser drawer—even his gun—and taped the box closed and labeled it, knowing perfectly good and well he would still be needing the contents right up to the end.

That afternoon, after Walter opened his empty dresser drawer and saw what she had done, he shuffled through the pile of boxes—you could hear him unstacking them and dropping them to the floor, making little thuds that vibrated through the house—until he found the one labeled "Walter's Top Drawers." He ripped the box open and began taking everything out and putting it back.

Mother ran into their bedroom, where he was undoing what she had done, and flung herself at him. "Stop it, Walter!" she shrieked. "It took me all day. . . ."

I was glad Roy and Benny weren't in the house to see it, but Melvina and I came down the hall just in time to see Mother pounding her fists against Walter, screaming at him, her face a fireball.

Walter slung that empty box across the room, where it bounced off the window but didn't break it. He snatched Mother's arms so she couldn't move. Stood with a white-knuckle grip on her wrists while she struggled to hit him. She was crying and Walter shook her hard, his teeth clamped together, like he was trying to shake some sense into her—but he couldn't—so he shook harder. "I hate you!" she screamed. Then he slapped her. Mother went limp. Walter slung her down on the bed, where she lay sobbing.

If Melvina and I hadn't stepped aside as Walter walked out of the room, he would have knocked us over. He didn't know any difference between us and the empty air. His footsteps echoed through the house, and when the screen door slammed I went to Mother.

Melvina stood in the doorway with her apron in her hands while I patted Mother like you do a cat asleep on a bed, so careful. Her face was buried in the bedspread.

"Now look what's done happened," Melvina said.

I sat down on the edge of the bed beside Mother and did not hear when Melvina left the doorway. When I touched Mother, I felt the quake of her insides—she made all the motions of coughing something up.

She wiped her hand across her face, pushed her hair behind her ear. Her eyes were hard red. "Repeat after me, Lucy. 'Everything is just fine. Everything is just fine. Everything is just . . .' "

Everything was out of order, the house, bare and cluttered both. Now Mother and Walter, mad. They went around like two bumper cars trying not to bump, heading straight at each other, then swerving at the last minute.

All the mirrors had been taken down from the walls and sat braced on the floor, so that when we went from room to room we could only see ourselves from the chest down. Headless. That's how it was. All of us.

Mother and Walter had gone deaf too. You could ask them a question and they forgot to answer you. "Where do you want me to put this?" you could say, then stand there the rest of your life holding the thing and waiting for an answer. It was scaring Benny. But I hated them for it.

It was Roy's job to make things worse. He started reminding Mother she had promised that he and Benny could camp out in the yard, *someday*. Now, unless it happened fast, we all knew there would never be a *someday*. "This is our last chance," Roy said like a scratched record. "This is our last chance. This is our last chance. This is our last chance." It would take killing him to get him to hush. Even when he got quiet the words were still there, because he had filled up the house with them. He begged Mother to let them camp out. He said one hundred times, "You promised." I listened to him pleading in the kitchen, "You can't go back on a promise. We'll make a tent. We'll make it up close to the house. You promised. You promised."

Any minute I thought Mother would scream for him to shut up, and list a thousand reasons why he and Benny couldn't sleep outside tonight or any night—ever. Not on California Street. I thought she would grab him by the shoulders and say, "Roy, what ever happened to that little bit of sense you used to have?" But she wore down easy.

"Okay, okay. Sleep outside if you want to." Roy and Benny let out happy screams and hallelujahs and bounded through the house like a couple of barking dogs.

"What's wrong with you, Mother?" I said. "Why did you do that?"

"Do what?" she said.

When Roy and Benny told Walter that Mother said they could camp out in the yard, he was dead set against it, just like Mother knew he would be. He didn't say one word, though. He sat in the truck a long time with the door open and listened to the news on the radio.

Roy and Benny pinned quilts to the clothesline, tent style. They made pine-straw beds inside and laid their bedspreads over them. They got canteens and filled them up with Kool-Aid and wrapped some saltine crackers in wax paper. It kept them out of Mother's way, all afternoon.

That night Mother fixed bacon sandwiches for supper, but Walter refused to come to the table.

"That's a bad sign," Melvina said. "I ain't never known a white man to refuse to eat."

"How many white men do you know?" Mother said. "One? Two? Sometimes you talk like you know everything, Melvina."

"I know trouble when I see it."

"You find what you look for," Mother snapped.

"Just closing your eyes don't make you blind."

"Just going around with your eyes open don't mean you see what you think you see either. Things aren't always what they look like."

258

"Eyes is better off open than closed."

"Maybe so, but a mouth is better off closed."

"I ain't said not half of what I *could of* said."

"Well, I don't know what stopped you."

"Because you couldn't of took it. Slightest bit of truth raise its ugly head and you all to pieces."

"Nothing ever bothers you, does it, Melvina? You're just a rock in a hailstorm, aren't you?"

"Get on out of my kitchen"—she waved her hand at Mother—"and let me clean up this mess."

"This is my kitchen—in case you forgot." Mother sat down in a chair, looked up at the ceiling, quiet. "You really had me fooled, didn't you? All this time."

"You the one's turned colors." Melvina pulled out a chair, sat down across from Mother, and took off her shoes. They sat in the hot kitchen for the longest time, looking out the screen door at the yard full of their children, Roy and Benny building a quilt monstrosity, Orlando throwing pine cones at Leroy and Nappy, seeing which one of them can get to the goal line without getting hit hard enough to cry.

When Walter came inside to rummage up something to eat, Mother and Melvina were still sitting there in silence. He looked at the bacon grease in the skillet, the sink full of dirty dishes, and then at the two women. "What's wrong? Somebody glue your fannies to those chairs?"

Long before dark, Roy and Benny were settled into their tent for the night, but as soon as it got dark Benny thought of Mopsy, and got scared and came back inside.

"You don't have any business sleeping outside in the first place," Walter told him.

Mother came and stood in the living room, where Walter was watching TV. "He can if I say he can, Walter."

"But I don't want to," Benny said. "I don't have to if I don't want to, do I?"

"They're my kids, Walter. They're not your kids."

I knew then that Mother had gone crazy. She wanted to
fight with Walter, make him mad enough to leave us. Walter
spit tobacco juice into his coffee cup and read the paper like
Mother was not in the room. Hardly even in the world.

"I'm sleeping outside with Roy," I said. I thought of Roy
outside in his pine-straw bed, Roy, who would not give up
and come in the house, no matter what. If lightning struck
him between the eyes it would not be enough to make him
give up. I went to my room to get my radio and the quilt off
my bed. But Mother had packed my quilt.

"Lucy," Mother shouted, "don't you dare . . ."

I ran past her with my radio in my hand and let the screen
door slam behind me, so glad to get out of the light and into
the darkness.

Roy and I lay in the tent with old George beside us,
smelling bad right up in our faces. I had come barreling out
of the house like somebody shot from a cannon, flung
myself through the tent flap and onto the ground beside
Roy. Cry was written all over me, but Roy refused to read
it out loud. He didn't ask me a single question. We just laid
there, the two of us, parallel as a couple of parked cars. We
both believed Mother would come after us and try and
make things right. We waited more than an hour until,
finally, we saw the light go out in Mother's bedroom.

"What you think's the matter with her?" Roy said.

"Walter, I guess."

"He ain't all of it."

Then Roy and I started talking—just fell into it like
talking was a deep hole that it would take us a long time to
climb out of. We hardly said one nice word about a single
person. It felt good. As right as rain.

"I'm glad we're getting away from a sorry neighborhood
like this," Roy said. "I bet over in Holly Hills people know
how to act half decent."

"Maybe," I said.

We heard Walter before we saw him. He squatted and

shined his flashlight in our faces. "Y'all ain't got no business out here."

"Mother said we could."

Walter shoved the flashlight to Roy. "Don't run the batteries down," he said, then went back in the house.

You don't have any sense of time out in a tent, crickets shrieking their heads off nonstop and you lose the sense of time. We heard a car horn honking. "There goes Alfonso Junior by Melvina's," Roy said.

It bothered me and Roy right up to the end that we never got inside Melvina's house. Deep down we held it against her. I told Roy the way I imagined Melvina's house looked inside. The way I imagined Old Alfonso would look in a white shirt and necktie—which we had never seen—how he would look dancing at the Blue Bird, how he would look close up when he was passed out on Melvina's porch.

"It's not too late," Roy said. He rolled over on his elbow to face me. "We could still get a good look at Melvina's house, and Old Alfonso, and all of it." Then he got quiet, his eyes lit like a couple of embers.

Old George didn't even wake up when we snuck out of the tent. Roy grabbed Walter's flashlight and I grabbed my radio. We ran barefoot through the woods, tree roots sliding like snakes under our feet. At Melvina's house a light was still on, so we edged up beside the window, trying to be quiet but knowing full well that the pounding of our hearts was too loud, that any minute someone would step outside to see who was beating drums in the yard.

I was boosting Roy up to look in the window when the screen door squeaked open. I dropped Roy to the ground. We scrambled up to run when we saw it was Skippy. "Shhhh," he said, and shoved us both back down underneath the house; then he scurried under there behind us. The three of us huddled in the pitch-black with the snakes and spiders.

At the second screech of the screen door Old Alfonso

came out and started down the back steps, not letting the door slam behind him but closing it carefully. He paused on the bottom step and fished in his pocket for a cigarette. He was so close to us that if I stretched I could have touched his shoe with my hand. The old man sat down on the steps and struck a match. It lit his face like a jack-o'-lantern.

We watched him smoke. My legs ached because of the position I was crunched into, squashed between Roy and Skippy, but nothing—except the wet tongue of a snake—would have caused me to make a move.

Old Alfonso was not drunk. He didn't smell of it or act it either. He made no move to burn the house down, get the wood ax after Melvina, or so much as strangle one of the yard dogs. Two of Melvina's dogs straggled over where he sat and lay down beside him. He didn't cuss, or swear, or sharpen his pocketknife to stab somebody with. No. Instead he cleaned his fingernails. And he hummed. Sat tapping his foot and mumbling a little piece of tune, just barely, just one step away from groaning, low and mournful and as personal as anything. I was ashamed, listening.

"He doesn't scare me," I whispered. Skippy clasped his hand hard over my mouth and didn't let go until Old Alfonso flicked his cigarette butt on the ground not a foot from where we were huddled, and walked out to the road in front of the house. We stayed put and watched him until he was vanishing around a bend in the road.

Skippy yanked Roy and me out from under the house. "What you call yourself doing?"

"We're going up to the Blue Bird," Roy said.

"Shoot, I say." Skippy spit the words.

"You can't stop us," Roy said.

Skippy stood looking at us. "Look, Roy's got a flashlight, and I got this." I pulled my radio from my waistband, turned it up louder than I meant to.

"Shhhhh." Skippy snatched the radio out of my hand and

turned it down. "You gon wake the dead." He took off running for the road with me and Roy fast behind him.

It doesn't look the same at night, that red dirt, that Florida sand; it's lit up, the way the moonlight ricochets off it. We ran until we were out of sight of Melvina's house; then Skippy made us stop so he could get a good channel on the radio. We sat on the roadside with the whole deserted world to ourselves, except for Old Alfonso strolling up ahead, two dogs loping along with him. I sat down beside Skippy, but Roy elbowed me—"Move over"—wedging himself between us. We waited in the shadows until Old Alfonso got a good lead, so we could trail him and he'd never suspect it.

It didn't take Skippy long to get in the spirit of the thing, fall right in with us. He sang with the radio, every song. I laughed at first, but then I started singing too—his heavy voice falling to the ground around our feet and my high one rising, floating in our hair. "Y'all stop," Roy said. "This ain't choir practice."

We skimmed along the road on the fringe of the shadows, just slow enough to keep Old Alfonso in sight but out of earshot. As he went along, dogs came from nowhere and followed him. Five or six, leaping all over the road, happy as frogs.

Three cars passed us. Each time we flung ourselves into the ditch, hiding just enough. Car headlights, too intent on the straight-ahead to notice the three of us on the edge, left dust clouds behind them, the tires spitting sand. Lit only by the stars and the yellow fingernail moon, the dirt road was spotted with occasional darkened houses but lined mostly with woods as good as jungle. The screaming insects pulsating through the darkness, the heaviness of the summer air bearing down like one quilt too many thrown over us, the tree branches where moss hung like unpinned lady's hair—all blended, making the road just as familiar to us this night as our own unmade beds at home. We were strangely unafraid.

"Look at Old Alfonso," Roy said. "Got about every dog in French Town with him. Wonder what makes dogs like him that way. They don't bark or nothing. Look up there."

Up ahead Old Alfonso was silhouetted against the cool shine of the road, his movements liquid, more flow than walk, and all about him that bunch of yard dogs, some high-spirited, some slack-tailed, rotating in circles like dancers around a Maypole. It was magic that only happened in late hours of the night in fairy tales you don't ever believe.

Skippy was walking beside me carrying the radio, holding it up to his ear, the music as warm as the night air, melting into us and stirring inside us too, pouring into me like ink in a cup of water, the way music does when it is perfect. In a bold moment, I began twirling around with my arms thrown out, thinking to keep on and on as long as I could, until I was too dizzy to stand it and dropped breathless in the dirt. I spun like an untalented ballerina, too heavy-footed, but lighthearted, laughing my songs into the night with Skippy beside me—then seeing immediately Roy's horror at my girlness. Me, too shy Lucy Conyers, spinning like a lopsided top.

Before I knew it Skippy felt it too, handed the radio to Roy, then got himself going, spinning like he could fly off in the air if he wanted to. I thought he would, any second. He made me scream silently. The two of us, him and me, dancing and spinning, not together exactly, but on the same road, to the same music, in the same darkness.

The only way Roy could get us to quit was to turn the radio off, like pulling the plug out of a sink of warm water. "Good God," he said, "quit. Y'all look like wild Indians."

Our first scared moment happened when the Blue Bird came into sight. Just seeing it changed my mind about going. It was dark and lit. Still and full of movement. This cinder-block box, assorted cars parked in the yard around it, laughing and fussing inside of it—we couldn't hear it but just knew it like we knew there were snakes in the woods. Didn't have to see to know.

We eased along quietly now, careful, stopping altogether to watch Old Alfonso holler something to people sitting in a car in the yard. He stuck his head in the car window and kissed a woman, then moved around to the front of the Blue Bird, where the only door was.

"We got to get around front where won't nobody see us," Skippy said.

"We don't need to get any closer," I said.

"You mize well do what you come for, girl."

"Lucy," Roy said, "if you ruin this I'll kill you."

"Follow behind me," Skippy said. He left the sentence hanging and turned to look at me. "I ain't got no idea what we out here looking for."

"Just colored-people things," I said.

"Ain't you come way out of your way for that?"

"Not colored people like Melvina and y'all," Roy said. "Real colored people."

Skippy looked Roy full in the face. "I'm gon try to pretend you ain't stupid." He took my hand. "Come on."

"Let go of her," Roy said.

"Shut up, Roy." I slapped at him.

I followed Skippy about as tight as a tick. The only thing scarier than keeping on was turning back—alone. Fear swelled in my belly, a growl with fire set to its tail. Soon my whole body was ablaze, hurting until it felt good, like when you stick your toe in the running bathwater and it's so hot it feels cold. I didn't know who I was, or who I had ever been. I leaped like a bony deer behind Skippy, on instinct, reduced to jerk-and-twitch movements in my scramble not to be lost from him.

Beside me Roy bobbed with more courage than agility,

his quick movements almost comical, but his face, when I caught a glimpse of it, dead serious. I was overcome with love for him. There was something sweet about Roy, his eyes blazing like a couple of stars on his face, like he was in sync with the natural order of things this one time in his life. Sweet Roy. I said a prayer to God, "Let Roy live forever."

And Skippy, who led me, this night boy, a black magnet that dragged two spindly, bobby-pin–legged kids behind him, I saw him more clearly than ever, blended into the darkness, the lines where the boy ended and the night began blurring into one thing that made sense. And his blood. I bet it is a beautiful red. I bet his bones are white as a picket fence. Running along behind him in spurts of stop and go, I went black as night too, and faded into the world the same as Skippy did.

The three of us hopped like crickets in the dark, darting sporadically along the outer edges of the Blue Bird yard, until at last we reached the shadowy spot directly across from the front door. We crouched along the back of an old car set up on cinder blocks, our hands rubbing the rusted fender like the rump of a horse, or like tag players safe and touching base at last.

The door to the Blue Bird was flung open, held in place by a rubber tire leaned against it. It took a minute before we could see inside. A couple of men sat along a counter, a Falstaff beer sign blinking behind them so that their faces turned on and off, yellow, black. The music was not loud every minute, sometimes sounding more like a steady stomping, now and then giving way altogether to the high-pitched laughter of some out-of-sight woman.

"Can't get closer than this without walking in the door," Skippy said.

We crouched down for a long time, ripe with expectation, monitoring the indistinct voices, the change of song, and mesmerizing ourselves in the on-again, off-again flash of the colored faces. The fear I had known earlier—with every kind of suddenness and love in it, and seeing through skin and bones—was gone.

"Say when you seen enough." Skippy leaned near. Up close he had a warm smell like Melvina. It's not like that salt-water smell me and Roy get. It made me think of earth after a hard rain, Skippy that close to me. I could touch him, say anything I wanted to him.

They were playing some song I never heard in my life. Music like water, like waves at the beach that come after you, try to pull you in and swallow you up. It was a slow song that somebody sad was singing, a sad woman, her powerful voice vibrating the ground where we stood. I put my hand on Skippy's shoulder and reached for him—to dance slow, the way you dance when the music isn't good enough for fast dancing. The way we had danced in my room that night.

"Stop that," Roy said. "Let go of him, Lucy. Skippy, get your hands off her." We ignored him and began to turn slowly, once, twice, like a couple of floaters on the ocean. We drifted with the current, riding music as clear and smooth as glass, as warm and light as a sea of breathing, and words, like waves, were breaking all around us, gentle and sweet.

"Y'all stop," Roy demanded. He yanked at my shirttail to stop me from spinning—but nothing could stop me. Skippy's hand on my waist, God. I felt his arm flex when we turned; his hand was warm and twice the size of mine as he wrapped and rewrapped it around my sweating fingers. Sometimes my bare feet stepped on his, and there were sandspurs too, but we didn't feel them. Just the music. Just the night. Skippy was real. He was handsome—and for a moment I was beautiful. The world was good. It's possible to fly with your feet on the ground. It's possible for two things to stir into one, the blur so excellent, the blending so easy.

"Let go of me!" Roy shrieked. "Get your hands off me!"

The music contracted like a muscle, Skippy and I were pulled under, brown arms grabbing us, clamping down, like a swarm of octopuses. I thought of drowning. My blood screamed at such a pitch it was deafening. *Fear drowns you in your own blood, Lucy.* I saw Roy wriggling like a worm on a hook. No amount of twisting and kicking could get him loose. He was fighting like crazy. Not Roy, I thought. It felt like the jumping-off place for dying. My blood was screaming, but my voice would not. All the things in my head came loose and were fast-falling to my feet, like an emptied bag of marbles, spilled out and rolling down. So this is what it is to die, I thought, and went out of myself.

"Ain't you got no kind of sense?" A sharp voice sliced into us. "Bringing white kids up here. You ain't got the sense God give a dead cat." In that instant I saw it was Alfonso Junior that had hold of Roy. Roy quit resisting so wildly, his eyes set right on me. I knew then, without looking, that those were Old Alfonso's knotted hands gripping my belly. He had grabbed Skippy and slung him to the ground, but he kept his arms locked around me. "What you doing bringing these kids up here, boy? You lost your mind?"

"It was us wanted to come," Roy said. "Skippy didn't have nothing to do with it."

"He ain't stopped you, did he?" Old Alfonso said. "Makes him as crazy as you." He loosened his grip on me so I could stand up solid, with him holding the back of my shirt.

Skippy stood up too and brushed himself off.

"What you think your mama would do if she knew y'all were out running around in the middle of the night?" Old Alfonso's voice sounded like a slow car on a gravel road, like he had rocks in his throat.

"She don't care," Roy said. "She wouldn't do nothing."

"Naw," Alfonso Junior said, "I reckon she gon like the idea. She gon think it's just the thing."

"We ain't hurting nothing," Roy said. "We can come up here if we want to."

Alfonso Junior snatched Roy up by the neck. "If you ever grow to fit that mouth of yours, you gon be a real large man."

I stepped closer to Skippy, who was standing across from me, but the old man jerked me back by the arm, his fingers clamped hard on my skin. "Where you think you going?"

"You better not kill her," Roy said to Old Alfonso. "You kill her and you'll be sorry."

I felt tied to a stake in a fire, the ropes going around my chest, too tight. "Shut up, Roy," I said.

Old Alfonso chuckled. "If I decide to kill somebody, what you gon do to stop me, boy?"

"We was about to leave," Skippy said.

"You ever killed anybody or not?" Roy said to Old Alfonso. "Did you?"

Alfonso Junior sucked air, laughing.

"I killed lotsa folks," Old Alfonso said, grinning. He was chewing on a toothpick. Alfonso Junior shook his head and kicked sand. Even Skippy smiled.

"Was they white or colored?" Roy said.

"Oh God, Roy. Shut up," I said.

"White, mostly," the old man said. "White people is the easiest kind to kill."

"What'd you kill them for?" Roy said.

Old Alfonso smiled. "Didn't like their looks."

"How?" Roy said. "How'd you kill them?"

"Killed them every sort of way. Killed them with variety. Ain't you ever heard it before, variety is the spice of killing?" Old Alfonso's voice rattled like something broken. He held that toothpick to his mouth, chewing on it at the same time, so he mumbled. He looked square at Roy.

"Did you stab them? Jab their hearts out? Slit their throats?" Roy said.

Old Alfonso nodded yes. "All them things."

"Does that go for rabbits too?" Roy said.

"Rabbits?"

"White rabbits? You know."

"White rabbits. White folks. Ain't no difference. I killed some of it all."

Alfonso Junior busted out laughing. Skippy smiled and looked at his feet. But the old man didn't crack a smile. "You ain't interested in getting yourself killed, are you?"

"Naw," Roy said.

"Or your sister here?"

"Naw."

"Then I better never catch you up here anymore," Old Alfonso said, " 'cause next time I catch you up here in the middle of the night, worrying your mama to death, we ain't gon talk it over. You get my intent?"

"Yessir," Roy said.

"Look around you," Old Alfonso said. "Y'all see a sign anywhere that says 'White Folks Welcome'?"

"Naw," Roy said.

"Well, don't you come back up here 'til you see a sign like that nailed to a tree. You hear?"

"We was just fixing to leave," Skippy said.

"Boy, I saw what you was fixing to do." Old Alfonso looked at me. "I think there's some things need explained to you before you find yourself bottom-up in a ditch."

"We're going right now," Skippy said.

"You ain't got sense enough to be turned loose," Old Alfonso said. "Get them kids in the car."

We said we could walk—or run—home if they wanted us to, but Old Alfonso wouldn't hear of that, nor Alfonso Junior either. They made us get in Alfonso Junior's liquor-delivering car. That tore-up thing. I was shaking.

Meanwhile Blue Bird people had come to the door and out into the yard to look me and Roy over, like we were a couple of sizable fish that got caught. They kept their distance, just eyeballed us, like people do any amazing sight. "I don't know what y'all think you see," Old Alfonso said to the crowd, "but if any y'all think you see two white chirren up here this time of night, you dead wrong. Understand me?"

Alfonso Junior dragged Roy to the car. I guess he knew Roy good enough to know he would tear off from there if he had a chance to do it. He shoved Roy into the front seat beside him, still gripping his shirt with one hand. Skippy got in the backseat, me right after him, and Old Alfonso next.

Alfonso Junior drove slow, like that car was a floating boat and couldn't go any faster than the breeze blowing it. It seemed forever—the ride through French Town, down those same dirt roads we'd walked earlier, with everybody still and quiet now, but especially Old Alfonso. He was like somebody who had disappeared altogether except for his skin and bones slumped into the backseat beside me. The closer we got to our house, the more Old Alfonso vanished. The more a ghost he got, the closer I edged to Skippy.

"Ain't nothing to be scared of," Skippy whispered. "I'm the one gon catch hell."

When we got in front of Melvina's house Alfonso Junior slowed the car to almost a stop and cut the lights off. "When I pull up in your yard you two get out quiet and get on in the house quick. You hear?"

"We're sleeping outside"—Roy pointed—"in that tent."

"Well, just get someplace, then," Alfonso Junior said, "and do it quick and keep quiet at it." His voice vibrated like a twanging guitar string.

The old car coasted down California Street, just as quiet as a moving thing can be. Alfonso Junior accelerated the slightest bit to ease the car into our yard, bringing it to a halt right about where Walter's truck was parked.

Old Alfonso sat up and leaned towards the front seat. Without realizing it, Roy and I had slid so low in the seats

271

we were out of sight completely. Only Old Alfonso's, Alfonso Junior's, and Skippy's heads showed.

"We gon open the door now," Alfonso Junior said, "and y'all get where you belong." I began shuffling over Skippy—then, before I was ready, Roy opened his door up front, which switched the light on inside the car. Then suddenly—quicker than a snake bite—a streak of lightning flashed through the car windshield and shattered it.

Before I could scream came another flash and another one, ripping through the windows, the noise sounding like firecrackers shooting off inside the car, glass busting and flying. Dear God, I thought. Walter. It was Walter.

I hear Alfonso Junior holler and reach across to the glove compartment for a gun of his own. It's slow motion. I hear him fire shots from his open car window in the direction of our house. Our good green house. Mother flashes through my head, her surprised face at the window, getting shot between the eyes. Who will tell Benny? The gunshots don't stop. I shrink, contract with the blast of each bullet, smaller, smaller. Melvina will be mad, I think, if Walter kills us. In my head she is running as fast as she can in her nightgown. Annie is calling her to come back. I even see Granddaddy, but he is too old to run. He stands still and cries. He doesn't have any arms or legs, just a swollen gray head with his hat on it. I think of dying. I think how easy dying is. The bullets are like stampeding horses, the noise. I cannot move fast enough. I hear Roy's voice, an ungodly scream more painful than any sound. His hideous shriek rips through me more fiercely than any bullet. God, I think, is Roy shot? Is Roy shot?

I cannot rise up to see. We are pressed down, Skippy and me both, pressed low onto the floorboard of the car under the weight of Old Alfonso's body. It is raining bullets. "Jesus Christ," Old Alfonso shouts, then goes limp. I cannot move. He is draped over us like a quilt, smothering us, and we are so tangled together, Skippy and me, unable to sort our arms and legs, unable to separate ourselves and come loose from one another. Then Roy goes silent too. Is Roy shot? There is not enough air to make the words. My head is pressed against Skippy's chest and his heart beats like a pair of running feet.

I feel it. For a minute it feels like when a baby pees on your lap—warm and insistent. I think of gravy, of that consistency as it pours, covering me, drowning me. I know immediately that it is Old Alfonso's hot blood. "Skippy," I whisper, and press hard against him, stabbing my fingernails into his flesh. He knows. Dying is easy, I think. It is easy enough. I quit struggling to get loose.

I don't remember the bullets stopping. I remember crying because Old Alfonso is so heavy. Just a small man like that, and I cannot get out from under him. Neither can Skippy. Old Alfonso is dead and burying us. Us. Then lights are going, lapping over us like dogs licking. But mostly I remember words breaking off everywhere. Snapping in two, all the broken words. Slices of night, like playing cards shuffled all out of order.

Then I am being lifted. I am gathered into a strong pair of arms and lifted. Words bounce against my face but cannot get inside, because I have closed myself. I am held very tightly and carried away. I think it must be God scooping down to get me.

*O*LD Alfonso was buried two weeks ago. None of us went to the funeral except Mother. She went even though Melvina told her not to. While she dressed in her Sunday clothes and took the pin curls from her hair, Walter said, "Sarah, I'm just saying this once. If you go to that funeral it's the end of us. I swear to God. It's over."

"Okay, then," Mother said. Ten minutes later she was pulling out of the driveway on her way to Good Shepherd Church. She was the first person there.

By the time the church was full it had started raining. Mother said she tried to be there without being there. "Have you ever been inside a tin-roofed church with lightning slapping everywhere, Lucy? You wonder if Melvina cried at her husband's funeral, and Annie and them too? God, yes."

When Mother came home from the funeral she looked like a woman who'd been baptized a few times too many. She spent the afternoon walking around the house wet-headed in her soaking clothes. "I stood in the back, Lucy, I kept saying, 'God, don't you think it's time for you to finally do something sensible,' then I looked at that rain slamming against the windows, drowning out all the crying inside that church."

At the funeral Melvina's sister Vernie, from Havana, Florida, said, "Look at that white woman back there with no hat on. What she think she's doing in here with no hat."

"She don't know no better," Melvina said. "Leave her alone." That was as near as Melvina came to acknowledging Mother, who stood tearing her Kleenex to shreds.

Mother went to the graveside too, which was one step too many, and stood in the pouring rain without any semblance of an umbrella, her clothes shrinking, clamping to her body, her hair flat to her head. She stayed so long the heels of her shoes sank deep in the mud and she had to step out of them and yank them out. The hungry earth made slurping noises. "Hush," Mother said, "you been well fed today."

Melvina didn't have any choice but to send Alfonso

Junior to lead Mother back to her car. "She's out of her head," Melvina said. "She acts like somebody wanted her here. She acts like she don't know whose pain this is."

"You'd think she the one shot the man," Melvina's sister said.

We haven't seen Melvina since Old Alfonso was buried. Annie came down twice to use the phone and once to borrow twenty dollars from Mother, but she wouldn't say what for.

Roy is still in Tallahassee Memorial. He had surgery to remove a bullet from his lower jaw. It ripped the skin off the side of his face, knocked out four teeth, and lodged in the bone below his ear. Now he'll have a scar where they sewed his face closed with skin from his leg. He also had a bullet removed from his shoulder, but that scar won't be any bigger than a polio vaccination. Mother cries every day when she goes to the hospital to see him. Sometimes the nurse gives her a tranquilizer and she sleeps in the chair in Roy's room.

Walter goes by the hospital every evening after work. Benny can't go at all because he's not sixteen. I'm not sixteen either, but Mother lies and says I am, and they believe her and let me in. I cried the first time I saw Roy, but not since. He's looking better. I kiss him when I leave, and he lets me. And the good thing about Roy is he doesn't act sorry for himself.

"The doctor says in a couple of years you can go to a plastic surgeon and he'll get rid of that scar altogether." This is what Mother keeps telling Roy.

When Walter goes to see Roy, he says, "Roy, son, I swear to God."

"I know," Roy says. "It's okay."

Walter stays in the hospital room until Roy goes to sleep for the night. He reads the newspaper up there and eats cheese crackers and feeds Roy milk shakes through a straw. When he comes home he goes straight to bed.

Two days after Old Alfonso's funeral Walter went up to Melvina's house with two hundred dollars. She opened the door but would not let him in. "What?" she said.

"I know you don't have money for a headstone." Walter shoved the money at her. "Take it."

Melvina let the money drop to the floor. "You can't buy forgiveness," she said. "I ain't selling forgiveness."

"I ain't asking your forgiveness. The police claim it was an accident plain and simple. I had a right to protect my property."

"Then don't come around here waving money in my face."

"Suit yourself." Walter bent down to pick up the money. "Pride is damn expensive, Melvina, if you don't know it."

"Don't say nothing to me about pride."

"Me offering this money don't mean I'm sorry—just like you taking it wouldn't necessarily mean you forgive nothing."

"You think your money gon cover things?"

"Don't misunderstand me. If the same thing was to happen tomorrow that happened that night, I'd act the same way."

"Shoot your own boy in the face again?"

"He knows I only shot that gun to protect him. Didn't have any idea—never mind that. There's two things I want to say to you, Melvina."

"I'm listening."

"One is, it was me shot that gun, not Sarah. I think you got sense enough to remember that."

"And what else?"

"I don't ever want her to know I was up here seeing you about this two hundred dollars."

"She ain't sent you up here with it?"

"Sarah don't send me nowhere. I decide where I go."

"This is like you stole all the water out Lake Jackson, then you come around and pour a cup of it back in, saying you're sorry. It's too pitiful."

Walter laid the money in Melvina's open hand. "You could make a down payment on a car," Walter said. "Maybe get you a job in town."

"Skippy been wanting to go to Memphis," Melvina said. "He's got a uncle there."

"Skippy?"

"Alfonso Junior is living at Virginia's house. Annie's got to help me raise these kids. But Skippy's got a chance to get away from here."

"You spend it how you want to."

"This don't pay for the toenail off Old Alfonso's foot."

"I ain't saying it does."

"He didn't die for just this little bit of nothing."

"It was an accident. I told you that."

"Yeah. You done told me."

"You're too proud to admit you're better off without him, aren't you, Melvina? I don't expect you to admit it. I'm not asking you to."

"I'm taking this money"—she crushed it in her hand, squeezing it into a knot in her fist—"but not to give you any relief."

"I'm not here after relief. But if you say a word about this to Sarah, so help me, Melvina."

"Go on now." She waved her hand to dismiss him.

"I never said I was sorry. You know that. Old Alfonso did everything but ask me to shoot him."

"I hope God can forgive you, because I never will. Not in a million years."

Annie told me all of this. She came down with twenty dollars to pay Mother back, but Mother wouldn't take it.

"Where's Lucy, then?" Annie said, and Mother sent her to my room. She came in and handed me a note.

"What is it?" I said.

"Read it."

Dear Lucy,

Meet me tomorrow evening
where we crossed blood.
Don't tell nobody.

Skippy

"Who wrote this?"

"Who you think wrote it? Skippy wrote it."

I held the note up to my face and cried into it like it was a handkerchief.

"What you want me to tell him?"

"Yes."

"Okay, then."

"I'm glad you don't hate us, Annie."

"I don't hate every one of y'all at every minute, because I ain't got enough time." She turned to leave.

"Nobody meant for Old Alfonso to get killed. Even Walter didn't."

"He's still dead just the same, ain't he?"

The next day when Mother was at the hospital with Roy, trying to spoon Jell-O into his mouth, Alfonso Junior and Skippy walked in. She stood up so fast, red Jell-O splattered like blood droplets on the bedsheets and the spoon clinked across the floor. Alfonso Junior was dressed to kill and Skippy had on a pair of long pants and one of Alfonso Junior's pressed shirts. "Goodness," Mother said.

"Mama sent this." Alfonso Junior handed her a quart jar of cream of tomato soup. "She said see to it he eats it all."

Mother took the jar of soup. "Look, Roy, what Melvina sent you. And look who's here."

"You ain't looking too pretty," Alfonso Junior said.

Roy tried to smile. The bandage twisted on his face.

"He can talk," Mother said. "You have to stand close."

They eased over to the bed, stiff as planks of wood. "What's all these wires going everywhere?" Skippy said. "They ain't trying to electrocute you, are they?"

"Naw," Roy said.

"We just come up here to make sure they treating you all right," Alfonso Junior said. "If any these doctors tries to give you trouble, then you let me know."

Roy smiled and held out his hand to Alfonso Junior. "They took you to jail?" he asked. Skippy put his hands in his pockets and Alfonso Junior looked out the window and rubbed his shoes together. "It was me and Lucy they should of took."

"They said if you get into any more trouble they gon drag you down there next. Didn't they say that, Skippy?"

"Fixing to make a poster with your picture on it. Pin it up in the post office."

Roy tried to smile, but his eyes betrayed him. Mother came over and pretended to fluff up his pillow.

"You gon be better in no time," Alfonso Junior said. "He don't look so bad, does he?"

"Naw." Skippy smiled. "He always was ugly."

When Skippy and Alfonso Junior were on their way out, Roy tried to sit up straight. "Walter's sorry," he whispered. "I swear to God."

"Roy," Mother said, "you know better than to swear."

"All them bullets," Roy said.

After Alfonso Junior and Skippy left, Mother told me, Roy had his first hard cry since the night of the accident. She said to him, "Thank God, Roy. Cry your heart out."

•

I was at the fort waiting to meet Skippy for probably an hour before he finally came. It had gotten dark.

It would be the first I had seen him since the night Old Alfonso died. The police had handcuffed Alfonso Junior and Skippy together and put them in the police car while they waited for the ambulance to come get Roy. Roy had to be peeled loose from Alfonso Junior he was hugged on to him so hard, bleeding bucketfuls on the front seat. The police pried Alfonso Junior loose and then Roy went unconscious. After the ambulance came the police took Skippy and Alfonso Junior down to the station. They stayed overnight.

I don't remember anything except what Walter told me. That the police had rolled Old Alfonso off me, laid him out in the backseat, dead, then unscrambled Skippy and me. Walter said my eyes were open but I was limp as a dishrag. He called my name, Lucy, Lucy, Lucy, but I don't remember it. They put Skippy in the police car, and Walter carried me inside to bed. I didn't wake up until the next day, didn't remember what happened until the day after that. "Roy's in the hospital," Mother said. "And Old Alfonso is dead."

"I swore I'd stay a hundred miles away from you."

"Skippy."

"It's not the first promise I ain't kept."

The night was throbbing with lightning bugs, like tiny flickering candles in the woods. The chorus of insects wailed a sadder song than usual. It was a hot night.

"Mama's talking about me going to Memphis."

"When?"

"Soon as she can get her mind settled on things here."

"I guess you're happy. I guess I should be happy for you. It's what you wanted, isn't it?"

Skippy took a step towards me. A twig snapped under his foot. "Come over here." I stepped towards him and he put his hand on my shoulder. "I come to say good-bye, Lucy."

"In the movies people hug," I whispered.

"This ain't a movie."

"No, but a movie sets a good example if you can't figure it out yourself."

"I can figure it out." Skippy slid his arms around me. I put my face against his chest and he tangled his fingers in my hair. I closed my eyes and listened to his heart make fists, his red blood pumping. I began to cry. I put my arms around his neck and held to him as tightly as I could, wanting this to be a skinless hug, where our blood would join and run together like crazy. I touched his hair, his ear, his lips. He ran his finger down the front of my nose. He pushed my hair back from my eyes. "Damn," he said. Then he kissed me. His mouth, hot and sweet, was moving slowly over mine, and I was lost in him. I opened my mouth to touch his tongue. He bit my lip gently, and I went out of myself at the taste of him, the way he pulled me towards him, the touch of his hands moving slowly over me. I clung to him like he was the truth and this was my only chance to ever know it.

It rained the day the moving van came. A mad, throw-a-fit rain. Rain, like a loud argument that we didn't have any part in but we still had to listen to. Heaven grumbling and spitting—in a dark mood. Thunder like doors slamming shut in the sky. There were three men with the van, and it didn't take any time to get things loaded up.

Rain or no rain, Walter sent Benny to get Skippy because they had to move the rabbit pen to Melvina's yard. Benny sprinted to get him, wet as a yard dog and shaking his head like one. Leroy and Nappy came too, just to watch. Walter got out in the rain with them. And I did. Like those people they talk about when they say, "Don't have sense enough to come in out of the rain."

Walter and Skippy thought they would carry the pen

intact up to Melvina's yard, but the posts were dug in good, and cemented too, so they wouldn't come up. Walter and Skippy fooled with it a long time. They talked to each other, and I heard Walter say "Old Alfonso" twice, but I couldn't hear the rest. Finally Walter gave up and got his saw to saw off the pen legs at ground level.

I was surprised Walter didn't make Benny go in the house and send Leroy and Nappy home too. He let them run stomping in the biggest puddles they could find, squealing and hollering like they did under the sprinkler on hot afternoons, only more so, because the rain was better.

Lightning would make them shriek and dive for the ground. They would run from the thunder, play chase with it, and tag, and last one down is a rotten egg, would swim through the heavy rain like three fish. Walter let them alone. He made Skippy and me hold the dumb rabbit pen steady and he sawed like a house afire. Skippy and I stood with our feet touching in the mud. Twice he placed his foot gently on top of mine. Both times it felt like a bolt of lightning was traveling up my leg.

Before long that pen was cut loose, and Walter and Skippy dragged it across the edge of the woods to Melvina's yard. Walter slammed the pen shut, double-latched it, and went inside the house—probably made Mother fuss, him dripping wet while she was trying to clean.

I sat out in the rain beneath a tree and watched the rain splat on the ground, make a slapping sound like hands clapping. Applause, you know. Clapping that doesn't let up, like after some wonderful event that makes people clap so long they're caught up in it and can't stop. Like that. Too wet is better than too hot. Too hot is what I had mostly known on California Street. The lightning acted like it had its eye on a tree in our yard, or a child. Fiery arrows pointing in the sky, flashing like neon signs, this way, this way, this way. A sky full of dynamite. The rain not drowning us exactly, just drowning out words we said.

I yelled for Leroy and Nappy to go home then: "The storm is getting worse!" I yelled for Benny to go inside too. "You have to come in if I do," Benny yelled back. I didn't hear what he said, but I knew because I saw his mouth moving. The sky was a river.

I looked at Leroy and Nappy heading through the woods home. Annie was at the door screaming, "Hurry!" They ran, hopping and leaping. Benny forgot to say good-bye to them. Probably didn't know he would miss them, waking up the next day in a new house in a new neighborhood. Leroy and Nappy wouldn't be waiting in the yard to play. But Benny didn't think about tomorrow and they didn't either. Those three little boys together almost every day of their lives, and they played in the rain on that last day like it was ordinary, splashed their way home, looking for nothing except the biggest puddles to jump in.

I felt like a thing that comes apart in a hard rain, disintegrates, like a bar of soap or a flimsy cardboard box. I looked across the yard at Skippy. The rain was so loud, a million words, not ours, pounding the ground, exploding with commas, periods, exclamation points. Skippy was standing by the rabbit pen, looking at the palm of his hand.

"What happened to your hand?" I yelled, but he couldn't hear me. I swam through the yard to him. I held his hand as though it were fragile. When I looked at his face to question him, the weight came into his hand, and his fingers folded gently over mine.

I love the rain.

"Wait here," I said, turning to run into the house and get what I was after. I had seen Walter set it on the top shelf of his empty closet with his chewing tobacco, the only things left in the empty room. He would think Mother had packed it. I stuck it inside my shirt and ran back outside.

Mother was in the kitchen fussing at Benny for tracking up the house with his wet feet. When the door slammed behind me, Mother called, "Melvina? Is that you?" All day she had been looking out the window—hoping against hope that Melvina would come down one last time. To say a decent good-bye. But it was useless. Melvina said good-bye to all of us the day of Old Alfonso's funeral.

Thunder crashed and made me jump. Skippy too. It sounded like the sky had split wide open. I handed him Walter's gun. "Never tell anybody," I said.

He held it in both hands and looked at it a long time.

"You said you wished you had one," I said.

"But this is the gun that shot . . ."

I reached up to kiss him, a shy kiss on the lips at first, then a slow, hot kiss designed to last a lifetime. Both of us were drenched, my hair flat to my head and darkened by the rain. His looking dry, raindrops sitting in it like tiny crystal beads. Our clothes were soaked, stuck to us like folds of transparent tape. I have never learned to say good-bye. The words.

"Lucy, you and Benny get old George into the car," Mother said. I was crying and didn't care who knew it. Benny didn't make fun of me either. It was like he wanted me to cry double time over to cover his part for him. Walter blew the car horn twice, three times, to hurry Mother. The thunder was so loud, the sky so dark, we felt almost cozy in our wet clothes, steamed-up car, and deep sadness. "Look at this rain come down," Walter said. "It's better than a free car wash."

Old George, wet, smelled terrible. Benny was holding his nose. I was watching the rain on the window, each drop rolling down the glass, dead-ending. "What is keeping your mama?" Walter said.

"She's still hoping," I said.

"Melvina's not coming. She might as well get it through her head." It was like Mother heard Walter. A minute later she came out. She locked the front door and walked to the car with her face buried in her hands. She got in and nobody said a word. Walter looked at her, then started the engine. He put the windshield wipers on and they slapped at the rain, made a song out of themselves, a broken record, slap, slap, slap, repeating something we already knew. Walter backed the car out onto California Street. The ditches were flooding, that red clay mixing in the water, thickening it, until it was like blood flowing. The water in the road was so deep Walter had to drive slow, going down California Street for the last time, floating down a blood river.

I write *I love you, Skippy* in the fog on the inside of the rear window.

Skippy is still standing in the yard. He holds the gun in his hand, raises it, pointing it at the sky, and fires a shot louder than all the thunder in the world.

Nobody hears him but me.